Steadfast Under Trial

FAIRCOURT FRIENDS SERIES
BOOK THREE

ALEXANDRA T ARMSTRONG

PARABLE PRINT

This book is gratefully dedicated to my cheerleader, line editor, and sweet
sister-in-law
Michelle Elizabeth Armstrong
Thank you for the blessing of your encouragement and support.

Blessed is the man who remains steadfast under trial, for when he has
stood the test he will receive the crown of life, which God has promised
to those who love him.
James 1:12

CHARACTER RECAP

FRIENDS

Marcus and Ava Van Zant: Interracial couple pushed out of a long-term pastorate before they were financially prepared. They are the parents of three daughters: Marley, Mia, and Marit – the latter two have cut their parents out of their lives. Ava is the part-time secretary of Grace Fellowship Church, and Marcus serves as an unofficial spiritual mentor to others.

Grant and Marie Renniger: Parents of twin sons, David and Daniel. Grant enjoys his part-time job at Grassy Fields Country Club as a golf starter and longs to be used by God there. Marie's involvement in the household includes responsibility for all things decorating and house-keeping. Unintimidated, she's slowly befriending her hateful neighbor Christine Williams.

Cal and June Sherman: A childless couple living on a rollercoaster of Cal's health challenges, which have recently improved. Cal is known for blurting his thoughts and praying faithfully for his friends and neighbors. June is the household peacemaker who has a soft spot for children and desserts.

Elodie Ford: This single black woman is known for speaking her mind and wearing colorful clothing. As Cal's health has improved, she's backed off mothering him and started teasing him again. She's also begun tolerating neighbor Bobby McBride, with whom she shares a love for big band music and swing dance.

NEIGHBORS

The Norman Family: Recently widowed dad Micah has a son, Chase, a daughter, Lovie, and a sister, Shelby. Shelby, reserved and recently converted, has moved in with the family and begun a relationship with the neighborhood mailman, Will.

Christine Williams: 70-something well-to-do widow who lives alone across the street and tends a prize rose garden. She manipulates her attorney brother, Luther, into doing her bidding through threatening letters. In order to maintain her membership at church and be buried beside her husband, she's become a semi-regular attendee at Grace Fellowship.

Bobby McBride: A handsome 70-year-old widowed black man with a cat named Rover. His son, DeShawn, is a strong believer who served a 20-year prison sentence and married, while incarcerated, Mariana. DeShawn and Mariana now live with Bobby and demonstrate authentic Christianity.

Jonathan Jefferson: The Pastor of Grace Fellowship Church, married to Kesha, and the father of four young sons. His best friend since high school is DeShawn McBride. Jonathan's biggest challenge is Christine Williams in his congregation.

Will the mailman: Divorced and disqualified from ministry, yet having a PhD in theology, Will is also the men's Sunday School teacher at GFC. He has two sons, Sam and Silas, whom he shares custody of with his remarried ex-wife. He's sweet on Shelby Norman.

Chapter One

Elodie halted at the arched kitchen entrance as she came upon the spectacle and held out an arm to keep Marie, who was just two steps behind, from continuing past her. Looking into the kitchen, they exchanged astonished glances and stifled eruptions of laughter. Marie snatched her phone from her trouser pocket and began recording video of Cal standing at the kitchen sink, gripping the counter's edge, and gyrating his hips in a rhythmic circle.

"If you add a grass skirt and speed it up, you could take that show on tour!" Marie suggested when he stopped.

Cal whipped around to face her, his ears flushing crimson.

"And I could be your road manager, Calico! I take 30 percent though," Elodie snickered.

"Your husband!" Cal pointed a finger at Marie. "Your husband stuck a handful of ice cubes down the back of my t-shirt. They stuck in my britches, and I was trying to work 'em out!"

"I don't see Grant," Elodie pretended to look around for him.

"I don't see ice cubes," Marie added. Although from where she stood, the kitchen island obstructed her view of the melting cubes at Cal's feet. "What I see is a video in my possession that has the potential to go viral on the internet," she held up her phone and taunted.

"Good!" Cal called her bluff, his face returning to its usual pallor. "Figure out how to monetize it and get millions of likes. Then I'll take my Junie on vacation away from you people!"

"Uh oh! We're 'you people' now," Elodie noted, unconcerned he might be seriously annoyed with them. She moved to the cupboard to retrieve coffee mugs for Marie and herself. "Have you had breakfast, Calorie?" she asked.

"I ate with Grant. He was giddy as a tipsy goat to be going back to work at Grassy Fields. I sure hope he dials down the spunk and sass on the . He was in a mood, for sure!" Cal held onto the counter's edge, bent over to pick up the ice cube remains from the floor, and tossed them into the sink.

"I'm sorry you bore the brunt of his enthusiasm," Marie apologized, taking a mug Elodie had filled with coffee for her and moving to the kitchen table where a box of cinnamon rolls lay open. "He's also happy because he had a pleasant conversation with our Daniel last evening. They patched up the falling out they had in Florida."

"Actually, we had a nice conversation too - before the icing incident," Cal recalled. "He asked me to pray that he'd follow through on his resolution to share the gospel at work. He didn't want to miss seeing opportunities or to chicken out if he did. Grant said he'd been praying about it since New Year's Day, and now it was D day. So, I prayed with him after we finished our coffee and rolls. Then he thanked me with ice down my back and headed out into the wide world to be an ambassador for Christ." Cal explained with a concluding snort.

"Nervous energy, I'm guessin'," Elodie slipped into a seat at the table and sipped her coffee.

"Yeah, probably," Cal agreed. "Well, I'm off to the Garage Cave. Gardening season will be starting up soon, and it'll be easier if you have sharp spades and pruners."

"Cal, that's so thoughtful of you! Thank you," Marie gushed, placing a hand over her heart.

Cal left the kitchen, and a few seconds later, the women heard a loud smack in the hall, which preceded Ava's entrance into the kitchen.

"What was that?" Elodie asked, eyebrows and vocal pitch raised.

"A high five. Cal held his hand up as we passed, and I high-fived him. He seems to be in a good mood," Ava answered, taking a seat at the table. She grimaced at the cinnamon rolls – not her favorite. "Good moods seem to be epidemic with the guys. First Grant, now Cal. How's your man's temperament today, Ava?" Marie queried with a grin. "Are we three for three?"

"I'm afraid we're not," Ava answered, shaking her head. She lowered her voice and continued. "I mean, I'm not sure. Marcus isn't in a bad mood, but he's not exactly himself, either. He hasn't been since the night we had Thursday Meeting in Elodie's room. I didn't notice it until Marley called and asked what was bothering Dad. Then I recalled that Meeting, and a few things clicked and confirmed she was onto something."

"Oh, I remember that Meeting. You told us Marit and Robbie were having difficulties, and Marcus said he didn't care. It was memorable for being so out of character for Marcus," Marie recalled, troubled.

"I hate Marley was more perceptive about her father's disposition than I was," Ava confessed. "Yeah, but we were all distracted and walkin' on eggshells over Grant and Marie fussin' with each other," Elodie blurted in consolation.

"You walked on eggshells?" Marie winced, horrified.

Ava and Elodie looked at one another and shrugged in affirmation.

"I'm so sorry we sucked everyone's energy into our marital spat," Marie apologized, dejected. She quickly righted herself and added: "I will not wallow. It's not constructive. What can I do to help you and Marcus?"

"Of course, pray for him. For us. I need wisdom. And courage. Please don't think I'm a horrible wife, but I haven't asked him what's wrong even though I'm sure there's something. My daddy always told Rae Jean and me never to ask a question we didn't want to know the answer to. He was talking about Momma and her mental issues, but those words have always stuck with me. Part of me – a big part – doesn't want to know what's wrong because then I can't un-know it, and I'm responsible for it. OK, I'll say it myself so you girls don't have to: I am a horrible wife. I'm not the partner to him that he always is to me."

"For the record, Grant is the better partner in our marriage by a factor of at least ten," Marie commiserated. "So, I have no stones to throw at you."

"Well, Ava, you makin' any plans to be a good wife to your husband and talk to him? Or should Grant or Cal do that for you?" Elodie pressed her.

"Ouch!" Ava flinched at the sharpness of her point.

"Yeah, yeah, the truth hurts. You expect me to sit here and listen to you admit you're not doin' what you know you should and just feel sorry for you? Marie's already covered that base."

"Ouch!" yelped Marie at her turn on the receiving end of a point.

"Come on, you two! Start actin' right." Elodie insisted.

"She's right," Ava conceded to Marie. "She's not all kindness and light about it, but she's right. I'll talk to Marcus and find out what's wrong."

"Now we're gettin' somewhere!" Elodie clapped her hands.

Ava got up from the table to drain the remains of the coffee pot into a mug as Marie and Elodie each set upon a cinnamon roll. The first notes of June's morning piano devotions wafted from the living room into the kitchen. She played *Have Thine Own Way, Lord*, which seemed apt for the moment.

Chapter Two

Bobby furrowed his brows as he surveyed the dingy upstairs bedroom and its closet, now brimming with boxes of unfamiliar things. But slowly, as an idea formed, a smile replaced his sullen expression.

DeShawn and Mariana had accepted Bobby's offer to live with him in the house DeShawn grew up in on Cedar Street. Bobby sweetened his proposal by having an architect acquaintance help him figure out how to convert the unused dining room off the kitchen into a small bedroom and bathroom so the married couple could have the entire second floor and their privacy. However, Mariana's greedy brothers demanded to sell their mother's house before leaving town after her funeral, and there were no other immediate housing options available.

"This must be God's provision for us for this season," Mariana convinced her reluctant husband.

Mariana moved into Bobby's home a week before her husband was released from the Kentucky State Reformatory. On DeShawn's release date, which coincided with his birthday, they departed for a five-year-delayed one-week honeymoon in a rented cabin at Red River Gorge in the mountains of Eastern Kentucky.

The downstairs renovations were still underway, but it occurred to Bobby that he should do something upstairs as well. He had only five days until his son and daughter-in-law returned home. He hurried down the stairs, past the plumber installing the sink in his new three-quarter bathroom, to the kitchen table to retrieve his cell phone. It wasn't there.

"Now, where did I set that thing down?" Bobby wondered aloud as he scanned the countertops.

He retraced his steps and returned to the upstairs bedroom he'd just come from, looking on top of the boxes, dresser, and bed where he might have laid the phone, unthinking. Not there either.

He sighed to himself in exasperation. *"I need a phone to call my phone,"* he thought, walking back down the stairs.

He checked the couch cushions in the living room to no avail and stood still, trying to remember. *"No sense checking my truck. I haven't gone anywhere today,"* he figured, growing frustrated. "Guess I'm gonna have to tie it to a string around my neck when I find it!"

"You talkin' to me?" the plumber asked, sticking his head into the hallway.

"No. Just grumbling because I can't find my cell phone," Bobby answered as he patted himself down. When his hand hit the hard object in his back pocket, he closed his eyes and exhaled. "Found it!"

Bobby sat on the couch and hit the contact call button for Elodie's cell. It was the first time he'd ever used it.

"Hello?" Elodie answered, pretending she didn't know it was Bobby calling. She also had him in her contact list and saw his name on the caller ID. She'd gotten his cell number from Marcus after the January ice storm on the grounds it might be needed in a future emergency.

"Miss Elodie, I need your help. Who's the interior decorator in your house? I want to freshen up the kids' bedroom before they get home – it just came to me to do it. But I don't have any ideas about colors and such. Your house looks put together. Who's the mastermind over there who can point me in the right direction?"

"Grant is our ace in that department. There's not a doily or knick-knack he hasn't personally curated," Elodie fibbed with an unseen smirk.

"I don't believe you!" Bobby declared.

"Then you're not as gullible as you look," she admitted with respect.

Bobby let go with a full-faced mega-watt smile, confident Elodie couldn't see the expression she loathed on him through the phone signal. But he was pleased with her comment, noting a shift from flat-out hateful meanness to a good-natured teasing kind of meanness – as one might tease a friend.

"Well, not gullible today anyway. But five minutes ago, I couldn't find my phone in my back pocket, so there's that," he laughed.

"One minute ago, I first picked up the television remote instead of my phone to answer your call," Elodie offered her own confession with a chuckle. "Marie's our decorating talent, if you must know. She's sitting right here. Would you like to speak with her?"

She handed her phone to Marie and listened to her make plans to go over to Bobby's house at one o'clock, right after lunch.

Marie walked around the rooms on the second floor of Bobby's house with a clipboard in one hand and a pencil in the other. Elodie, who'd accompanied her, gamely followed behind.

"All the rooms need painting. You said they'd have the entire floor for themselves, right?" Marie directed her comment to Bobby, who stood in the upstairs hall while the women wandered.

"Uh, yeah. I, uh, I won't have to come up here at all," Bobby stammered in surprise at the suggestion of an increase in the project's scope.

"Then you should freshen all the rooms at once. Painters will show up for a larger job quicker than for smaller ones spread out. Do you know what color Mariana likes?" Marie was relishing the opportunity to make these neglected rooms pretty.

"DeShawn asked me to send her peach-colored roses for Valentine's Day because that's her favorite color flower," Bobby answered.

"Lovely! We can pick a pretty shade of peach at the paint store and an accent color for the curtains and bedding – I'm thinking a fern green or light turquoise. We can paint the other two bedrooms off-white, a neutral color. One could be a television room with a sofa, and the other an office-type room with maybe a nice second-hand desk. Furniture takes months to order, so we'd have to find things in stock or thrifted. A quick trip to a home store, and we can pick up a few pictures for walls and do-dads for accessorizing. Why not paint the bathroom too? Then, we can get coordinating towels, a bath mat, and a shower curtain in one color we pull from the bedroom, and it will all look brand new. We can do this!" Marie was confident and writing furious notes on her clipboard.

Elodie stepped into the hall. "Should have warned you; she also knows how to spend money," she apologized to Bobby in a low whisper.

"Yeah, but I like her vision. I'm sure the kids will like it too – they're certainly not expecting it. Do you think we can do it all?" he wondered.

"If your bank account can handle it, Marie can handle it," Elodie assured.

"Well, ladies, let's go shopping!" Bobby cheered, indicating with a sweep of his hand toward the stairs that they should proceed.

He followed the ladies down the stairs with a skip in his step - energized by the prospect of delighting Mariana, which he was sure would make DeShawn happy, too.

Chapter Three

Marie was beside herself. She'd been on the phone all morning trying to hire a contractor to paint the upstairs rooms of Bobby's house and gotten nowhere. Every one of them was booked several weeks out. As an act of desperation, she'd even generously offered – with Bobby's resources – a 30% bonus to move to the head of their schedules. She still had no takers because the project was still considered a small residential job.

"Why did I assume painters were just holding their breath, waiting for my call? It was stupid of me not to consider there'd be a lead time to get scheduled. But the paint's purchased, and Bobby's expecting this to happen this week! What am I going to do?" Marie lamented at the kitchen table. An egg salad sandwich sat before her, untouched.

"You really put the cart before the horse this time," Elodie stated the obvious, unhelpfully.

"I'm sorry, Marie. What a tough spot," June soothed, licking her finger and picking crumbs of potato chips from her plate.

"We could do it," suggested Cal. "But when I say 'we,' I mean 'you all,' actually. I can't climb those stairs, or paint anything. Of course, Ava and Grant are tied up with their jobs," he reminded them.

"I wouldn't mind helping," Marcus offered, wiping his mouth with a paper napkin.

Marie bounced a leg absentmindedly, brightening at the possibility of a resolution to her dilemma.

"There's a reason we didn't paint this house ourselves when we moved in. None of us are painters," Elodie cautioned.

"Well, we weren't chicken keepers when we moved into this house either, but we figured that out," Marie argued, nodding toward the sandwich in front of her as proof of her claim.

"I get it's not rocket science, but what if we mess up the man's house?" Elodie had drilled down to her genuine concern.

"It's only paint. Worst case, we'd have to go over some places," June was warming to the idea.

"If you ladies paint da trim and cutting in, I could roll da walls," Marcus proposed.

"We don't even have to paint the trim! All we need to do is wipe it down with a wet rag to clean it up. Yes! We can do this ourselves. Will you girls help Marcus and me?" Marie appealed to Elodie and June with pleading eyes.

"I will," June agreed.

"Oh, stop lookin' at me like you got caught passin' gas in church," Elodie scolded Marie. "I'll help, but I won't be blamed for shoddy workmanship. You're gettin' what you pay for, and I'll say the same to Bobby."

"Calm your conniptions, girl! We both know you could spill a can of paint on Bobby's hardwood floors, and he'd say you improved them," Marie rebuked her friend.

A trace of a smirk appeared on Elodie's face in acknowledgment of the comment's probable truth.

"I'm happy to have helped you solve your dilemma, Marie." Cal huffed a breath on the fingernails of his right hand and buffed them on his overalls.

"Cal, you are a problem-solving machine," Marie chuckled. "I'll tell Bobby his painting crew will be there tomorrow at 8 am!" She finally dug into her sandwich with relish.

"Can we make it 9 AM?" Marcus requested. "Some of us have piano devotions around 8:15," he advocated for June and her routine, smiling at her.

"9 AM it is," Marie mumbled with a mouthful of sandwich.

Marie and Marcus ended up doing 100% of the painting project over two days while Bobby worked around them with a rented steam cleaner, covering and uncovering sections of carpet protected from paint splatter with plastic film. He also re-glazed the original bathroom sink, pitted with a century of chips and wear.

Instead of painting, Elodie and June scoured second-hand stores for a decent desk and chair for the office and end tables for the television room. When they located acceptable items, Cal drove his truck to the shops to have them loaded and transported to the house. There, Elodie and June gave the pieces a thorough cleaning and polishing, dodged by the men delivering the brand-new sofa. And in lieu of Thursday Meeting that week, Marie and Elodie accompanied Bobby to pick out new draperies at a department store in Louisville. At the same time, Marcus and Grant mounted a 55" flat-screen TV in the television room and installed new curtain rods in all the rooms.

By Friday evening, Marie's vision and Bobby's hopes became a reality: a lovely suite of rooms transformed the upstairs of Bobby McBride's house. It was a cohesive arrangement of subtle peach and creamy white with accents of light turquoise and a dab of contrasting burnt orange – colorful, yet soothing; stylish, but inviting.

Surveying each room through its open door, they stood in a cluster in the small second-floor hall, illuminated by polished ceiling fixtures with new LED bulbs: Bobby, Marie, Grant, Marcus, Ava, June, and Elodie.

"You all did a beautiful job! I'm only sorry I didn't get to be part of this team effort and transformation," Ava complimented the group.

"You made lunch and supper for us today while we put everything together. That's not nothin'," Elodie remarked.

"Your son and his wife are going to love this space!" June gushed to Bobby.

"That's the hope! I mean, how could they not?" he responded with a satisfied smile.

"This is really a nice thing you've done for them, Bobby," Grant affirmed.

Bobby lowered his shoulders. "Nice, yes. But was it the right thing to do?" He suddenly second-guessed himself.

"What do you mean?" Elodie asked, taken aback by Bobby's question.

"What if DeShawn thinks I did this to manipulate him somehow into staying here?"

"Did you?" Marcus challenged him, raising a single eyebrow.

Marie and Ava exchanged glances. "You know, why don't you guys delve into the meaning of life or whatever heavy conversation you're about to have while we ladies wander back home and into our pajamas? We're tired," Marie reacted, thinning the herd of observers for Bobby's sake.

The women took their leave, and the men, at Marcus's initiation, moved into the television room and seated themselves on the new burnt orange linen sofa.

"Am I trying to manipulate my son?" Bobby restated Marcus' question. "This morning, I would have said 'no' – probably 'heck, no!' But now, I'm not so sure. And maybe DeShawn will see it that way, and it's too late to undo it. And..." he left the sentence unfinished, having worked himself into a knot of self-doubt and agitation.

Marcus left the silence alone, and Grant followed his lead.

"I love Mariana," Bobby began again. "She's a great girl. But a wife was the last thing I expected to get between DeShawn and me. I wanted time to get to know my son again, and that won't happen now. I wanted time alone with him to do things together."

"Sounds like you wanted to go on the honeymoon with him," Grant teased, nudging Bobby's shoulder.

Bobby laughed out loud. "Yes, I did! I guess I did!" he continued laughing. "Maybe I just had to admit that and get it out of my system." He stood up and laughed again, trying to shake off his worry. "He's going to love this setup here! And I'm doing the best I can."

"That's all a man can do," Marcus assured him.

"Besides, who gets mad when the Sherwin-Williams fairy shows up to slap a fresh coat of paint on your digs?" Grant wondered aloud.

"No one," Marcus answered the rhetorical question for Bobby's sake.

Chapter Four

Will whispered 'Goodnight,' planted a kiss on Shelby's cheek, and headed out the front door of the Norman's home.

Every other Friday evening for the last six weeks – on the weekends he didn't have sons, Sam and Silas - he'd been invited to supper with Shelby's family and play a board game afterward. Tonight, they'd played Faircourtopoly, the local version of the classic game, and Will mercilessly bankrupted the entire Norman clan except for seven-year-old Lovie, who refused to play 'that boring game' and watched a kid's movie instead.

Shelby hesitated before returning to the dining room to put away the game. She leaned her back against the front door, a dreamy expression enveloping her countenance.

"You tired, Aunt Shelby?" Lovie asked as she passed through the front hall on her way upstairs to get ready for bed.

"Nope. Happy," Shelby stretched her arms overhead and grinned.

"Since you're happy, do you want to have a sleepover with me in my room tonight? We haven't done that in a loooong time! And if you say 'yes,' then we'll both be happy," Lovie wheedled her angle with pleading eyes.

"That's a marvelous suggestion, Lov!" Shelby gamely agreed. "Go put your pajamas on and brush your teeth. Remember, your dirty clothes go in your hamper, not on the floor next to it! I'll be upstairs after I put the game away and say 'goodnight' to your father and brother."

"Yay!" Lovie cheered, racing up the staircase.

"What's the little toad yelling about?" Chase asked his aunt as she returned to the dining room to find him sorting the play money into organized piles.

"I've accepted her invitation for a sleepover tonight," Shelby informed him.

"Oh."

Sensing some disappointment with her answer, Shelby suggested: "Maybe you could invite your dad for a sleepover in your room."

"Are you kidding? I hear him snoring through my wall. You think I want that thunder in the same room with me?" Chase laughed, dismissing the idea.

"Good point." Shelby gathered play pieces and folded the gameboard into the box.

Chase stretched his neck toward the living room and saw his father in his preferred chair, enjoying a European soccer match on television.

"Aunt Shelb, can I ask you a personal question about you and Will?" Chase made his request in a low voice.

"Perhaps. Can I hear the question, and then I'll decide if it's appropriate to answer?"

"How come Will always comes over here for your dates? How come he doesn't take you out? Is he a cheapskate?" Chase was blunt.

Shelby sputtered and let out a bellowing laugh. "You want to know if Will is a cheapskate?" she repeated, trying to rein in her surprise and amusement.

"I'm almost done with eighth grade. This summer, I'll be in high school and might find a girlfriend. But I thought girls wanted you to take them places and spend money. Will has a job and makes money, so why doesn't he take you places?"

"Okay. I see." Shelby regained her composure after realizing Chase had been observing her and Will and making mental instructions for dating.

She slid the game box toward Chase so he could put the piles of money in and add the cover, and then she pulled out a chair and sat.

"I'll accept the question. Have a seat." She nodded to the chair beside her, and Chase sat in it.

"The short answer to your question is: No, Will is not a cheapskate. The longer answer has a few parts to it. Do you want the long answer?"

Chase eagerly bobbed his head up and down.

"First, not all girls are the same. Yes, some like to go places – maybe out to eat or to do an activity – but not all girls do. Or at least not all the time. They're more of the homebody type. Now, me? I like to go out and eat and do fun things. And I could do that all the time!"

She saw Chase's face contort into puzzlement at the disconnect between what she said she liked and what they did.

"But there are other things to consider," she continued. "Eating out and entertainment are expensive. You realize that. Will and I have done those things a few times because we both have jobs that make money. But we also think it's important to spend our funds wisely. So, we often choose to have dinner and play games at home so we can save our money.

And here's another thing: time we spend just having fun doesn't help us get to know one another as much as interaction in a natural family setting. If we're distracted with being entertained, then we're not communicating or learning about one another. I mean, how would we have learned that Will is a stickler for following directions, that he has to keep his temper in check when competing, or that onions make him gassy if he didn't spend time at our house?" she added a smile to her commentary.

"Do you ever go to his house, I mean, apartment?" Chase asked.

"No," she answered forthrightly, dreading the follow-up question sure to come.

"Why not?" And there it was.

Shelby shifted in her chair and wondered if her brother, presently engrossed in a soccer game 20 feet away, should be part of this conversation. She looked Chase in the eye and plunged ahead, anyway. This was an opportunity to teach him what she hoped her brother would approve.

"It's not wise for a woman to go to a man's apartment alone because there might be a great temptation to play kissy-face." She noticed Chase burying a grimace at the thought of her playing kissy-face with their mailman and left the point there. "But also, a godly man is responsible for protecting a woman's reputation and his own as well. He shouldn't allow the opportunity for anyone to accuse them of sin. Do you know what I mean?"

"I know what you mean," Chase broke eye contact, cheeks blushing.

"That's why, if we're not at church or out in public, Will and I spend time here with my family. In fact, he's told me I'm not welcome at his apartment, and I love him for that. I love that he protects my reputation, and I hope someday you'll be a godly young man who protects his girlfriend's reputation, too."

"You said you love him," Chase pointed out her wording without further comment.

"I do," Shelby answered, her freckled cheeks blushing.

"I don't," Chase responded curtly, making his aunt frown. "He's not my type!" he guffawed and gave her a playful punch on her arm.

"Aunt Shelby? Are you coming?" Lovie hollered down the staircase.

"Be right there!" Shelby hollered back, standing to her feet. Before she turned to go, she said to Chase: "I love you, too. Always have, always will."

CHAPTER FIVE

"Welcome home!" Bobby shouted out the back door to DeShawn and Mariana as they emerged from Mariana's silver compact sedan in the driveway.

"Thanks. It's good to be home," DeShawn tried to sound convincing to his father and wife. He still harbored reservations about living as a saved, married man in his unsaved father's house. The last thing he wanted was marital or parental friction; he simply didn't know what to expect. Although he reminded himself that was true about most things now that he was a free man.

"Need any help with your bags, son?" Bobby offered as they climbed the few back porch steps.

"He's got 'em," Mariana answered for her husband, leading the way into the house.

"Something smells good," DeShawn complimented, ducking his 6'2" frame, stepping through the kitchen door, and sniffing the air.

"Got a roast in the crock pot for supper. I plan to make some corn pudding, too," Bobby was pleased with himself. "DeShawn, do you remember your momma's corn pudding? I'll make it just like she did."

The younger man stopped in his tracks, recalling. "Oh, wow. That was our comfort food in the cold months. That, and her mac and cheese. What time do we eat?" he asked with genuine enthusiasm.

"A couple of hours – about five o'clock, I guess. Is that too early?"

Bobby answered.

"No, that's fine, Dad. That'll give us some time to unpack. So, we'll just go upstairs now and tend to that."

Mariana took a step and peeked at the progress of the renovation off the kitchen. "Your new room looks like it's always been here – so comfortable and inviting. You even have your furniture moved in and clothes hanging in the closet!" she noted through the open door.

"You like the gray walls with the navy bedding? I'm pleased with it. And I won't miss climbing those stairs, that's for sure. That's for young legs! There's still a minor problem with the shower, but the contractor's coming back Monday to fix it and do some touch-ups on the paint where it got scuffed by workers," Bobby rambled.

"If you're happy, I'm happy for you," Mariana squeezed her father-in-law's arm gently.

She led the way as the couple headed down the hallway and up the staircase to their second-floor bedroom. DeShawn tightened his jaw and grip on the suitcases as he realized his father was following along behind them on the stairs. It was his understanding that this wasn't supposed to happen.

"What have you done?" Mariana screeched when she reached the hall at the top of the stairs.

DeShawn, primed to be frustrated with his father, turned back and shot him a glare.

"It is beyond beautiful and beyond generous!" Mariana continued, stepping forward to survey the view beyond each open door. "Honey, look what your father has done!" she captured her husband's attention.

"How did you do this since last week? Oh, it's perfect! I love the colors – like an August day at the beach! Did you hire a designer?" Mariana gushed over the transformation of the rooms.

Relieved his wife was delighted and not angry with whatever had transpired in their personal space, DeShawn stepped forward to view the rooms he hadn't seen in 20 years.

"Dad, you renovated up here, too? For us?" he asked in amazement, soft eyes replacing the former glare.

"Not a renovation. It was just freshening up with paint, curtains, and a few pieces of furniture. Our neighbors helped me. Consider it a wedding present," Bobby answered.

"You replaced the sink," DeShawn noticed, stepping into the bathroom and trying to take in everything at once.

"No, not replaced. Just re-glazed the original. It's the same one as before."

"Well, it looks brand new," DeShawn responded with admiration.

The couple walked from room to room, appreciating each thing that captured their attention – the luxurious off-white bedding, the office set-up for DeShawn's future studies, the new sofa which they sprawled on to try out, and the beautiful coordination of all the rooms in their private retreat. Mariana opened a closet door and located where her cardboard boxes of clothing and possessions had been hidden away.

"I want to unpack everything and put it in its new place. I just love this so much!" Mariana squealed, draping herself across their beautiful queen-sized bed. "I've never lived in one room as pretty as this, let alone three rooms and a bath!" She patted the place beside her on the bed, inviting her husband to join her. And when he reluctantly did – because his father was in the room - she startled him with a proper kiss on his mouth.

Taken aback, DeShawn jumped up from the bed and addressed his father. "D – d- Dad," he stammered. "Thank you so much! We never expected…"

Bobby cut him off. "I only came upstairs this time to see your reaction. I hoped you'd be pleased with it, and I'm glad you are. You all take your time unpacking. Or get another kiss if you can, son! I'm going downstairs. Got to get my ingredients together for that corn pudding."

He gave them both an approving grin, turned, and went downstairs to the kitchen.

Bobby had never made his late wife's corn pudding recipe, let alone could guarantee it would come out the way she'd made it. He just hoped he could, for DeShawn's sake. He was digging in the back of a kitchen cabinet, trying to locate Julia's old recipe file, when his cell phone rang in his back pocket.

"Hello, Miss Elodie!" Bobby answered her call.

"Did they love it, or did they love it?" El asked eagerly.

"Oh, they loved it alright. They're upstairs right now unpacking from their trip and sorting Mariana's things out of the boxes – settling in and making this their home."

Elodie could hear the joy in his voice. "Bobby, I'm happy for you. You'll enjoy havin' family under your roof."

"I'm sorry you don't have a family, Miss Elodie," Bobby responded.

"No, I don't have children. But I have a bunch of brothers and sisters in this house who are, for sure, my family! They're a great comfort that, though I'm single, I don't have to be alone in my golden years." Elodie was emphatic.

"Well, that's true," Bobby acknowledged. "You know, I only have one sister. Always wished I'd had a brother, too," he mused.

"Well, if Marie wouldn't pitch a fit, I'd let you take Grant off our hands for nothin'," she chuckled.

Bobby echoed her laughter and added: "At the moment, Marie might be more useful. I'm trying to make corn pudding over here, and I can't find Julia's recipe box."

"Trust me when I tell you, you do not want Marie tryin' to help you make corn puddin'. You'll end up with a corn brick. But I can make it if you're needin' help," Elodie offered casually.

"I got a roast in the crockpot, and I promised DeShawn his momma's corn pudding like I make it every other week or something. But the truth is, I've never made it. Don't know what got into me, except I just want to make him happy. I'm in a fix without that recipe, and if you could help me out of it, I'd be grateful."

"Well, now that I know you lied to him, I shouldn't help you at all!" Elodie threatened.

"You're right. You probably shouldn't," Bobby admitted.

"But if you're willin' to give up your deceptions, I might be willin' to extend some grace," she challenged him playfully.

"I'm willin'," he repeated her phrase with relief.

"Okay, then. I'll be over in ten minutes," she assured with a smile in her voice.

After rummaging through her closet for a fresh blouse and poking a few stray hairs back into her braids, Elodie crept down the stairs and out the front door like a burglar. She wanted to keep this errand off the household topics for discussion.

CHAPTER SIX

C hristine fidgeted with the laminated florist card she kept in the pocket of her sweater and watched the commotion from an upstairs window. On the sidewalk across the street, the young man and woman who moved into Bobby McBride's house were being introduced to neighbors by that impertinent woman, Elodie Ford. Christine knew who the young man was. She remembered him as the troubled McBride boy sent to prison for robbery and murder. It horrified her to know a convicted felon was living mere yards away from her house.

She watched the group, oblivious to the danger, meander down the street, picking up the woman and young boy from the Norman residence along the way to Grace Fellowship Church. Although it wasn't the first Sunday of the month – the one Sunday she attended - Christine checked her gold watch and calculated she still had time to apply a dash of makeup, arrange her hair, and make it to the church service if she hurried. Someone needed to alert the Pastor to the riffraff infiltrating the congregation.

June was unpacking art supplies in the pre-kindergarten Sunday School room to prepare for Junior Church, and Marie was dawdling in conversation with Anna Cramer after the Senior Ladies' class, but the rest of the household witnessed the shocking confrontation in the foyer. Christine Williams, uncharacteristically present in the middle of the month, had cornered Pastor Jefferson at the Visitor Center desk.

"There's an undesirable in our midst who needs to be shown the way out!" she barked at the Pastor, expecting his immediate concern and action.

Pastor Jefferson exchanged glances with Marcus, with whom he'd been conversing prior to Christine's interruption. Then he chuckled and said: "Mrs. Williams, if all the undesirables have to leave this building, please turn off the lights after we're all gone."

"I see! This is a laughing matter to you. A thief and murderer is living across the street from me, and now he's invading my house of worship. We are not safe in our own neighborhood," she glared at Marcus with haughty eyes, daring him to oppose her view before continuing her harangue against the Pastor. "And now this entire congregation is at risk because you think our safety is a joke!"

Ava and Elodie, chatting with Kesha Jefferson and Shelby Norman near the staircase, and Cal and Grant, opening the doors for departing members and visitors, turned at the sound of Christine's shouting.

"I can assure you, Mrs. Williams, the spiritual and physical safety of this congregation is of utmost importance to me," Pastor Jefferson patted the air with open palms, attempting to calm her.

"I'm glad to hear that. So, you'll remove the felon, then?" she lowered her shoulders and relaxed.

"I can't do that, Mrs. Williams."

"I'm sure you can do it, but you won't," she corrected tersely.

"I guess it's both. I can't, and I wouldn't if I could. DeShawn McBride committed a serious crime when he was 18 years old. He served 20 years in prison for that crime and is now free to move about in society. He is as welcome in this congregation as any other repentant sinner, and I expect he and his wife will become members shortly. I appreciate that his history puts you ill at ease, but I'm confident when you get to know him, you'll respect him for the godly man he's become."

"A jailhouse conversion, was he? And you believe that and are ready to embrace him as a paragon of virtue now? Furthermore, you expect everyone else to be as naïve as you. Well, I will not because the Good Lord has given me common sense. It's a pity the leader of this church should lack it," she insulted.

Pastor Jefferson glanced at Marcus again and sighed. "Mrs. Williams, might you be happier and more secure at another church with a pastor who possesses the common sense you require?

"Without a doubt! But unless I can be buried in this church's cemetery – next to my husband – without membership in this disastrously run institution, we're stuck with one another," she shot back.

"There's another solution available to you. Your husband could be re-interred elsewhere," Pastor Jefferson suggested in exasperation.

"Dig him up? What..?" she shrieked, horrified by the suggestion. At a complete loss for further words to express her outrage, she reared back and slapped the pastor's face.

"Mrs. Williams!" Marcus intervened and stepped forward. "Dat was uncalled for."

"There was never a situation where it was more called for! Imagine a so-called man of God suggesting the removal of a man's mortal remains from his resting place like it was akin to moving a sofa across a room. It's blasphemous, that's what it is!"

Christine Williams turned and marched toward the front doors like she couldn't escape the place fast enough. Grant, who'd been riveted to the drama at a safe distance, opened the door to facilitate her exit.

The friends took turns ladling chili from the crockpot on the kitchen island into their bowls, except for Grant, who despised chili and heated a can of chicken noodle soup at the stove. They each grabbed a piece of French bread from a platter next to the crockpot and took their usual places at the dining room table for Sunday after-church lunch. No one said a word until they were finished, and then the comments flew like machine-gun fire.

Elodie started it. "If she can throw hands like that, why should she fear DeShawn?"

"Just when I think I've seen it all in church, Christine Williams performs a new trick," Ava shook her head.

"Pastor Jefferson literally turned the other cheek. Did you see that?" Cal asked, impressed by his display of self-control.

"I don't tink she knows da meaning of da word 'blasphemous,'" Marcus noted.

"I don't think she knows the meaning of the word 'no,'" emphasized Grant.

"I feel so sorry for poor DeShawn and Mariana. It won't be the last time someone complains about their attendance at Grace Fellowship," June sympathized.

"I feel sorry for Christine Williams. She's a desperately unhappy and frightened woman," Marie commiserated.

Everyone looked at Marie and then nodded their heads in agreement as the truth of her assessment grew obvious.

"That's still not a license to go around slappin' faces," Elodie argued, starting another round of comments unfavorable to the neighbor across the street.

Chapter Seven

Although he wore an emerald green Grassy Fields Country Club fleece-lined windbreaker and a coordinating Scotch plaid newsboy cap, Grant rubbed his hands together to generate warmth against the early morning chill. He reminded himself that 7AM starts would be more pleasant in May than they were in March.

Grant checked his watch and noted it was now 7AM, and the first scheduled foursome hadn't arrived at the tee. Looking toward the clubhouse, he saw two players struggling with a bag that had fallen off their cart and strewn its contents on the path. Their partners laughed at them from a cart a few yards behind. The group made it to the first tee several minutes late.

"I hope your game goes better than the loading of your clubs, gentlemen," Grant welcomed the jovial men he recognized as semi-regulars from last year.

"It's probably an omen of our success, but who cares? We stopped keeping scorecards a few years ago," admitted the spokesman for the group, a short and sprightly 80-year-old named Larry.

"Well, just keep having fun then. Off you go!" Grant directed them onto the tee box. As he watched each man take his first swing, he mentally affirmed their decision not to keep score. The lot of them belonged on the public par-three course in neighboring Henry County.

"Hey, Grant! I heard you busted some ribs at the end of last season –

tough luck. Glad to see you back on the job," Joe Jacobs greeted him.

Grant first knew Joe as the attorney from whom he and Marcus sought help in responding to Christine Williams' accusation that they were running an unlicensed senior care residence. Their acquaintance renewed when Joe, a season pass holder, frequently appeared at Grassy Fields in a foursome of Main Street business owners.

"Where's your sidekick today?" Grant inquired, speaking of Joe's usual cart partner, Wilson Appleby, who owned The Copy Shoppe on Main Street.

"I guess you didn't hear. Wilson had the widow-maker on Christmas Day. He dropped dead in front of his whole family at the dinner table," Joe tried to sound clinical and detached, though the death of his friend was painfully personal.

"No, I didn't know. I'm sorry for your loss, Joe. It must have been a shock – he was about your age, right?" Grant responded.

"Forty-five – one year older than me. Thank God his kids are older – college age – and not in grade school like mine," Joe shuddered.

Grant was not one to usually pick up on such things, but for some reason, it struck him that Joe had referred to himself twice when sharing these details about Wilson. He wondered if the Holy Spirit helped him see that.

The rest of Joe's foursome, including Wilson's replacement, stood near their carts, using clubs to stretch their backs while waiting for the prior group to move off the fairway. Grant quickly said a silent prayer, asking God for courage and wisdom to share the gospel with Joe, with whom he stood shoulder to shoulder.

"It's sobering to realize that one minute we can be carving a Christmas ham, and the next minute we can be on the other side of eternity. Would you be ready?" Grant turned his head toward Joe.

"I've been thinking about that a lot since Wilson passed. Of course, I've got all the legal documents my wife would need: a will, living will, and power of attorney. If I'm gone, there's a nice life insurance policy to care for her and the kids. But it still feels like something's missing. What am I missing?"

"Got your debts covered?" Grant inquired.

"I bought mortgage insurance for the house. There's no other debt besides that," Joe answered proudly.

"What about your debt to God? Who's paying for that – you or Jesus?"

"What?" The question caught Joe off guard, and he cast a nervous glance up toward his golfing buddies, who were still stretching their muscles.

Grant decided to use legal language that Joe, as an attorney, would be comfortable with. "A good judge cannot simply dismiss crimes because there'd be no justice. His community would throw him off the bench. It's the same with God. Our sins against Him – of which we're all guilty - require justice. The fair sentence for crimes against God is eternal separation from Him because no sin against Him is petty. He is holy, and His standard of law-keeping is perfection. That's the bad news. The good news is that in His mercy, God provided a judicial remedy. He accepted Jesus' death on the cross as a substitute payment for our sins – for anyone who would repent and believe.

"I'm listening," Joe responded when Grant paused.

"That's really the sum of it. Fair warning: the evidence of authentic repentance is a distaste for sin. It doesn't mean we're perfect. Far from it. But if we're converted, God will send His Holy Spirit to help us fight our sin," Grant assured. "The focus of our life will be pursuing God instead of pursuing our rebellion to Him."

The stretching friends returned their clubs to their bags and approached.

"You've given me something to consider, Grant. Are we good to tee off?" Joe changed the subject.

Grant saw that the previous group was replacing the flag pin in the hole. "Yup, you're good to go. Have a great game, fellas!" he encouraged the players.

The foursome moved to the tee box when Grant was startled by the sound of a cough right behind him. He spun around, coming face to face with Buddy, the golf ranger.

"How long have you been standing here?" Grant asked, wanting to gauge how much of his conversation with Joe Jacobs Buddy had overheard.

"Long enough," Buddy answered tersely and routed the conversation in his preferred direction. "There's some kind of doodle-mutt running around the back nine. I couldn't catch it because it's a skittish thing. Thought I'd warn you in case it wanders up here. You probably want to give your next group a heads-up, too. Sheesh, people need to control their animals better and not leave them wandering around. Somebody could shoot it," Buddy warned, pushing a long stray lock of his comb-over hair back into his golf cap.

Surprised by Buddy's suggestion the dog could be shot, Grant responded: "Well, it's not like it's a rabid coyote. I don't think people shoot at mutts – especially those sweet-tempered doodle things."

"Well, I'd shoot it. Might have to if it won't leave. Take it seriously, Grant," Buddy ordered and drove off.

Grant shook his head in disbelief as he watched him drive away. He'd keep an eye out for the dog, which, apparently, needed protection from the golf ranger. But even gruff Buddy couldn't dampen Grant's internal joy. He'd just shared the gospel with Joe Jacobs, and inside, he was praising God.

Chapter Eight

"These winds are crazy!" Marie exclaimed, settling on the couch for Thursday Meeting.

"Our daffodils will be destroyed," Ava lamented, sitting next to Marie and tucking a foot under her bottom.

June stood, peeked out the living room window, and surveyed the patch of flowers at the end of the lilac hedge. She noted hopefully, "Maybe they'll bounce back. But right now, they're lying on the ground."

"Are we ready to start da meeting?" Marcus asked without enthusiasm.

June reclaimed her seat in a chair next to Cal.

"Ready!" Grant exclaimed. "And I'll start us off. I'm happy to report that with the Good Lord's help, I was able to share the gospel with someone at work this week – a season pass holder. I didn't even have to be awkward and force the conversation; it just kind of came up naturally. And it wasn't as scary as I feared it would be."

"Good for you, Grant!" Cal encouraged. "That's an answer to prayer, dear!" Marie shouted, surprised this was the first she had heard about it.

"He didn't drop to his knees and say the Sinner's Prayer or anything, but he said I gave him something to think about," Grant explained.

"The rest is up to the Holy Spirit. He'll either give the man a soft heart and the gift of repentance or let him go on his way. But you were obedient, Grant. You did your part, and I'm proud of you," Elodie affirmed.

Grant looked at Marie to confirm he wasn't hallucinating the rare compliment from Elodie. She gave him a little wink in acknowledgment.

"Thanks, El. Well, that's all I have. Who's next?" Grant finished up.

Ava jumped in. "I got to see DeShawn and Mariana at the office today. She's taking someone's weekend shift at the hospital, so she has today and tomorrow off. I guess that's neither here nor there. Anyway, DeShawn came to see Jonathan and borrow a book, and I chatted with her for a few minutes. She said Kesha told her about the ruckus Christine Williams caused over them on Sunday, and, to their credit, it doesn't seem to be scaring them away. They prepared themselves for disapproval and resistance to their attendance since this is DeShawn's hometown, and everyone knows his business. I was hoping we could have them over for dinner one evening soon. We might offset some of the awful they have to experience with neighborly hospitality."

"That's a great idea!" June agreed. "Let's ask them for next Saturday."

"That's the Saturday before Easter," Marie recalled. "But there's no reason it wouldn't work if no one objects."

No one did.

"Anything else to discuss?" Elodie asked after a lull.

The friends looked from one to another and came up with nothing until Marcus asked in a muted voice: "What happens if someone in dis household tinks they've made a mistake in joining it?"

Every head snapped in his direction except for Ava, who lowered hers. She'd kept her promise to the women and spoken to her husband about what was weighing on his mind, so she anticipated what was coming.

"I thought our setup was like a Roach Motel. Once you check-in, you can never check out," Cal blurted, waving an index finger like a clock pendulum.

Elodie chuckled. "Hey, Marie! Remember when you were wantin' a name for this house? I think ole' Calculator has stumbled upon something here. The Roach Motel!" and she guffawed again.

Looking around, Elodie noticed no one else was laughing – their eyes sadly riveted on Marcus. "Oh, look what you made me do!" she lunged, taking a swing at Cal's arm and missing, faulting him for her untimely remark. "Sorry, guys," she apologized and sat back in her chair.

"Do you think you've made a mistake, Marcus?" June asked softly.

Alarmed, Grant interjected: "There's no way for any of us to take our money out now!"

"We know that, Grant," Ava answered curtly. "Nobody needs that reminder ever again."

Marie glared at Ava, her husband-defense system primed and ready to launch.

June's eyes widened as the tension escalated, and she reached for Cal's hand, gripping it. For a moment, the only sound was the wind howling outside.

"I don't know what I'm doing here," Marcus said, raking fingers through his wiry hair.

"Does anybody know what they're doing here? We're all figuring it out," Marie was blunt as a butter knife.

"Da opportunities are passing by! After dey let me go from da church, I didn't even consider dere would be anoder ministry position somewhere. But since I've been here, I've been contacted tree times. It was impossible wit what we were going tru last year, but I'm ready to tink about da future. I mean, I tink we're ready," Marcus corrected himself.

"I have questions." Elodie raised her hand as a signal she was going to speak rather than a request for permission to do so. "Will any future 'opportunity' guarantee you success and happiness? Cause it doesn't always turn out like we hope. And what part of a new 'opportunity' will be an upgrade to what you have here? A paycheck? A title? Fifty hours a week at 90 miles per hour? What exactly do you want from a new 'opportunity'?" She used finger quotes each time she said the word 'opportunity' to express her contempt.

Neither Marcus nor anyone else responded.

"And another thing," Elodie wasn't finished. "If you're lookin' for greener pastures because you're bored or unchallenged here, perhaps you should think about fixin' that. And that's all I'm going to say."

"Good, because you've said enough!" Ava barked at her, finger pointed at Elodie's nose.

June squeezed her husband's hand tighter. Marcus rose and trudged up the stairs to his bedroom, leaving those remaining in the living room in a wake of tension.

When she heard their bedroom door close, Ava stood, walked over to Elodie, and held out a fist for her friend to bump. A look of confusion passed over Elodie's face.

"Thank you for asking those questions and saying what you did about addressing his discontent here," Ava spoke quietly. "I can say the same things to him, and it doesn't register. It just hits differently coming from someone else. Tonight, you gave me a chance to be his defender instead of his challenger, so, thanks for that," she explained and smiled gratefully.

She turned and trotted up the stairs to console her husband.

When she was gone, Cal turned to his wife: "It's safe to release your death grip on my hand now."

June released both her husband's hand and the breath she'd been holding. "I hate drama," she muttered.

"Me too! I need a cookie," Grant slumped in his chair.

CHAPTER NINE

"Good to be back in the Garage Cave, gentlemen!" Bobby declared, strolling to the Friday evening game through the open overhead door.

"Sure is. I didn't mind picking up twigs in the yard this afternoon when the trade-off was being able to do it in short sleeves. Yesterday's wind blew us in some nice temperatures today," Grant replied, concentrating on wiping winter dust from the folding table and chairs with a damp rag.

"What do you have dere?" Marcus noticed Bobby had a covered foil pan in his hand.

"DeShawn made us a batch of lemon squares for our 'party' tonight," Bobby chuckled.

Marcus turned away, uncharacteristically disinterested in a dessert.

"We never called it a 'party' before, but he can call it what he likes if he's baking for it," Grant eyed the pan with great interest.

"How does he like using his 'Italian Masterpiece,' as my Junie calls it?" Cal inquired as they all chose a seat.

"He's thanked me for that stove a half-dozen times since he's been home. You know it was meant to be his high school graduation present, but it arrived after..." Bobby's voice dropped off.

Cal and Grant expected Marcus to jump in, but when he didn't, Cal tried to fill in.

"It arrived after he went on 'vacation,'" Cal suggested, pulling the foil covering off the pan.

Bobby chuckled. "Vacation, huh?"

"It was all-expenses-paid, wasn't it?" Cal quipped.

"It was that. But we should call it what it was: prison. It just hurts to put my son's name in the same sentence with that word, more so now than before he was released. I want him to be able to move on with life and not look back. Guess that experience might always lurk over his shoulder. I inadvertently heard parts of a conversation DeShawn and Mariana were having – something to do with an unpleasant neighbor." Bobby was fishing.

"Don't look at us!" Grant asserted, a hand raised as if stopping traffic.

"Oh, I know where to look if the subject is an unpleasant neighbor," Bobby responded bitterly, tossing his clean-shaven chin toward Christine William's house.

"She's probably unhappy. Marie reminded us da oder day dat she's also frightened. She's old, alone, and dere's a felon who's done hard prison time living across da street from her now." Marcus, now engaged in the conversation, tried to give a sympathetic explanation, avoiding retelling the scene at Grace Fellowship. He suspected the inflammatory details of that spectacle were just what Bobby wanted to find out.

"I should have let the old biddy have a stroke over her roses last summer. Maybe this year, I'll pull them off their stems like our little buddy Chase did," Bobby grumbled.

"And who do you tink she'd blame for dat?" Marcus argued.

"You're right," Bobby sighed. "Anything bad that goes down in this neighborhood will be blamed on DeShawn."

"Yes. Anoder ting to consider is dat DeShawn is a grown man. He doesn't need – and probably wouldn't welcome – any interference by you. You mean well, but he's not a boy. Show him you respect dat. It reminds me of something da Bible has to say:

Whoever meddles in a quarrel not his own is like one who takes a passing dog by the ears. Proverbs 26:17"

"Gonna get bit!" Bobby chuckled. "I didn't know the Bible said stuff like that. That's pretty practical advice."

"You should read it. I'll bet a lot of tings in dere would surprise you," Marcus suggested without pressure.

"Hmm," Bobby gave polite but minimal consideration.

"Don't mean to change the subject," Grant began, "but I'll forget what I want to say if I don't. The 'passing dog' verse reminded me there's been this skittish little dog – well, not that little, about 40 pounds – running around the golf course this week. Someone said it belonged to a couple who lived near Grassy Fields, but they moved and left the poor thing behind. No one can get near it cause it's wily. Our golf ranger, who has zero compassionate bones in his body, is threatening to shoot it."

"Wile E.? Like the coyote, Grant?" Cal asked, amused.

"Let's bag da Garage Cave and go catch it!" Marcus suggested impulsively.

"I thought you were pouting because you can't run away and join the circus," Grant jabbed the newly revived man sitting next to him.

"What?" Bobby twisted his head, puzzled.

"Don't listen to him. Are we going for adventure, guys, or sitting at home?" Marcus challenged his friends.

Grant, Cal, and Bobby exchanged shrugs.

"Adventure awaits!" exclaimed Bobby.

"Go get DeShawn. We're going to need some young legs. Also, grab some of Rover's cat food." Marcus was taking charge. "Cal, let's take your truck. It'll fit all of us and a dog."

"Do we need a net?" Cal inquired.

The men, rising from their chairs and wondering if a net was appropriate, responded with blank stares.

"Perhaps dynamite?"

The blank stares transformed into appalled grimaces.

"Or spring-loaded shoes from the Acme Company?" Cal added with volume, thinking louder might help his slow-witted friends catch the joke.

"We're trying to catch Wile E. here, aren't we?" he shouted with some frustration at last.

Finally, the guys got the reference to the old Looney Tunes cartoon character he'd mentioned less than two minutes ago and began to chuckle.

"That's a good one, Cal!" Grant remarked, grabbing the pan of lemon squares to take with them.

"Not if you have to explain it," Cal muttered in response, walking to retrieve his truck.

Chapter Ten

Cal's white F150 rolled in front of the Norman house when Bobby, from the right side of the back seat, yelled: "Stop!"

Cal reacted and hit the brakes, sure that Bobby had spared him from hitting a child about to dart in the street or something with equal potential tragedy.

"Hey! There's Micah. Let's enlist his young legs in our mission, too!" Bobby suggested.

"Hey!" Cal blurted in exasperation from behind the steering wheel; his voice pinched into a higher pitch. "Bobby nearly scared the driver to death with an imaginary crisis."

"My apologies, sir. Let me rephrase my request: 'Would you kindly decrease the velocity of your mechanical conveyance for the purpose of extending an invitation to our esteemed neighbor, Micah Eugene Norman, to partner with us in our endeavor?' I should have said that instead," Bobby responded sarcastically and lowered his window.

"By da time you said all dat, we'd be a block down da street," Marcus noted.

DeShawn, seated next to his father in the back seat, lowered his head, hoping his grin wouldn't evolve into audible laughter. He was enjoying the older men's sassy banter.

"Micah! Come here a second," Bobby shouted to the neighbor, who was arriving home late from work.

"His middle name is Eugene?" Grant asked over his shoulder from his front passenger seat as Micah approached.

"No clue. Just made that up in the moment," Bobby admitted.

"What's up, guys?" Micah asked, surprised to see Cal's truck packed with neighbors.

"We're going to catch a stray dog wandering Grassy Fields Country Club and could use your help. Are you game?" Bobby asked.

"Aww," Micah began to decline. "I'm just getting home from work, and I've got Chinese takeout for supper. I'm not dressed right, and it's been a rough day."

"It's a men's adventure!" Marcus yelled from the far side of the back seat, trying to sell the scheme.

A smile crept across Micah's face as he reconsidered the offer. It had been a long while since he'd smelled adventure, let alone tasted it. "Okay! Let me drop this food in the house for the family, and I'll be right back."

Cal parked in a corner of the country club parking lot, and the men formed a loose circle on the pavement.

"What's the plan?" DeShawn asked with a glance toward the fading light of the evening sky.

"The plan is to catch the dog," Cal responded simply.

"Find da dog, lure da dog, capture da dog, get da dog out of here," Marcus embellished the explanation with vague details.

"There's six of us," Bobby took control and organized them. "Let's divide into three groups of two and try to locate the pup." He opened a plastic bag of cat food and gave each man a handful. Next, he passed out lengths of clothesline rope for makeshift leashes.

"We can narrow our search to the back nine holes over to the right. That's where it's been hanging out," Grant pointed toward the setting sun.

"What's it look like?" Micah pitched out what he believed to be a reasonable question.

"Are you thinking you might encounter a pack of dogs out here and have to choose one out from among them?" Bobby mocked him. "If you see a dog, that's our dog!"

"It's a curly-haired mutt about 40 pounds. Tan and white," Grant offered.

"That's actually helpful, Grant. Why don't we search together?" Micah suggested, turning his back toward Bobby.

"Come on, DeShawn! You're my partner," Marcus claimed his help.

"Guess that means you're stuck with me," Cal nodded toward Bobby.

Forty minutes later, Grant and Micah returned to the truck, leading the frightened dog on a clothesline leash. Cal and Bobby congratulated them on their success but wore sheepish expressions of discomfort.

"You guys alright?" Micah asked with a furrowed brow.

"We fell into a sand trap," admitted Bobby.

"We weren't out there five minutes before we walked over the lip of a bunker. Just didn't see it. We fell in, rolled around trying to find our feet, and got sand in places where the sun don't shine," Cal explained, shaking a leg hoping to dislodge more sand.

"Kind of put an end to our adventure," Bobby added miserably.

Grant and Micah, imagining the scene, laughed.

"You're not hurt, are you?" Grant asked through his chuckles.

"Just our pride," Cal moaned.

"Hey, he's a handsome fellow!" Bobby bent to pet the cowering dog.

"Nope. She's a pretty lady," Micah corrected.

"Where's DeShawn and Marcus?" Grant looked around the truck and then into the pitch-dark course.

"They haven't come back," Bobby responded.

Grant handed the dog's leash to Micah, pulled out his cell phone, and called Marcus.

"Hello!" Marcus answered brightly.

"We got the dog. It's time to go home," Grant advised.

"Got just a bit of a problem wit dat. We're lost."

"Where are you?"

"In da middle of a golf course! I don't know where or how to even answer dat question?"

Grant rolled his eyes and took a deep breath. "They're lost," he whispered to Micah, Cal, and Bobby, who snickered unsympathetically.

"Okay. Go to the nearest tee and tell me what number is on the marker. I'll come to get you," Grant instructed.

"Dat's da place where da grass is short, and dere's a hole where a flag is supposed to be? Dere's no flags out here!" Marcus was entirely unfamiliar with golf and slightly panicked.

"No, that's a green. The tee is where you take your first shot."

"Dat is also not helpful!"

Grant took another deep breath. "Have you seen a bench in your travels?" he asked.

"Yes! We're sitting on one now."

"Near the bench will be a post with a number on it. What's that number?"

"What's da number on dat post, DeShawn?" Marcus sent his partner to find out.

"Da number is 10!" Marcus reported into the phone.

"Oh, good grief! Turn around and look for my phone flashlight. You're only 50 yards away from the truck!"

DeShawn and Marcus trudged across the ninth green and back to the truck, Marcus holding up his hand, pleading there should be no snarky comments directed toward them. Everyone got in the truck; the dog sat on Grant's lap in the front seat.

"So, where are we taking the mutt now that we've saved her from the ranger?" Micah asked.

"Home," answered Grant, stroking the dog's back to calm her.

Chapter Eleven

"Look what we found!" Grant exclaimed to the ladies making decaf coffees as he led the canine orphan into the kitchen by her clothesline leash.

"Where'd you find it?" Marie asked, hands firmly on hips.

"Not important at all," Grant responded. "Isn't she sweet?" He looked over his shoulder to Cal and Marcus for backup, who nodded their affirmation.

The grungy dog stepped forward and sniffed at the feet of the women, its matted tail wagging ever so slightly.

"We saw you leave in the truck," Ava informed the men with an accusation in her tone.

"It was Marcus' idea! He said we should have an adventure. The next thing I knew, we were at the golf course!" Cal caved under the pressure and sang like a snitch.

"Next thing he knew! Like his truck drove itself there," June needled her husband's excuse.

Marcus cuffed the back of Cal's head for ratting him out.

"We had to rescue this abandoned little girl before the golf ranger shot her as he threatened to," Grant appealed to Marie with puppy dog eyes of his own.

Elodie gingerly bent down to pet the dog, mindful of her painful lower back, and the pup rolled onto its back in submission.

"You want a belly rub, huh?" El cooed to the dog and obliged her.

Marie bent down next to them to give a little scratch to the dog's head, and Grant took this as a promising sign.

"She smells," Marie observed, wrinkling her nose. "She needs a bath." Marie stood again, tapping Elodie on the shoulder to follow and offering her an arm for support as she rose.

"This dog wouldn't be in our kitchen if you guys didn't want to keep her. We understand that," Marie began.

"But here's the deal," Ava followed up. "We're not certain if she's right for our household or we're right for her. So, she's on probation for a week. We'll decide next Thursday Meeting, and it has to be unanimous."

"Right now, we're not prepared to care for her. You guys need to go to Big Mart and get her food, bowls, a proper collar and leash, a brush, and a bed. Oh, and flea shampoo!" June insisted.

Grant put the clothesline leash in Elodie's hand, and the three men wordlessly darted out of the kitchen toward Cal's truck.

"Mercy!" Marie laughed when they were gone. "I guess they really want to keep this pup. But I have to admit, I've missed having a dog to take on my walks."

"She's a cute one, too!" Elodie agreed.

"She'll be cuter once she's had a bath," Ava added, wrinkling her nose.

"Mercy. I think that's a good name for her," June suggested.

It was after 10 PM by the time the dog was bathed, blow-dried, and brushed – a job undertaken by the Rennigers, Van Zants, and Elodie in the upstairs hall bathroom. When the task was complete, they took the fluffy dog downstairs to show her off to the Shermans.

"Come in!" June responded to the knock on their bedroom door.

"We know you guys are night owls and thought you'd like to see the finished product." Marie said, opening the door wide.

The dog bounded up onto the bed between June and Cal.

"Mercy!" June laughed.

"June, you're right. That name is perfect for her," Ava concluded.

"Mercy? No, her name is Wile E. like da cartoon coyote," Marcus insisted.

"It's kind of perfect for her," Grant agreed with him, nodding.

"She was hard to catch!" Cal informed the ladies.

The women exchanged grimaces among themselves.

"Please, no!" Ava pleaded.

"That's a horrific name for such a sweet girl," June objected.

"I hate everything about it," Marie frowned.

"Hasn't the poor dog suffered enough?" Elodie demanded.

"Dey seem to have a strong and united opinion about dis name. I guess 'Mercy' also suits her. It's girly, and she's a girl dog," Marcus conceded.

"I could live with it," Grant shrugged, happy to have the women invested in the dog's name.

"Aww. You guys are giving up too easily! 'Wile E.' is a hilarious name for a dog!" Cal mourned the impending loss of his name choice.

Marcus walked around the bed to Cal's side and gave him another cuff on the back of his head.

"Owww!" Cal wailed this time.

"First ting, you cannot talk about anyone else giving up too easily when you spilled your guts about us going to da golf course to get da dog, and it was my idea. Second ting, you are da man who wanted to give Grant a horse and name it Hoof Hearted, proving you have no aptitude for naming animals anyway," Marcus scolded.

"So, we won?" June asked timidly.

"Have 'Mercy'!" Ava introduced the dog by its new name with arms dramatically outstretched toward her.

Chapter Twelve

In the middle of the prelude, Christine Williams sauntered up the center aisle of Grace Fellowship Church to claim the front-row seat no one else wanted. It was the second Sunday in a row she had attended, and she was acutely aware that every eye in the congregation was riveted on her. She didn't crave the attention, but it did not bother her.

For the first time in her life, Christine wanted to be among the congregation, and it was now her intention to attend weekly and fully participate in the affairs of her church. At first, she hadn't appreciated the young pastor's ultimatum to put in a minimum monthly appearance or lose the church membership she neglected. But now that she'd complied, Christine determined to wield whatever influence her membership afforded. She believed her input was sorely needed to remedy the sloppy governance she'd observed and protect her interest in the church cemetery. Thanks to her, it would be a long time before the Pastor suggested re-interring anyone else's loved one.

Christine also wanted to keep close tabs on the McBride felon, whose release had disrupted her comfort, security, and nerves. If he were going to occupy her neighborhood and church, she'd be vigilant to detect any infraction that would send him back to where he came from. Grace Fellowship Church would be a handy venue to aid her purpose.

Beth Ann Sharp concluded her instrumental piece at the piano, and Pastor Jefferson approached the pulpit for the opening prayer. Bracing his hands on either side of the large wooden lectern, he bowed his head and prayed that God would reveal Himself and glorify the Son through the preaching of His word. As he did so, Christine Williams had a different conversation with God:

"It's a good thing I'm here. Better late than never, I guess. This church is in trouble, but I'll do what I can, God."

At the end of the service, Shelby turned to Chase to let him know she wouldn't be walking home with him and the neighbors. She and Will were going for lunch on Main Street. Latte Da returned the sidewalk table set-ups when the Spring weather arrived, and Shelby convinced Will it was the perfect way to ease back into patronizing the establishment after their disastrous first date there.

"Do you need a chaperone to keep your reputation pure?" Chase suggested impishly, hoping for a free cafe lunch.

A smile spread across Shelby's face, and she gave her nephew's hair an affectionate tousle. "I'm sure there will be other patrons to monitor us, but I appreciate your concern," she answered him.

"See you later, bud," Will grinned at Chase as he took Shelby's hand.

Will led Shelby to his car in the church parking lot and drove the few short blocks to Main Street, where he secured an on-street parking spot across the street from Latte Da.

"You know, you're running the risk we get tossed out of this place. I'm sure they still talk about me here," Will cautioned as they crossed the street toward the two-story red brick building with pink and white striped awnings.

"Oh, yes! I know for a fact you're a legend here," Shelby teased. "So what? I'm happy to make a return visit and show off the progress of our relationship. They'll be very impressed if I don't inspire you to toss your cookies again."

"Sure. Nothing says 'progress' like not running out on a date covered in vomit!" Will agreed, his feet shuffling toward the cafe. "But we are sitting outside, right?"

"It would be a sin to waste the Vitamin D available on a pretty day like this," Shelby confirmed.

They seated themselves at an unoccupied bistro set on the sidewalk and ordered sweet tea and chicken salad sandwiches on sourdough bread from the waitress attending outdoor customers.

"It was nice to see Christine Williams in church for a second week in a row," Shelby commented off-handedly as the waitress departed.

"Was it?" Will challenged.

"Wasn't it?" Shelby replied, perplexed.

"I'm not sure. Of course, I can't read her heart, but I don't get a strong humility vibe from her. Actually, I don't even detect a weak humility vibe. Humility springs from a repentant heart that understands the gravity of its sin against our Holy God. If there's no humility, there's no repentance. If there's no repentance, there's no salvation. And if there's no salvation, there's absolutely no indwelling Holy Spirit working Christ-likeness into us," Will explained.

"But isn't church the best place for unsaved people to be?" Shelby wondered aloud.

"Maybe yes, maybe no."

"Why on earth would it not be?"

"Jesus told a parable about the kingdom of heaven being like a man who sowed pure wheat seed in his field, but unbeknownst to him, his enemy came and sowed weeds that grew up with the wheat. The man instructed his workers to let the weeds grow until harvest, so the wheat would not be pulled up inadvertently. Jesus explained to his disciples that the wheat seeds were people who belonged to His kingdom, and the weeds were people who did not – the unbelieving unsaved. And even though they grew together in the same field, there would come a day of separation when the weeds would be thrown to the fire." Will paused to let her picture the imagery of the story. "Shelby, who do you think the enemy in the parable is?"

"Satan?" she guessed, tilting her head.

"That's right. In the story, the one who sows the weeds that stress the wheat is our Great Enemy, Satan. My concern is that, sometimes, the church becomes its own enemy by sowing the weeds ourselves. But our good intentions have a way of sprouting unintended consequences."

"Are you saying you think Christine Williams will bring unintended consequences to Grace Fellowship Church?"

"I'm saying anyone without the indwelling Holy Spirit of God working to make them like Jesus has significant potential to create havoc in the church," Will answered and sighed heavily. "She's already slapped Pastor Jefferson across the face. There's no telling what might be next."

A light breeze blew a strand of Shelby's strawberry blonde hair across her face, and she smiled as she pulled it away. "For some reason, I always imagined Satan never stepped foot in a church – like it had the same effect on him as daylight to a vampire. How foolish to imagine he waited outside until services were over and the people came out before he harassed them," she chuckled at her own naivete before growing serious. "It's a bit of a jolt to learn he doesn't stay in his own fields."

"He thinks every field is his," Will warned.

Chapter Thirteen

"Hey, Calzone!" Elodie, shuffling into the kitchen, greeted her breakfast partner.

"Hey, yourself, El Camino," Cal looked up from his bowl of bran flakes and smiled at her from his seat at the breakfast table. "What kind of trouble will you be causing today?"

Elodie scanned the room as if fearful of being overheard. Then she answered in a hushed voice: "Marie and I are plannin' to knock off a bank this mornin' - your June's our getaway driver. Then we've got an afternoon heist at the art museum. Followin' that, I have to work out what I'm makin' Saturday when DeShawn and Mariana come for supper. It's my turn to cook."

"Sounds like a full day," Cal remarked, unconcerned, and took a bite of bran flakes.

Elodie poured herself a cup of coffee and a bowl of peanut butter puff cereal. She joined Cal at the table and, grabbing the jug there, doused both cup and bowl with milk. Before digging in, she tapped a bit on the screen of her cell phone and replaced it in the pocket of her circle denim skirt.

"Morning!" Ava said chipperly, entering the kitchen dressed in her overalls, a cornflower bandana encircling her head, and with Marcus at her elbow.

"Gardening today?" Cal inquired as he reached down to pet Mercy, who'd walked in with the Van Zants and padded to his side to give him a sniffing once-over.

"We're tinking about gardening," Marcus corrected.

"We're at least going to the garden center to find inspiration – and possibly some cold-weather greens to plant," Ava clarified. "Really, we're just having a day-date," she added with a cheery grin.

"Coffee?" Elodie, her mouth full, nodded toward the pot on the counter. "Oh, rats! I dribbled on my good yellow blouse," she complained, wiping at the small stain with a paper napkin.

"Not today, tanks. Taking da wife to Latte Da for breakfast before garden center wandering," Marcus answered, ignoring Elodie's mishap.

The sweet notes of the hymn Softly and Tenderly wafted from the living room as June began her piano devotions an hour earlier than usual.

Cal noted his friends' surprised expressions at the change. "She's been having trouble sleeping," he explained.

"Does anyone in this house sleep through the night?" Ava laughed. "Of all the betrayals our bodies commit, I think that one hurts the most. I miss getting a solid eight hours like I did in my fifties," she lamented.

"Ah, the memories," Cal agreed.

"On dat note, we'll be off – before you bot convince me to go back to bed," Marcus took Ava's elbow and guided her toward the kitchen door.

Marcus almost closed the door when they heard Ava shout: "Moving truck! Look, Marcus, there's a moving truck across the street!"

Cal and Elodie exchanged hopeful expressions as Ava returned to inform them: "It appears the renters are moving out of the gray house across the street from the Normans."

"Aww," Elodie groaned as she and Cal lowered their shoulders in disappointment. "Thought it was ole Christine Williams packin' bags."

"Haha. No. The house next to hers has a moving truck parked in front of it," Ava confirmed. After sharing her news with her friends, Ava returned outside to join her husband for their day date.

"Well, perhaps the folks who move in will be more sociable than the ones leavin'," Elodie hoped.

When Cal didn't reply to her comment, Elodie addressed herself to Mercy as if talking to a baby: "Isn't that right, girl? Don't we want some more friendly neighbors? And maybe they'll have a doggy friend for you!"

Wagging her tail, Mercy understood Elodie's words as an invitation to approach and be petted. Elodie happily obliged her.

"You're not wearing that, are you?" Marie snapped at Elodie as she breezed into the kitchen.

Cal reacted involuntarily, raising his eyebrows in alarm at the condemnation in Marie's tone. He pretended to scrape nonexistent remains of bran flakes from his bowl while glancing side-eyed at Elodie to witness her reaction.

"Don't be ridiculous! I'll change into somethin' more suitable before we leave," Elodie reassured her.

"Good," Marie affirmed. She searched the cupboard for the pink mug with yellow flowers she favored. Once located, she squeezed a teaspoon of honey in the bottom and filled it with coffee. After a quick stir, Marie took a satisfying sip and seated herself at the table.

Cal was just about to excuse himself from the ladies' company when Marie turned to Elodie and whispered with just enough volume for him to hear: "I've got my black slacks and turtleneck laid out on my bed. But I can't find the ski masks! They were in the attic. You don't think June already got them, do you? I'll ask her when she's done at the piano. I'm so excited about our first big jobs! Two in one day, and they'll never suspect old ladies. But we need those ski masks!"

The color drained from Cal's face as he looked up and stared at the women who couldn't be planning what they appeared to be planning.

Elodie, disbelieving Cal's gullibility and her own success, couldn't keep it together and burst out: "Bwah ha ha ha!" She rose, leaving the kitchen and her dishes where they lay and laughing all the way down the center hallway.

Cal frowned with his entire face and turned to Marie. She slid her cell phone in front of him, which displayed a text from Elodie:

"Told Cal you, me, & June robbing bank & museum today. Play along."

"I was starting to trust that woman!" Cal was indignant. He rose, gathering his breakfast dishes and utensils.

"And now you know that was a mistake," Marie chuckled and sipped her coffee.

Chapter Fourteen

As far as spring days go, it was perfection – a cloudless sky and a warm breeze stirring the scents of lily-of-the-valley and peonies across the front porch. June sat alone on the glider, waiting for the school bus to arrive and deposit children on the grassy median between the sidewalk and street curb. She was hoping a particular child might stop for a chat before running home.

Punctual as a German train schedule, the school bus pulled up to the Cedar/Tamarack Street corner at exactly 2:50 pm and let two familiar children off the bus. Chase and Lovie chattered to themselves as they crossed Tamarack and headed home.

"Hello, Chase! Hello, Lovie!" June shouted to them.

"Hey, Miss June!" they responded in unison.

"Tell Aunt Shelby I stopped to say hi to Miss June," Lovie instructed her brother before peeling onto the walkway to her neighbor's front steps.

June, delighted her wish had come true, grinned as Lovie climbed the few steps onto the porch, plopped down on the glider beside June, and tossed her backpack haphazardly next to it.

"This pretty day has just gotten prettier since you've stopped to visit me!" June gushed to her young visitor.

Lovie smiled shyly in response, unusually reserved.

"Did you hear we have a new resident living in our house?" June tried to pique her interest.

"Really? Did they get the pink guest room?" Lovie responded and followed up quickly. "I hope it's a lady, then.

"Well, it is a lady, but she doesn't get her own room. Stay right here while I get her so you can meet her," June rose from the glider and opened the front door. "Mercy!" she called.

The shaggy dog obediently responded to June's call and trotted to the front door.

"Come on, girl," June beckoned her onto the porch.

"You got a doggie!" Lovie squealed, jumping from the glider and rushing to the dog, which was hugging June's leg.

Lovie crouched down and patted the dog, who responded by licking her face.

"Oh! She likes me!" Lovie swiped the short sleeve of her blue t-shirt over her mouth but was delighted.

"She does!" June agreed. "But we're not sure yet if she's a permanent or temporary resident. Mr. Renniger found her at the golf course, and we're trying each other out for a bit. It's a big decision."

"If you don't keep her, I'll ask Daddy if I can keep her!" Lovie offered, still stroking the dog's back.

"Ok, but I think we all like her," June changed the subject quickly. "I saw the big moving truck across the street from your house yesterday."

"Yup. The ghost family moved somewhere else!"

"Ghosts!" June exclaimed, feigning alarm.

"That's what Chase and Daddy called them. We never saw them outside – don't even know how many there were. But there were lights on at night," Lovie added.

"We saw their lights, too. Mr. McBride mentioned they didn't give out candy to Trick or Treaters at Halloween. Not friendly ghosts, were they?" June chuckled.

"Let's see if your dog will glide with us," Lovie suggested.

They returned to their seats on the glider, and Lovie patted the spot between them, inviting Mercy to hop up. The dog jumped up so quickly that Lovie barely had time to pull her hand out of the way. And the three of them swayed gently.

"She's so smart and friendly. What's her name?" Lovie asked.

"We call her Mercy."

"I like it," Lovie affirmed.

"And how was school today?" June inquired, interested.

Lovie sighed and remained quiet. She petted Mercy's head again.

"Something wrong?" June frowned, concerned.

After another moment of silence, Lovie answered. "Addy and Lena went on spring break together. Now they're best friends, and I'm not. They ignored me at recess and played by themselves – yesterday and today!"

"Oh, honey! I'm so sorry. I'm sure that hurts your feelings," June sympathized. She looked over the dog's head and noticed a tear sliding down Lovie's cheek.

"Trade places with Mercy," June instructed. Without waiting for Lovie to move, June gave Mercy a little push off the glider, scooped Lovie close to her side, and told Mercy: "Up, girl!"

When they were all situated again, June wiped the tear on Lovie's face with the hem of her pastel-striped tunic. Lovie leaned into June's side and replaced the erased tear with several more.

"Chase said it happened to him before," Lovie sniffled. "But he said it will be worse for him after the summer when he has to go to high school because he doesn't know who will be his friend after the summer changes everyone. Why do the summer and vacations have to change everyone?"

"I'm not sure," June answered off the cuff, trying to squeeze the memories of what it was like to be thirteen, like Chase, to the front of her mind. "I guess everyone grows up some over the summer months," she reasoned aloud. "But just because someone says their hurt might be worse than yours, it doesn't make you feel better, does it?" June returned to her immediate concern for Lovie.

"No!" Lovie agreed emphatically.

"I know Addy and Lena are being rude and unkind right now, but I'll bet it doesn't last. Sometimes friendships go through rough patches, but after the rough patch, you'll still be friends – often even better friends than before," June consoled, stroking Lovie's blonde locks.

"I hope so. And I hope this patch doesn't last too long. That awful Joey John might try to spit on me on the playground again if he thinks I don't have my squad to back me up," Lovie worried, tapping a foot in the air.

"I'm going to pray for you, sweetie," June promised.

And Lovie, not knowing what to say to that, decided it was time to go home. She wiped her cheeks with the palms of her hands, then wiped her damp palms on Mercy and laughed. Grabbing her backpack, she headed down the steps and hollered over her shoulder: "Remember, if you don't keep Mercy, I'll take her!"

"I'll remember," June hollered back to the little girl hopping down the walkway.

Though the visit had concluded, June continued gliding with Mercy, thinking about her young neighbors' worries concerning their friendships. It hurt her heart to think of theirs hurting.

Chapter Fifteen

Ava and Cal settled themselves in the living room and smirked as they observed Grant bolt up the stairs toward a bathroom, returning from his after-dinner constitutional.

"He's always quick and on time for Thursday Meeting. You've got to give him that," Cal snickered.

"He's got his system regulated like a Swiss watch," Ava agreed.

"I should be dat blessed!" Overhearing the conversation as he entered the room, Marcus contributed his two cents.

June, followed closely by Mercy, joined the friends in the living room, choosing a seat on the couch by her husband. She was about to invite the dog to occupy the space between them but hesitated.

"Is she allowed on the furniture?" June directed her question to no one in particular.

"I guess we'll decide dat after she's granted permanent citizenship," Marcus answered confidently.

Grant and Marie descended the staircase together and sat in the remaining chairs. Grant patted his lap to get Mercy's attention, and she left June's side and hopped onto his lap.

"No El Camino?" Cal noted it was time to start the meeting and Elodie's absence.

"No. Her back is bothering her. I told her to take an ice pack and go to bed," Marie explained. "But she gave me her proxy vote for the matter at hand," she added, reaching over to pat Mercy's head.

"So, do we hate this sweet girl or what?" Ava asked sarcastically.

"If we do, there's something wrong with all of us," Marie, leaning over, cooed close to Mercy's face.

"So, who are the heartless monsters who vote we should put her back on the mean streets?" Grant's question dripped with accusation. He mulled over putting the vote in those terms early that morning and had been practicing saying it all day.

No one raised their hand.

"Even mean old Elodie wants you to stay," Marie addressed the dog, assuring her it was a unanimous decision.

"I told you it wasn't going to be a problem," Grant spoke in Mercy's ear and tousled the fur on her head.

"Good! We're keeping da dog. June had asked earlier if we would allow her on da furniture," Marcus said with a question in his voice.

"Well, she's already up in Grant's lap," June noted with a hint of approval.

"Aww, I hate to be the party pooper, but I'd rather we didn't start that. The crewelwork chairs in the study would get ruined, and it wouldn't be good for the couch either," Ava bravely offered her honest opinion.

Grant nudged Mercy off his lap, and she gamely sat at his feet.

"Though I do love to cuddle a doggie during a movie on the couch, you make a good point, Ava," Marie supported her.

"I'll let you cuddle me on the couch!" Grant offered, twitching his thick eyebrows up and down.

"Me too!" Cal agreed enthusiastically, eyes shining.

Everyone turned to stare at him, and June swatted his shoulder with a heavy backhand.

"Oww!" Cal whined. "I agreed with Marie that I like to have a dog up on the couch when I watch television – not that I wanted to cuddle with her!"

"Well, you should have been a little quicker with your comment because we all heard you say you wanted to cuddle with Marie!" June admonished him.

"Moving right along," Marie, shaking her head, was eager to change the subject. "Grant said he saw a man putting a 'For Rent' sign in front of the gray house across the street. We should start praying for our new neighbors – whoever they might be."

"I hope it's a family with children to be friends for Chase and Lovie," June shared her hope. "They need friends close by over the summer."

"I never would have thought of that. I'm sure you're right," Marie nodded.

"Chase is worried about starting high school, and Lovie has drama with her little friends, Addy and Lena," June explained.

"Hmm," Ava was thinking. "I know there's an organization that promotes prayer around school flagpoles at the beginning of a new school year. Kids might need it just as much at the end of a school year because so much can happen to them over the summer.

"I'm not for starting a new organization, but what if we did it ourselves – met outside the school and prayed for all the kids?" Marie expanded on Ava's idea.

"Dat would be a good witness for Christ and a way to tell da kids we care," Marcus was getting on board.

"I bet I could put it in Grace Fellowship's bulletin, and we might recruit a few other parents or grandparents," Ava suggested.

"Plan it for a Monday or Friday when I'm off work, and I'll come too," Grant offered, not wanting to miss out.

"OK, we've got something new to do on our calendar," June said, pleased. "Do we have any other business to discuss?" she asked, taking uncharacteristic charge of the informal meeting.

"DeShawn and Mariana are coming for dinner Saturday evening. Does anyone know what's on the menu?" Grant asked, always interested in opportunities for special meals.

"Eye of Newt, I believe," teased Ava.

Grant rolled his eyes at the unserious answer and responded listlessly, "Eye of Newt, again? We just had that last time you cooked."

Marcus chuckled, and the look his wife shot him made him regret doing so.

"Elodie is supposed to cook – if her back is up to it. She said she was making her fried chicken and cole slaw," June reported.

"Now, that's what I'm talking about!" a smile returned to Grant's face at the prospect of Elodie's fried chicken.

"Not so fast, dear. Her back pain is a real problem, and it seems to be getting worse," Marie tried to temper her husband's enthusiasm. "If she's not doing better on Saturday, you'll get fried chicken made by the second stringers."

"Marcus, you got any clergy connections with healing oil?" Grant implored, only half-joking.

"That's sacrilege!" Cal fussed at Grant with a pointed finger.

"And so's your wanting to cuddle with my wife!" Grant snapped back, trying to stifle a grin.

"Why do you think I pointed out your inappropriate? To cover my inappropriate." Cal admitted with a smirk.

"You're welcome, then," Grant nodded at his friend. "Guess we're all done here."

CHAPTER SIXTEEN

Mercy announced the arrival of her neighbors with two sharp barks a few seconds before they twisted the old-timey bell in the antique front door. She skittered through the hall to greet them at the door, and Marcus followed.

"Hello, hello! Come right in," Marcus greeted DeShawn and Mariana, who had dressed nicely for the dinner invitation. He wore a light blue dress shirt and navy Dockers, and she wore a yellow belted shirt dress that contrasted with the wavy black hair that fell around her shoulders.

Marcus ushered them through the door and into the house. "Come on back to da kitchen."

"Your house is beautiful!" Mariana admired, scanning the study, center hall, and living room as she passed them.

"All da credit goes to da women," Marcus acknowledged.

The Shermans, Rennigers, and Ava greeted them in the kitchen, halting their dinner preparations to welcome their guests. DeShawn noted Elodie's absence.

"Miss Elodie have something better to do this evening?" he asked lightheartedly.

"She'd rather be here than where she is," June responded.

Marie provided more detail. "She's laid up in bed with sciatica. Poor thing can hardly move."

"Is she alternating ice and heat?" the nurse in Mariana kicked in.

"She is, and on pain meds," Ava confirmed, picking up a butter bell from the counter.

"I'm sure her bed is comfortable, but she needs to walk," Mariana advised.

Cal's hand flew to his mouth in reflex to her suggestion, but it didn't prevent him from blurting: "Oh, I hated when the nurses in the hospital would make me get up and walk after surgery. That's the meanest thing in the world when you already feel terrible."

"I get it," Mariana took no offense. "But you need to circulate the blood to help the incision heal and prevent blood clots. A stroke on top of what you have going on would be much worse. So, nurses insist that patients who don't want to walk, walk anyway. It's part of the job."

"Well, I insist we all walk to the dining room. Dinner's ready," Ava directed cheerfully.

They settled at the dining table, which Marie had taken care to decorate for Easter. It was draped with a robin's egg blue tablecloth and set with everyday white dishes on burlap placemats. Down the middle of the table, Marie had placed three glass vases filled with bouquets of pink, yellow, purple, and white tulips she'd purchased from Big Mart. And scattered among the vases were pastel-foiled chocolate eggs.

"Fried chicken!" DeShawn exclaimed when his eyes landed on the platter sitting on the buffet.

"It's Elodie's recipe, but not her hands that made it. It would taste better if it had been," June apologized, smoothing her apron.

"That woman can work miracles with a chicken leg," Grant said wistfully, grieved by the loss of her skill for this evening's meal. And then, not wanting to offend Ava and June, added: "But I'm sure this will be good, too."

"It's ok, Grant. God gave Elodie fried chicken as a spiritual gift, and we don't try to compete with it," Ava laughed. "Just choke it down the best you can."

"Well, it looks and smells marvelous, and I can't wait to sink my teeth in," DeShawn declared.

"I think just one piece for you, baby. Your stomach is not used to oily foods," Mariana cautioned.

Grant and Marie exchanged glances at the comment before Marcus suggested they give thanks for the food before it got cold.

Marcus prayed: "Holy Fader, we tank you for dis meal and dese new friends at our table. Most of all, we tank You for da Resurrection Sunday we'll celebrate tomorrow, and because of dat, da hope for our own resurrection someday. We give you glory for providing da Savior, Jesus, in whose name we pray. Amen"

"Amen," sang a chorus of friends and neighbors.

June rose from her seat and handed out the platters and bowls full of chicken, coleslaw, buttermilk biscuits, mashed sweet potatoes, and buttered green beans to be passed around the table. The triple-layer coconut cake decorated with jelly beans around its base remained on the buffet for dessert.

"Mariana and I would like to thank you all for everything you did to help Dad fix up the upstairs rooms for us. Honestly, we were blown away by your generosity, which continues with this wonderful dinner. I want you to know it means a lot to us," DeShawn commented as the chicken platter reached him. He took a single piece and passed it on.

"It was our pleasure," June assured.

"I love to decorate. You can believe it scratched a creative itch for me," added Marie.

"So, you're back from your honeymoon and settled. What's next for you, DeShawn?" Marcus had an urge to explore.

"Oh, he's going to look for a job and save some money for school," Mariana answered quickly.

"Oh," Marcus tilted his head. "And DeShawn," Marcus continued, looking directly at him, "your fader told us you're interested in Biblical studies. Have you tought about where you'd like to apply?"

"Jonathan Jefferson is campaigning hard for Southern, but we haven't decided that yet, have we, baby?" Mariana responded again.

Ava and Marie exchanged simultaneous glances and then looked to June, whose eyebrows were knit in a furrow.

"Nope. No decision about that yet," DeShawn confirmed. He then leaned toward his wife and consulted in a whisper: "Is the honey on the table for the biscuits or the sweet potatoes?"

"Either," she instructed.

After they'd said good night to their guests, the friends worked together to clean dishes and put away leftovers. Elodie sat in her purple chenille robe at the kitchen table, eating coconut cake and listening intently to the conversation swirling around her.

"I see trouble on the horizon," June shook her head.

"She treats him like a baby," Ava said, stopping to put her hands on her hips.

"She actually calls him 'baby,'" Grant recalled.

"Maybe he is a baby. He hasn't been in the outside world since he was 18," Marie tried to defend Mariana from accusation.

"Ha!" scoffed Cal. "Which place do you think is tougher on a man, the friendly Faircourt community or prison?"

"Well, there's that," Marie admitted. "But he didn't seem to resent her speaking for him."

"He will," Marcus, Grant, and Cal agreed in confident unison.

Chapter Seventeen

Cedar Street appeared to be hosting an Easter Parade. Dressed in their Sunday best, Ava, Marcus, Marie, Grant, and June were joined on their walk to Grace Fellowship Church by DeShawn, Mariana, Shelby, Chase, Lovie, and Micah. The latter two were guilted into coming by new believers Shelby and Chase, who claimed it was more important to go to Easter service than Christmas and reminded them they'd attended Christmas Eve service. It didn't hurt that Shelby bought Lovie a new outfit for the occasion – a light pink cotton dress smocked at the collar and embroidered with white rabbits holding orange carrots with green tops. New lace-trimmed ankle socks and white Mary Jane shoes completed the ensemble. Lovie vowed she would never wear anything else when she dressed that morning.

Cal and Elodie met them in the church vestibule, as they had driven to church in Cal's truck.

"I'll try to sit with you, but I'll probably end up standin' in the back of the sanctuary to ease my back," Elodie warned Marie.

"I'm surprised you're here at all. You do what you have to do, girl," Marie encouraged.

"Never missed an Easter service in my entire life. Today's not gonna be the first," Elodie determined.

The contingent entered the sanctuary except for DeShawn and Mariana, whom Jonathan Jefferson stopped at the Welcome Center. The pastor grabbed DeShawn and gave the larger man a bear hug.

"We waited a long time for this to happen, didn't we, brother?" Jonathan asked in a low voice, a bit choked up.

"That's right. So, you better preach a barn burner, friend. I didn't come to take a nap," DeShawn replied, giving him two sharp claps on his shoulder blade.

DeShawn released his Pastor and turned to escort his wife into the sanctuary.

"What was that? This isn't the first time you've been to a service since you've been home," Mariana asked, seating herself in the row behind the Norman family.

DeShawn slid next to her and answered: "All the years he visited me or talked to me on the phone while I was serving, we'd often look forward to the first Easter service I'd be able to come to Grace Fellowship. I guess we kind of agreed Easter is the culmination of the church calendar, and my first attendance would represent the culmination of God's purpose for my prison sentence. We picked an Easter service to look forward to. This service."

"You never told me that. It's sweet," Mariana tucked a hand under her husband's arm and gave his beefy bicep a squeeze.

Pianist Beth-Ann Sharp played *Christ The Lord Is Risen Today* as the prelude, which, as the people of GFC were becoming accustomed, coincided with Christine Williams' march down the center aisle to her front-row seat.

"Is it just me, or does Christine appear less haughty today? Her face seems a little less pinched than usual," June whispered to Marie.

"I don't know. Maybe," Marie strained to see what June saw, hoping she was right. "A little humility would look good on her. On all of us, actually," she corrected herself.

"True," June agreed, convicted by the accuracy of Marie's conclusion.

Pastor Jefferson moved from his seat on the dais to the pulpit and opened the service with a prayer of confession of sin and the need of, and thanksgiving for, a Savior. Then, he led his congregation in singing the triumphant hymn, Christ Arose.

Micah didn't sing the unfamiliar song, but his eyes fixed on the words on the hymnal page:

[1] Low in the grave he lay, Jesus my Savior.

Waiting the coming day, Jesus my Lord.

Chorus: Up from the grave, he arose,

with a mighty triumph o'er his foes.

He arose a victor from the dark domain

and he lives forever with his saints to reign.

He arose! He arose! Hallelujah, Christ arose!

2. Vainly, they watch his bed, Jesus my Savior.

Vainly, they seal the dead, Jesus my Lord. (Chorus)

3. Death cannot keep his prey, Jesus my Savior.

He tore the bars away, Jesus my Lord. (Chorus)

The words on the page conveyed reality and truth to Micah, and they struck him as ominous in contrast to the joy and comfort he sensed those around him found in the lyrics. He was relieved when the song ended, and Pastor Jefferson began his sermon. Unfortunately, his relief did not last.

The Pastor's text was 1 Corinthians 15:12-25 in which Paul addressed those who did not believe in bodily resurrection, likely because their culture had influenced them to believe separation from the physical world was superior. Pastor Jefferson explained from the text Paul's argument that bodily resurrection was inseparable from faith in Christ. It is only because Jesus was raised that we also have hope of a physical resurrection of our bodies.

It was only the second sermon he'd heard in his life, the first being the

---

1. Christ Arose, by Robert Lowery (1826-1899) Public Domain

one he'd heard Marcus deliver when they had the ice storm.

Micah understood the concept of death too well. But this business about a physical resurrection at some point was entirely new. He thought Christianity taught only a person's soul survived death, and he was iffy about believing that.

But the verse that arrested Micah's attention was verse 22:

For as in Adam all die, so also in Christ shall all be made alive.

As Pastor Jefferson preached, Micah understood that *only* those in Christ would be made alive because of his resurrection. And like the words of the hymn, it seemed threatening to him, and he felt the hairs on his arms raise. He wouldn't have known how to verbalize the reason for his discomfort if anyone asked.

He fidgeted purposelessly, looked at his watch, and wondered how much longer this uncomfortable service would last. Then he looked down at Lovie seated next to him. She caught his glance and rolled her eyes, wordlessly indicating her boredom. He was relieved she didn't seem to grasp the sermon's terrifying content. But he noticed Chase riveted to the pastor and that he wore a hint of a smile. Micah shook his head in disbelief.

It was over in another five minutes, and Micah relaxed. His only worry now was that his son would fish for a favorable comment on the sermon as they walked home.

Waiting his turn to shake his pastor's hand after the sermon, DeShawn overheard Christine's parting rebuke to him: "The women at the tomb is the traditional and appropriate text for an Easter sermon," she sniffed and exited the church with no expectation of a rebuttal.

"I enjoyed your Easter sermon for its freshness. Absolute fire, brother! The guy sitting in front of me was squirming like a worm on a fishhook."

Jonathan gave his friend a friendly jab with his free hand. "Seeing this day finally come was the best, man," he said, his eyes welling.

"He is risen," DeShawn responded with a wide grin.

"He is risen, indeed," Jonathan replied.

The moon, though not full, was bright enough to cast a patch of horizontal shadows across the ceiling of Micah's bedroom. He'd forgotten to close his blinds before going to bed, and now he stared at the pattern above, unable to sleep.

"Death cannot keep his prey," the phrase from the hymn he'd read, haunted his thoughts. He supposed it seemed good news in some way when the phrase applied to Jesus, but it seemed terrible news when applied to himself. If Pastor Jefferson was right and all people would one day rise from their graves to receive commendation or condemnation based on their standing with Jesus, Micah knew he would receive the latter.

"So be it," Micah said aloud to the shadows. He would go to hell and be reunited with Dahlia. He rose from his lonely queen-size bed, retrieved a bottle of bourbon from the shelf in the closet, and downed two sizeable mouthfuls. Whether it was to strengthen his resolve or weaken his fears, Micah wasn't sure. It didn't matter.

Chapter Eighteen

Marcus, sipping a mug of steaming black coffee as he entered the study, was startled to see Marie perusing the bookshelves before breakfast. She was looking over his theology books.

"Looking for someting in particular?" he asked.

"Good morning, Marcus. I was wondering if there might be something on these shelves that would help me be more people-y," Marie turned to look at him.

"Is da leopard trying to change its spots?" Marcus chuckled and seated himself behind the desk.

"It's that or give up. Why are you sitting? You're supposed to be pulling a book off the shelf that will help me," Marie protested.

"Tell me what being 'more people-y' means to you, and den I might be able to help you," Marcus was digging.

Marie released an impatient sigh and sat on one of the matching crewelwork chairs under the window.

"I was quite focused on finding a book, and I find it an irritating interruption to sit for a chat before that can happen. Doesn't that tell you everything you should know about my need to be more people-y?"

"It gives me a symptom, not a root cause," Marcus answered, undeterred in his quest for deeper conversation.

Marie sat back in the chair and crossed her legs, the synthetic fabric of her wide-leg camel-colored trousers dangling neatly. She thought for a moment before beginning.

"I understand God commands me to love my neighbor, which is people in general. And I don't have any problem serving them, other than..." Marie hesitated before admitting, "I don't love it. I mean, I get satisfaction from accomplishing something for someone else, but I'm not so heavy on the feelings for people themselves. Except for Grant, my boys and grands, and the people who live in this house, I'm not so emotionally invested – not like June is, anyway. Her heart melts over everyone else's problems. I tell myself God's word doesn't command us to be "emotionally invested," but to love; and love is action, not emotion. But everyone else seems to have this connection to other people that I'm lacking, and I'd like to fix that if I can. Is this making sense, or is it more symptoms? I'm hoping a book could help me find that root cause if you'd just point me to it," Marie suggested with a wry smile.

"I'm going to put you out of your misery and tell you dat book doesn't exist in dis library. And if you find it somewhere else, let me read it when you're done because I'd like to be more people-y, too," Marcus confessed.

Marie raised her eyebrows. "Well, you're not a ten like June, but I had you figured for a solid nine on the rating scale of people-y-ness."

"I give myself a six at most," Marcus stated. "I only lean in dat direction. I'm not a paragon."

"Had me fooled! Take, for instance, what you're doing now – making me talk when I meant to do something else. I've seen you do that over the decades with anyone who will stand for it. I thought you loved making people talk and bare their souls because you were some kind of relational junkie," Marie theorized.

"I'm a problem-solver. It takes drilling down to da root to properly discern a problem. Only when you get to da root, can you fix it. I like to fix problems, and it doesn't matter whose," Marcus shrugged.

"So, underneath all that apparent concern beats a heart as cold as mine?" Marie smiled.

"No. Nobody is as cold as you are," Marcus replied somberly, watching Marie's smile fade and her shoulders stiffen. And then, he burst out laughing.

"That was pretty cold," Marie's mirth joined his, and she stood to take her leave.

"On second thought," she sat again. "I'm not going to kid either of us that I want to solve your problem or that I could even if I wanted to. But I'm curious. Scratch that. I'm interested in how you're doing. Have you resigned yourself to gutting it out with all of us in Faircourt?"

It was Marcus' turn to sit back in his chair and ponder a question put to him.

"What if I never do anyting more significant for God's kingdom dan being da pastor dat I used to be?" he asked in response.

"Okay. What if?" Marie was game to travel the imaginary road.

Marcus frowned. "Dat was not what I expected you to say. I tought you'd try to encourage me."

"Welcome to the unexpected. Now, answer the question," Marie insisted.

"I can't," Marcus said, turning his head to look out the window behind the desk.

The study remained quiet for several moments except for the muted noises of those breakfasting in the kitchen at the back of the house. After a while, Marie spoke.

"I was reading my Bible upstairs earlier. I'm starting First Kings. King David is old and cold, and a beautiful virgin is brought in to warm and tend him. He's not even aware that his son, Adonijah, is usurping his throne. The last thing of note that he does is ensure Solomon is crowned as his successor while he's still alive. So, Solomon is king and David's in his last days, however long they lasted, just trying to keep warm."

"Are you saying I should lower my expectations to survival level?" Marcus turned back toward Marie, peering at her over the rim of his silver-framed glasses.

"I don't know whether you should or you shouldn't. What I'm sure of is that God didn't love David any less in his declining years than He did in David's productive years. Yes, David had a heap of victories piled up from his youth and, maybe like you, he longed to add to them in his later years. But no matter how many victories he amassed, none of it is the basis of his position in heaven today, and neither will yours. Whether you have served 35 years as a pastor or whether you have 10 more years to give, all that matters is what Jesus has done and none of what we've done."

"But I want to store up treasure while I can," Marcus said. "I want to do someting!"

"So do I, and we should," Marie agreed. "But I suspect my motives aren't always purely for future reward. Pride is my nemesis. I wonder how many of my good works will go up in flames when tried by heaven's fire because they were riddled with pride. Perhaps it's good to have a season of purifying stillness before God gives us our next assignment.

Marie stood again, realizing Marcus was not resigned to rooting where he'd planted himself and that she, indeed, couldn't fix that.

"I don't do da season of still very well," Marcus admitted.

"I don't know anyone who does, except maybe Elodie, who thrives in low gear," Marie responded and smiled. "For whatever it's worth, Marcus, everyone in this house loves and values you, and I'm going to pray you'll find treasure right here in godliness with contentment. I promise there's only a bit of self-interest in that prayer."

Chapter Nineteen

"Good morning, Buddy!" Waiting for the first foursome to arrive, Grant greeted the Grassy Fields ranger from his station at the first tee with a wave.

Buddy stopped his golf cart on the path and shouted back to Grant. "Heard that stray dog lives at your place now," he said with a hint of accusation.

Grant approached and rested a hand on the cart's roof. "That's right. We took her in, and now she's part of the family."

"What right did you have to do that?" Buddy demanded, his eyes narrowing and nostrils widening.

"I'm sorry. Uh, were you planning to take her?" Grant asked, astonished, and promptly withdrew his hand from the cart.

"I was planning to deal with the situation, but it appears you intend to do my job as well as your own."

"I assure you that was not my intention. I felt sorry for the poor dog being abandoned, and we just wanted to help. That's all," Grant explained.

"We?" Buddy raised a patchy arched eyebrow.

"Just some friends and me – I couldn't catch her alone."

"After club hours, I assume?" Buddy sought clarification and raised a brow.

"Yes," Grant admitted, realizing too late he'd broken employment rules by coming onto club property after hours and worsened the in-fraction by bringing others with him. The rule was written to deter teen employees of the club from after-hours shenanigans, but, to be fair, it applied to every employee.

"That's what I hate about you Christians – you're quick to tell everyone else their sin deserves punishment, but your sins are exempt because the rules don't apply to you. Well, you're a hypocrite, Grant Renniger, and that makes you worse than Joe Jacobs, who I overheard you preaching at last week. If anyone is going to hell, it's you," Buddy spat his words and drove his cart away in a fury.

Grant slumped onto the bench near the tee box, grateful Buddy's tirade had happened before the first golfers teed off. He was shaken and needed a minute to process the dressing-down he'd just received. Reviewing the conversation in his mind, he identified two things he'd done to make Buddy angry. He shared the gospel with Joe and violated employment rules to rescue Mercy. Furthermore, he recalled Buddy say-ing he hated Christians. Hated. He'd never heard anyone he knew assert that so bluntly, and it shocked him.

Grant formulated a plan to rebuild the relational bridge. After all, he had to work with the offended man, and he couldn't hope that doing nothing was an option. Perhaps the resolution might be as simple as asking Buddy what he expected him to do from now on. He decided he would search for the ranger after his six-hour shift and try to appease him.

"You look like you dropped your ice cream cone in the dirt," Joe Jacobs said, sitting on the bench beside Grant and playfully slapping his shoulder.

"Do I? Uh, er, just ruminating," Grant stammered, startled from his thoughts. He looked over and saw the rest of Joe's foursome beginning their stretching routine at the cart. They'd be occupied with it for a minute or two.

"Say, I'm glad we have a second," Joe began. "I was pondering what you said to me last week. I asked my wife, Allison, if she thought we should start taking the kids to church to give them some religious education, and she was all for it. She said she used to go regularly as a kid with her parents but had drifted away from church in college. Her family was Baptist. Anyway, she told me she'd been thinking about returning to church for some time but wasn't sure how I'd react. She said she was amazed that I brought it up, so she's gung-ho. I don't have a church background and don't know the first thing about picking out a church other than to search online. Could you recommend one? Can I ask where you go?"

Grant felt the heaviness in his heart fly away, and a smile crept across his mouth.

"Our whole household goes to Grace Fellowship Church on Sycamore Street. Jonathan Jefferson is the pastor and an excellent Bible teacher. We'd love to meet your family there this Sunday," Grant enthused.

"Jonathan Jefferson, huh? He was two years behind me at Faircourt High and best friends with a kid sent to Kentucky State Reformatory," Joe recalled. "Since he's a pastor now, I guess he's a little choosier about his friends."

"Not so much," Grant felt bad about Joe's assumption. "You'll see the kid who went to KSR at our church because he and Pastor Jonathan are still best friends. DeShawn was released last month."

"DeShawn McBride. That's right; that was his name. Wow. He sure did a long stretch." Joe tried to recall specifics of his case, which escaped him. He was a college sophomore away at Syracuse when DeShawn's case reached court.

"Church is the place for people who need forgiveness and second chances. I have to be on my thousandth chance," Grant said, trying to balance defending DeShawn and not alienating Joe.

Joe grinned. "Yeah, I guess church would be the place for that."

"Here comes your crew," Grant noted as the three men walked toward them.

"Grace-something, you said?" Joe requested repetition as he stood.

"Grace Fellowship Church on Sycamore. Hope to see you there," Grant obliged and waved the men onto the tee box.

It was a steady day on the golf course, with one group following another throughout Grant's shift. When it was over, he set out to look for Buddy in a cart he borrowed from the clubhouse. He drove around the entire course and discovered Buddy was nowhere to be found. Before giving up, Grant drove to the Pro Shop to inquire whether the attendant there had seen him. Indeed, she had. She'd seen Buddy clock out hours ago. He'd gone home early.

"This is a disaster!" was Grant's first thought, assuming Buddy's temperament would be inclined to dwell on and magnify his offenses before Grant could address them. His second thought was to pray.

"Father God, Your word says I shouldn't fear what man can do to me, but I admit being concerned about what this man, who says he hates your people, may do. He seems so irrational. So, Father, I pray you would help me, by the power of Your Holy Spirit, to put all my confidence in Your sovereignty and goodness. Perhaps in Your wisdom You know this isn't the time for me to talk with Buddy and have worked this out for my good. I'm sure that wherever Buddy is, You see him. Father, in Your mercy, melt his stony heart and draw him to Yourself. This spiritually dead man cannot be reborn by effort of his own. So, I ask You to give him new life for the glory of Your Son, Jesus Christ, in Whose name I pray. Amen."

Chapter Twenty

A bit of gardening therapy was just what Marie needed after a light supper of Ava's homemade French onion soup and potato rolls. The stretch of perennial shade garden between the house and the driveway needed to be thinned, and Marie had been cooped up in the house all day, engrossed in preparing her Sunday School lesson. So, when her husband set out for his post-supper walk, and the other ladies headed for the front porch to take in the evening air, Marie gathered gardening tools and set to work dividing lily-of-the-valley and hostas.

She could see Christine Williams across the street from her position on the side of the house, fussing with her roses. Marie waved when she thought her neighbor was looking her way. Christine raised her hand almost imperceptibly in response and turned back to her work.

"Hmm. At least I'd beat her hands down in a who's more people-y contest," Marie mused to herself and grinned. She continued to work, setting aside thinned lily-of-the-valley plants on the driveway, thinking of starting a new patch on the shady side of the Garage Cave.

"Greetings, neighbors!" Marie heard Ava's voice boom from her seat on the front porch.

"Good evening, ladies," Bobby's voice responded.

"Hi, girls," Mariana answered playfully. "Someone's missing," she observed quickly, climbing the porch steps followed by her father-in-law.

"Oh, Marie's around the side of the house digging up flowers," June answered, pointing toward the driveway.

"Hello, Miss Elodie," Bobby nodded toward her, singling her out for special acknowledgment, yet careful not to smile.

He received a simple nod from her in return.

"How's your back feeling today?" Mariana asked her.

"Well, I'm outside and upright, so I guess it's not too bad," Elodie answered, confident her response would not elicit further medical suggestions from the zealous nurse.

"Then you should be walking. It's the perfect evening for it," Mariana advised.

Elodie scowled, but Bobby saw an opportunity.

"I'd be pleased to offer you an arm to aid in your physical therapy," he piped up and took a few steps toward her chair.

Elodie glanced at Ava and June before responding to the invitation. "Well, since you're here," she stood with a hint of a smile at one corner of her mouth and placed a hand on Bobby's shirt-sleeved arm.

He helped her navigate the few porch steps and ambled down the walkway to the sidewalk, where they turned right. When they reached the driveway, Marie, who had heard all the porch conversation unseen, shouted at Bobby: "Have her back before midnight!"

"I will!" Bobby played along while Elodie threw her free arm in Marie's direction and hissed: "Hush yourself!"

Marie walked down the driveway until she stood at the side of the porch.

"Did you ever think you'd see that sight?" she asked the women whose eyes were still watching Elodie and Bobby walking down Cedar Street.

"You could knock me over with a feather," June declared.

"Hell must be having an ice storm," Ava shook her head in disbelief.

"What's so unbelievable about DeShawn's daddy and Miss Elodie taking a walk?" Mariana was perplexed.

Marie, Ava, and June erupted in spontaneous laughter.

"What?" Mariana demanded, placing her hands on her hips.

Marie approached, walking past the boxwoods surrounding the porch, and climbed the steps, sitting next to Ava on the glider. She motioned for Mariana to sit in the chair previously occupied by Elodie.

"She's been horrible to him," Marie winced.

"Didn't like him from their first meeting and wouldn't give him the time of day afterward," June continued.

"But something's changed," Ava added brightly.

"Well, she's been friendly to him since I've known her. She came over to the house when we got back from our honeymoon and helped Dad make corn pudding for us," Mariana submitted this evidence for her case.

"She never did!" June slapped her own knee.

"She slipped that past us," Ava raised her eyebrows.

"She didn't tell us. That rat!" Marie grumbled.

"Now that I think about it, she's been less hateful to him since about Thanksgiving," Ava recalled.

"And wasn't her New Year's resolution something about treating certain people better and being more Christlike?" June wondered aloud.

"Tell me, is Dad McBride sweet on her or something?" Mariana wanted to know.

June, Ava, and Marie looked amongst themselves for an answer, and June came up with one she thought they would agree on: "I don't know if he's sweet on her exactly, but he's always a gentleman to her."

"And kind," Ava added.

"That's just how DeShawn treats me – so very kind. Guess he learned it from his daddy," Mariana gushed.

Marie responded intentionally: "Oh, no! Then it will be even harder for you to accomplish Romans 12:10 – that verse that says we're to outdo one another in showing honor." She added a lilting laugh to her comment so it wouldn't sound preachy to the young wife.

Mariana smiled at first and then pursed her lips. "Maybe he should level down a bit. Then, I might stand a chance. The problem is, I can't seem to stop being his advocate and voice now that he's out of prison. That was my role for the past five years – to speak for him and handle things on the outside. I'm having difficulty stepping back and letting him answer for himself now. It's a bit of an issue at the moment if you want to know the truth," she admitted and lowered her head.

June scooted her chair closer to Mariana and put an arm around her shoulder.

"That makes sense," Ava began. "Of course, it would be hard for anyone to make that adjustment, and it'll take time.

"How mature of you to recognize the problem and shine a light on it by sharing it with us. I'm impressed," Marie encouraged Mariana. "This is one thing the Body of Christ is meant to be for one another – a safe place to share our struggles. Satan loves darkness, and when we hide our struggles in the darkness like a shameful secret we have to keep, then he can keep accusing us about them. But when we bring them out into the light, he flees and takes his awful influence with him."

Mariana's countenance brightened as she lifted her head. "Thanks," she whispered.

At that moment, Grant sped up the walkway, bound for his regular destination upstairs. Through quick breaths, he managed to ask before he walked through the front door: "I passed Bobby and El walking down the street. Are we in the new Heaven and new Earth right now?"

The ladies on the porch giggled.

"Well, I'd better get back to my little patch of shade garden," Marie said as she stood and brushed dirt from the tops of her wide-leg jeans. "I've pulled some lily-of-the-valley out to give the others some breathing room, and now it's time to tackle the hostas."

"Lily-of-the-valley was my mother's favorite flower," Mariana smiled at the memory.

"You must take the ones I've pulled out!" Marie insisted.

"Really? I can have them?" Mariana felt elated. "Oh, but I guess I should ask Dad if digging up a spot for them is okay. DeShawn's mother, Julia, planted the pink azaleas in front of the house. They have fat buds on them now and will be gorgeous soon. Dad said he wouldn't mind if I added flower boxes to the front porch to keep the color through the summer. I love her color choice of pink flowers against the yellow house. It's so cheerful. Anyway, I've never gardened before, and between flower boxes and a patch of lily-of-the-valley, I'll get my feet wet."

"Your father-in-law won't deny you, girl," Ava assured.

Mariana followed Marie around the corner of the house to retrieve the flowers.

"We were wrong about her," June admitted in a low voice.

"We forgot it's hard to be newly married, which they are even though their license says it's been five years," Ava acknowledged.

"I'm going into the house to practice honoring my Cal," June rose from her chair.

"Poor guy won't know what hit him," Ava chuckled.

Chapter Twenty-One

Grant flinched at the piercing ring of the cell phone on his nightstand as he was tying his shoes at the edge of the bed. He reached for the phone and then locked eyes with Marie, sitting up in bed with her open Bible in her lap. They shared an unspoken understanding that calls this early in the morning were unlikely to be good news. And with Grant's mother nearly 95 years old, they lived with dreaded anticipation of a bad news call from Pleasant Pond Retirement Village.

"Hello," Grant answered the phone on its third ring, although he sat right next to it.

Marie strained, unsuccessfully, to hear anything coming from the speaker at her husband's ear. Grant listened without comment for a minute before responding to what he heard in staccato sentences.

"Yes, I understand. I'm very sorry. Goodbye."

He tossed the phone back on the nightstand in frustration, and it slid across the polished wood and fell to the floor. Then he kicked off the sneakers he'd just put on and faced his wife.

"Not going anywhere now. I just got fired by the Club Manager," he informed her as his shoulders drooped.

"What on earth? Why?" Marie was dumbfounded.

"Proselytizing players seemed to be the main complaint, but bringing the guys on the course after hours to rescue Mercy sealed my fate. I know the golf ranger blew me in to the boss." Grant drew his feet up on the bed and laid down with his hands folded across his abdomen as if positioned by a mortician.

"They fired you for sharing your faith?" Marie was incredulous.

"Apparently, that creates a hostile environment for club patrons and other employees," Grant spoke to the ceiling.

"Oh, honey, I'm so sorry! I know you loved that job. Aww," Marie set her Bible on her nightstand and snuggled up to her husband.

"I thought I was doing the right things for the right reasons," Grant lamented.

Marie propped herself on an elbow. "Would you change what you did?" she challenged.

Grant pursed his lips and shook his head from side to side in quiet response.

"It's never wrong to do the right thing for the right reasons," Marie assured him.

"I guess. But it doesn't feel great now." Grant was glum.

Marie rolled away from him and stood up, sliding her feet into pink fuzzy slippers and wrapping her pink and white-striped bathrobe around her.

"Just stay right here. I'm going downstairs to make your tea and honey. Let me serve you on the first day of your second retirement," she instructed cheerfully. "I'll be right back."

Grant listened to Marie's fading footsteps as she descended the staircase. Besides the tea, it occurred to him that something else might be helpful. He checked the time again on the nightstand clock and debated with himself for a few moments. Eventually, he stood, retrieved his phone from the floor, and sat in one of the white leather recliners at the foot of the bed. Then, he called his mom.

"Who's dead?" G-Lu answered brightly after noting her son's number on the caller ID. She'd obviously been awake for some time.

"Mom, you are a piece of work. Sorry to disappoint, but no one's dead. I just wanted to talk. I got fired from my job this morning," Grant blurted into the phone.

"Oh, that's too bad," G-Lu soothed pragmatically. "What happened?"

"I created a hostile environment by sharing the gospel, and I broke a club rule," Grant recited his crimes.

"You say you were fired for sharing the gospel at work?"

"And breaking a club rule."

"But you proclaimed Christ?"

"I did."

"Son, I'm so very proud of you. That's the best reason to get fired from a job. If you get another one of those starter jobs, I hope you'll get fired from that one for the same reason. You should start looking today. Don't let grass grow under your feet about it, you hear me?"

Grant couldn't stifle a chuckle. "If I'm hearing you correctly, your advice is to get fired from another golf course?"

"Well, no. It doesn't necessarily have to be another golf course. But I know those places offer your preferred employment because of the benefits. As far as I'm concerned, you could get fired from a burger joint for sharing the gospel just as well," G-Lu clarified.

"Duly noted," Grant replied, searching for more to say.

After a moment, G-Lu picked up on what was left unsaid: "It wasn't supposed to turn out this way, was it? You thought God would bless your evangelism efforts with souls and success, didn't you?"

"I guess I was hoping that's what would happen," Grant confirmed, though slightly defensive.

"We all do, dear. There's nothing wrong with wanting to see fruit from our labors. But God doesn't guarantee we always will, at least on this side of heaven. But don't worry. You know He is building His church and will not fail. The only part we're responsible for is faithfulness in proclaiming His gospel, and you did that. That's why I'm proud of you, son. By the grace of God, you did your part."

Grant smiled, encouraged by his mom's words. "You're right. It was by the grace of God, Mom. I'm not a natural or gifted evangelist, though I've always admired the ones I've known who were. But gifted or not, I still wanted to share the gospel and prayed for the opportunity at the country club. One day, God brought this guy that I sort of knew to the first tee, and we talked about death. I knew it was a wide-open door to share the gospel. And I did. It might not have been eloquent or professional, but with God's help, I did it. And guess what? I saw the guy yesterday, and he said he might bring his family to Grace Fellowship." Grant was growing animated.

"Well, how about that!" G-Lu exclaimed. "You may see that fruit after all."

"Yeah, I forgot to tell Marie about that part," Grant remembered.

"You forgot to tell me what?" Marie walked into the bedroom carrying a bed tray with coffee for herself, Grant's tea, and two peach scones made by June.

"I hear your Marie. Tell her I love her, and we'll catch up soon," G-Lu was ending the conversation. "But Grant," she continued with a parting reminder, "don't forget to look for another job to get fired from!"

"We'll see, Mom. I love you. Bye."

Marie set the tray on the edge of the bed and handed Grant his tea and scone.

"By the amused look on your face, I gather a chat with your mom was helpful?" Marie guessed.

"She has her way," Grant acknowledged with a broader smile.

"Indeed, she does. Now tell me what you forgot to tell me," Marie insisted, sitting in the matching recliner with her coffee to listen to her husband's story of God's work in Joe Jacob's family.

CHAPTER TWENTY-TWO

"What's up, neighbors?" Bobby greeted his friends as he strolled through the raised doors of the Garage Cave on the overcast mid-April evening, his cat, Rover, marching along at his side.

"My weight!" Cal looked over his shoulder from where he stood, puttering at his workbench and grinning. The success of his cancer treatments had stimulated his appetite, and no carbohydrate was safe in the house if Cal could get his hands on it. "Look-y – my britches fit me again." He turned, slid two fingers inside the waistband of his overalls, and tugged at the denim to demonstrate its snugness.

"If he keeps it up, he'll be able to play Santa Claus at Faircourt's tree-lighting event dis year," Marcus suggested.

"If he keeps it up, you and I are going to look trim in comparison, and then our wives won't watch our snack intake like line judges at a tennis match," Grant hoped.

"Good point," Marcus noted, pulling out a chair and sitting at the card table.

The other men joined him and spent the next ten minutes figuring out how to play a card game called Five Crowns, which G-Lu recommended to Grant, extolling it as the popular game at Pleasant Pond. They finally commenced play but quit halfway through because everyone of them kept discarding valuable wildcards, forgetting the wildcard changed with successive hands.

"How do people in the old folks' home enjoy this game? It's maddening," Bobby complained and tossed his cards on the accumulated mound in the center of the table.

"My mother has probably figured out a way to supplement her income by playing with the residents who have poor memories," Grant chuckled.

"She'd have made a killing here with us," Cal admitted. "I mean, hypothetically, if we gambled, that is."

Bobby sat back in his chair and stretched his legs under the table. "It's tough, this business of aging. If I don't write it down, I'll forget it. Even that's not foolproof because sometimes I forget where I've put what I've written down. See what I have to do?"

He pulled his cellphone from his back pocket. Attached to it with a rubber band were a small notepad and pencil. He held it in an outstretched palm for the others to view.

"You realize you can just type notes for yourself on da phone. Dere's an app. Den, you could get rid of dat paper and pencil," Marcus suggested.

"You're funny, Marcus. I suppose it's theoretically possible, but with my limited technology skills, it's not bloody likely," Bobby retorted, shaking his head.

"Somebody's been watching British television again," Grant teased, changing the subject.

"Well, not me. I just overhear through the heat registers what Mariana's watching upstairs sometimes," Bobby explained.

"Got your ear to the ceiling, do you? Overheard anything interesting?" Cal prodded with a sly grin.

"No, sir! Do you think I'd want to eavesdrop and overhear something I don't want to know? Nope. Don't want to hear what my son and his wife say to each other in private – not even a little." Bobby was adamant, shaking his head vigorously.

"You've repeated what da wisest man in da Bible says about dat subject," Marcus remarked. He always looked for ways to introduce Scripture into conversations with Bobby and to show him areas he agreed with.

Bobby responded with a raised eyebrow, which Marcus interpreted as an invitation to explain.

"King Solomon said:

Do not take to heart all the things that people say, lest you hear your servant cursing you. Your heart knows that many times you yourself have cursed others. (Ecclesiastes 7:21-22)

You're right not to want to eavesdrop on private conversations because you've probably said things you shouldn't have and wouldn't be glad for others to know about," Marcus elaborated for Bobby.

"Oh yeah," Bobby agreed. "Me and King Solomon know what's up."

Grant winked at Marcus in silent recognition of the minor accomplishment with Bobby while Cal gathered the cards into their tin and regretted fishing for gossip about the young couple.

"Hey, Cal, since you're back to dabbling at your workbench again, what would you charge to make me a couple of flower boxes for my porch railing? Mariana wants to add a feminine touch to the old bachelor pad and asked if she could put up flower boxes," Bobby asked, providing his motive.

"Just bring me two eight-foot boards of teak or cedar, and I'd be happy to make them for Mariana at no charge," Cal answered, grateful for the opportunity to make up for his previous error.

"I'll pick them up at the hardware store and have them to you tomorrow afternoon. Thanks, Cal, I appreciate it."

"If you want some company to go to the Man Mall, I'll be happy to go with you. Marie says she'd gotten used to my getting out of the house, and getting fired from the country club has cramped her routine," Grant offered.

"You got what?" Bobby didn't believe what he had just heard.

"Canned. Axed. Kicked to the curb," Grant elaborated, long-faced.

"Why?" Bobby requested an explanation.

"He shared da gospel wit a golfer," Marcus informed him.

"They fired you for that? It doesn't seem right. I'm sorry, Grant," Bobby sympathized.

"Don't be sorry. He'd do it again," Cal assured and shrugged his shoulders.

Bobby didn't doubt it. As the guys moved their conversation back to the delights of the hardware store, otherwise known as The Man Mall, Bobby reflected on the solid commitment to Jesus demonstrated by these men over the past year. He understood they prioritized their relationship with Him above anything else and would bet his truck on their continued faithfulness. He'd never known anyone like them. And now, he thought, maybe it wouldn't be so bad if DeShawn was like these religious neighbors.

CHAPTER TWENTY-THREE

Grant, Marie, Ava, Marcus, and June stood on their porch dressed in their Sunday best, waiting for DeShawn and Mariana to begin the three-block parade of neighbors to Grace Fellowship Church. Elodie had pleaded with Cal to leave early and drive them to church before Mariana had a chance to pressure her to walk for her back's sake. He agreed after extorting a promise from El to make her chicken pot pie this week.

"Here they come," June announced, peering between branches of the large magnolia tree in the yard to see DeShawn and Mariana crossing Tamarack Street.

Mariana looked like a picture of Spring itself, wearing a cap-sleeved cotton dress of tiny pink roses and white polka dots on a Robin's egg blue background with bits of white cotton lace on the Peter Pan collar and short sleeves. She held hands with her husband, who wore a mint green, lightweight sweater, navy chinos, and a broad smile. It was identical to the one his father frequently flashed before Marie told him to knock it off if he wanted to be friends with Elodie.

The friends on the porch joined the McBride couple on the sidewalk, exchanged greetings, and assimilated Shelby and Chase Norman into the contingent when they reached the bottom of their driveway. Eager for a catch-up chat with Marcus, Chase wheedled his way between Marcus and his wife, forcing Ava off the narrow sidewalk. Used to this maneuver,

Ava good-naturedly ceded her position and moved back to walk with June. As she turned, a glimmer of gold caught her attention on the other side of Cedar Street.

"Don't look now, but I think Christine Williams is walking to church this morning," she said in a stage whisper so the group could hear.

In mass disregard of Ava's instruction, every head turned to the left to see if it was so. And it was.

"I think I'll go over and walk with her," Marie announced, stepping away from Grant's side onto a grassy median between the sidewalk and curb.

"No!" DeShawn insisted, stopping Marie and everyone else in their tracks. "Let me do it. I've got to talk with her – show her I'm not a threat to her." Despite his phrasing, DeShawn wasn't asking the group's permission but informing them of what he intended to do.

Marie returned to her spot next to her husband, and DeShawn crossed the street toward Christine Williams.

"Fools rush in..." Ava shook her head and left her comment unfinished.

"I can't watch," Mariana winced.

"Maybe I should go with him. She told me I was 'tolerable,' and that might be enough social currency to help," Marie suggested.

"I'd like you to stay here with me, if you don't mind," Grant reached for his wife's hand.

"You're not scared, are you?" Marie teased.

"Of her? Yes, I am!" Grant confessed. "Not for myself, but for you. Okay, a little for myself, too."

Marie squeezed his hand. "Okay. He's on his own, then."

"Mrs. Williams!" DeShawn called out when he was only 15 feet away from her.

Christine came to a halt and jumped off the sidewalk onto the lawn of the gray house next to hers when she saw the man approaching her.

"Don't come any closer!" she shrieked at DeShawn.

DeShawn came to an abrupt halt and raised his hands as if surrendering. "Mrs. Williams, I just want to speak with you for a moment," he pleaded.

"I don't need to speak with you; I don't want to speak with you; and I don't have to speak with you," Christine retorted and stepped back onto the sidewalk to reclaim her space, regretting she'd let him see her momentary fear.

"You're right, you don't. But I wish you would. I just want to tell you…"

"Aht!" Christine cut him off and held her palm up to him. Then, she turned her back on him and proceeded to walk away.

"I just want to tell you, 'I love you,'" DeShawn finished what he had to say, even if it was to her back.

Christine kept walking, but her mind was reeling. She wondered what had possessed the felon to say those words. Absentmindedly, she reached into the pocket of her cashmere sweater and fingered the laminated florist card there – the one she'd gotten last summer that contained the words 'I love you' and was signed LYE. It would be a cruel disappointment, she thought, if DeShawn McBride had been the one who'd sent her the card and flowers.

"Impossible," Christine muttered to herself as she hurried her pace to Grace Fellowship.

DeShawn crossed the street again, back to his sympathetic wife and neighbors, who had heard the entire exchange.

"Well, dat was not received so well," Marcus stated the obvious.

"You're a glutton for punishment," Shelby rebuked DeShawn with a wink.

"Why did you tell her you loved her?" Mariana asked, genuinely surprised.

Marie jumped to DeShawn's defense: "That's what we're supposed to do to our enemies."

"Well, there's that," DeShawn smiled gratefully at Marie. "But to tell you the truth, I have no idea why I said it. I wasn't planning to say it. I just wanted to let her know I'm no threat to her – maybe show off a little of the McBride charm. I thought I'd appeal to her as a brother in Christ. But when she wouldn't let me speak, I just blurted out what came to my mind that summed it all up."

"You're a bigger man than I am," Grant said with sincere admiration.

"Me too. I would never have the guts to do that," Chase looked back at DeShawn in awe.

Mariana placed her hand back in her husband's, and the group continued their walk to church. Eventually, all crossed Cedar Street, walking several paces behind Christine Williams for the final block.

When the neighbors reached the church parking lot, a voice rang out. "Hey there, Grant!"

When Grant looked across the lot to identify who had hailed him, he spotted Joe Jacobs striding toward him with his wife and children in tow.

At the end of the worship service, Pastor Jefferson brought DeShawn and Mariana McBride to the front of the sanctuary and recommended them to the congregation for membership. When the show-of-hands vote was taken, Christine Williams, from her front-row seat, not only raised her hand in objection to their admittance but stood. Emboldened by her assertive action, two other women and a man joined her. In the church's 90-year history, no one had ever objected to receiving a new member recommended by the Pastor.

The the other 95 percent of adult members present outvoted the naysayers, but it was an unfortunate blight on the unity of the church body at Grace Fellowship Church.

CHAPTER TWENTY-FOUR

"G rant Renniger is reading a book?" Ava feigned shock at finding him sitting in one of the crewelwork chairs in the study with a volume of Jonathan Edwards in his hand. She'd never known Grant to be much of a reader.

"Well, I'm holding a book. Can't say I've read any of it. Doesn't Marcus own any sports biographies or mystery novels?" Grant wondered, thinking he might choke down something in those genres.

Ava gave him a side-eyed expression of rebuff. "You're kidding, right?"

"Ah, wishful thinking, I guess."

"Mind if I come in?" Ava asked politely.

"You wouldn't be interrupting anything," Grant admitted. "Come on in."

Ava sat in the matching chair on the other side of the round table and tucked a foot under her bottom – a position her flexibility allowed and that she found comfortable. She leaned her head backward and exhaled to the ceiling.

"I went into the living room to watch television with Marcus, El, and Cal while June works on dinner, but my husband has discovered The Munsters. I didn't care for that show 50-whatever years ago, and I doubt it's improved with age. So, I fled," Ava admitted.

Grant would've put up a vigorous defense of The Munsters, which he enjoyed, if his curiosity had not been piqued by other information Ava provided.

"Do you know what June's making for dinner?" he asked with bushy eyebrows raised.

"We're swimming in eggs at the moment. The chickens are laying faster than we're consuming, so she's making quiche and a Greek salad," Ava answered.

Grant raised and lowered his eyebrows in quick succession to signal his approval. Mercy, passing by and seeing occupants in the study, sauntered in and lay down at Grant's feet for a nap.

"You're bored without your job, aren't you?" Ava guessed.

"Out of my ever-loving mind."

"But you can still play golf, right?

"I could, but it would be awkward to play at Grassy Fields, and I don't have the emotional reserves to get myself off my you-know-what and find a place and a foursome to fit in. It's tiring just thinking about it."

"Okay, I'll change the subject then. Marcus and I were delighted that Joe Jacobs and his family attended church on Sunday. That was thanks to your efforts and God's grace."

Grant brightened at the mention of Joe Jacobs. "He didn't see us at our finest with all the membership drama going on at the end, but he told me he was glad they came when we met again in the vestibule. So, I guess he wasn't completely turned off."

"Glad to hear that," Ava was relieved. "Pastor Jefferson was wondering about them at the office today. Were you aware that they knew one another in high school?"

"Yeah, Joe told me Jonathan was a grade or two ahead of him. Or was it behind him? I don't remember. Aggh! It doesn't matter, but I hate that my mind's not the steel trap it once was. I can remember the big information chunks, but fine details fall through the mental sieve and into oblivion."

Ava shifted in her chair so she could face Grant. "I woke up this morning at something ridiculous, like 3:30 am, and couldn't fall back asleep. And it's funny you should bring up the trouble older people have with forgetting details because I was thinking this morning that's something we have in common with little children. My granddaughter, Emily, is nearly four now, and I'm sure that I'm erased from her memory. There's a chance I still exist as a mist in the minds of her brothers."

"I'm sorry, Ava. What Mia's done has been cruel to you and Marcus and to her own kids. I'm dumbfounded she doesn't understand that, and if she understands it, it's worse because it means she doesn't care."

"Vengeance blinds people. Mia can't see anyone but herself. Her sister, too. But where I was going with the memory thing is that, it might be a mercy, after all, at least in this case with these children. As I lay in bed, I wondered if that is God's way of protecting them from missing us as much as we miss them."

"Possibly," Grant offered weakly, unsure of God's purposes in this area. In truth, he was hesitant to speak on any matter discerning God's purpose.

"Here's a question I have," he wondered aloud. "If you would have asked me three years ago if the people living in this house were spiritually mature, I would have said 'yes.' Absolutely. Wouldn't you? But that's not my question. This is my question: How long do you have to walk with the Lord before you start counting your trials as joy, the way James says in the Bible? Because, based on our recent history, none of us long-timers are doing so good at that, especially myself."

"You're talking to the lesser qualified of the Van Zants to answer that question," Ava demurred, taking no offense at her inclusion in Grant's assessment because it was true. "But you're right, and it's a good question. In light of your observation about us, I'd ask it this way: why weren't we better prepared to face our trials with joy?"

"Exactly!" Grant agreed with her rephrasing.

Ava quoted the verse Grant referred to deliberate on it.

Count it all joy, my brothers, when you meet trials of various kinds, for you know that the testing of your faith produces steadfastness. And let steadfastness have its full effect, that you may be perfect and complete, lacking in nothing. James 1: 2-4

"I once heard a radio preacher say we can count our trials as joy – be thankful for them – only in life's rear-view mirror. When we get past the trial and see that God has given us something better than what we lost, we can rejoice. But this verse in James says to count it all joy when we meet the trial. That's on the front end of it, not the back end," Grant reflected.

"Hmm," Ava added her thoughts. "And in Romans 5, Paul says that we rejoice in our sufferings, not after them. I'm not sure where your radio preacher based his doctrine other than in unsanctified human nature. Even the unsaved can recognize and appreciate when something lost is replaced with something better. But they sure can't do what Paul and James command us to do when our trials begin."

"Pastors don't preach enough about trials and suffering. If they did, we might be better prepared to glorify God at the start instead of falling on our spiritual backsides," Grant suggested, rubbing a hand over his bald head and down the back of his neck.

"Perhaps," Ava was thinking. "Then again, is it really suffering if we can handle our deepest trials like a walk in the park? And if we don't suffer, how can we gain the benefits Romans 5 lists – endurance, character, and hope? And honestly, I don't know if a thousand sermons on suffering could have prepared me for the heartbreak God ordained for me."

"Hmm. I guess some trials can be met with joy and faith that God will work them out for our good on the front end, and others are meant to put us on our spiritual backsides for a season of refining. In either case, remaining steadfast and faithful in His strength will bring glory to God," Grant reflected.

"Dinner is ready!" June shouted from the kitchen.

Grant clapped his hands together. "And on that joyous news, I will elevate my physical backside and enjoy my dinner," he said, rising from his chair and offering a hand to Ava to help her from hers.

"I still wish I'd handled my trial better on the front end," Ava admitted as they walked to the dining room.

"Me too with getting fired. I had to call my mommy, for Pete's sake," Grant grimaced.

Chapter Twenty-Five

"Girls night out. Woot! Woot!" Kesha Jefferson announced their entrance with a circling fist high in the air as she stepped into a bustling Latte Da with Shelby and Mariana on a Friday night.

Shelby cringed and hid behind Mariana at the unexpected demand for public attention by her Pastor's wife. Introverted Shelby preferred to blend in rather than stand out. She was relieved that the audience of amused faces smiling in their direction retreated quickly to their own affairs. Mariana turned to catch Shelby's eye, looked toward heaven, and shook her head at Kesha's bold display, signaling her mutual embarrassment.

The ladies moved to the counter to place their orders.

"Medium house decaf, skim milk, no sugar," Kesha ordered, paid, and stepped aside.

"Cuban espresso," Mariana ordered without looking at the menu board.

"What is that?" asked the puzzled barista with bright pink hair, listening over the cashier's shoulder.

"Espresso with brown sugar," Mariana explained.

"Oh. Okay. Can do," the barista nodded.

After Mariana paid for her espresso, Shelby ordered. "Around the holidays, you all had a Coconut Snowball special. Can you still make one of those?" she asked.

"Can we make a Coconut Snowball?" the cashier shouted to the barista making the Cuban espresso.

"Afraid not. We're out of coconut syrup."

"Oh, that's disappointing," Shelby, overhearing the answer, extended her lower lip. "Well then, make it a medium caramel latte with whole milk. No, skim milk," she corrected.

The ladies collected their coffees and sat at the last unoccupied table in the middle of the dining area.

"Jonathan used to buy his drugs here," Kesha mentioned as the women settled and sipped.

"You don't say." Shelby's eyes widened, though she tried to appear unaffected at this glimpse into her Pastor's history.

"So did DeShawn – and his daddy," Mariana laughed at Kesha's attempt to shock them. "DeShawn told me Latte Da used to be a drugstore when he was a kid. Got his candy here, too."

Shelby exhaled, relieved. She gave Kesha a side-eyed smirk. "You got me," Shelby groaned.

Kesha smiled. "In fact, this is where Jonathan and I courted. I had an after-school job here during my junior and senior years of high school. That boy used to hang around here so much I was always getting fussed at by the pharmacist. I would have been fired, except I showed up every day and worked. So, he tolerated Jonathan – but just barely."

"I got saved here," Shelby informed Mariana, as she knew Kesha was already aware.

"No way!" Mariana exclaimed, disbelieving.

"Sure did. Marie Renniger can verify I prayed to receive Christ as my Savior right over there in that chair," Shelby pointed to a stuffed chair under a front window, now occupied by a gray-haired gentleman.

Mariana looked around the coffee shop and commented: "What a coincidence that both of you have a significant attachment to the same place. DeShawn and I don't have a 'place' unless you consider the prison 'our place,' which we definitely do not."

"So, consider 'your place' on the horizon of your future, just waiting to be identified," Shelby suggested.

"And speaking of the horizon of one's future, is there any movement on the horizon with you and Will?" Kesha asked boldly.

"You'd have to ask him. I'm content to go at his pace now. At my age, it's not like I have to be concerned about my biological clock because that clock is wound down with a few springs sticking out of it at odd angles," Shelby made light of the loss of her fertility.

"I just might ask him!" Kesha was unsatisfied with the information she sought and turned her attention to Mariana.

"Is it going well living with DeShawn's father? I see the gray house across the street from Shelby is still for rent," Kesha hinted.

"It's going very well, so we're not in the least bit interested in our own place right now. DeShawn would say the same thing if he were here. His dad respects our privacy and is so good to us. I can see how much he loves having us with him, and DeShawn is delighted to be able to do things around the house that have gotten difficult for his father. He just uses his hunky, muscular body to lift or push things around like its nothing. The two of them are really getting on as the weeks go by, and it makes me happy to see them happy," Mariana answered with contentment.

"Now it's your turn to answer, girl," Shelby insisted to Kesha. "What's going on in the life of 'the life of the party'?"

"'The life of the party?' Where'd you get that idea about me?" Kesha was dumbfounded.

Mariana and Shelby exchanged incredulous glances.

"I don't know. Maybe it was the 'Everybody look at us! Woot! Woot!' entrance you made into this place. Do you think it could be that, Kesha?" Shelby asked sarcastically, crossing her arms.

"Oh, that. Okay, I can't be held responsible for my actions when I get away for some child-free-me-time. I just don't know how to behave,"

Kesha giggled. "At home or at church, I'm dull as a celery stalk."

"In my world, a crisp celery stalk is much too tantalizing. When I make ramen noodles for Chase, Lovie, and myself, I don't put the flavor packet in mine? Sometimes, bland is my favorite flavor. Now, that's dull," Shelby chuckled at herself.

Not to be left out of the competition for the dullest of them all, Mariana confessed: "DeShawn has asked me to please talk to him about something other than my quest for the perfect sensible shoe. I'm on my feet all day as a nurse, so it's important to me, but it doesn't make me a sparkling conversationalist."

"I got a cordless iron for Christmas and squealed like a 3-year-old over a new dolly," Kesha admitted.

"My favorite hobby is knitting, and the yarns I prefer are cream or gray because other colors are too exhilarating and give me heart palpitations. I'm a 44-year-old 85-year-old," Shelby lamented.

"I find cable management thrilling. I got to do Dad's entire house when I moved in," Mariana boasted.

The women sat back in their chairs and, compelled by the discovery of a common uninspiring kinship, burst into uproarious laughter, which nearly caused a scene to rival their entrance.

CHAPTER TWENTY-SIX

DeShawn and Mariana sat shoulder to shoulder in front of the secondhand computer, a hand-me-down gift from Jonathan Jefferson, on their study's desk. Marianna was trying to help her husband navigate the online application for theological studies since computers and software had been practically reinvented since he had been first exposed to them 20 years ago.

"The next thing you have to do is write a testimony of your conversion. Type it in this box right here," she pointed to a corner of the monitor. "Just keep it under 500 words."

"I'm supposed to count how many words I use?" DeShawn asked, slapping the table beside the computer.

"No, no. Look here; it will count your words as you type."

"Okay. That's good," he answered, relieved but nervously shaking sweaty hands before the keyboard to air-dry them. "So, basically, I just write that my best friend visited me in prison and explained that I was paying for a sin I committed on Earth, but Jesus, by His death on the cross, paid for all the sins I would pay for eternally? And I tell them I believed, repented, and was baptized at the Kentucky State Reformatory?"

"That's your story, and you should stick to it," Mariana responded with an encouraging squeeze of his bicep.

"Do you think they expect me to disclose what I was convicted of?" DeShawn asked, turning to face his wife and scratching his head.

"I'm not sure what they expect, but you have nothing to hide. Everything is public record, baby," she reminded him. "And if God is for you, who can be against you? If you wonder if they'd want to know it, then be transparent and include it."

DeShawn began typing his less-than-500-word testimony while Mariana went downstairs to forage for a snack in the fridge. After a quick scan of its contents, she pulled out a snack-size bag of raw baby carrots and a container of red pepper hummus – two things the inside of Bobby McBride's refrigerator had never seen until he learned of his daughter-in-law's affinity for them. Now Bobby made sure baby carrots and hummus were always in stock.

"Hey, Miss Banana!" Bobby boomed his greeting with a wide smile as he entered the kitchen door. He'd started calling her 'Miss Banana' when she tried to correct his pronunciation of her name from 'Mari-ahh-na' to 'Mari-anna.' "Rhymes with banana," she'd said and sealed her fate.

"Hi, Dad! Did you have a good day at the lot?" she returned his smile, stepped to his side, and gave him a kiss on his cheek - which she knew he loved her to do because the first time she did it, he touched the spot afterward as if to keep it from flying away.

"Yes, I did. I finally sold a trike that's been sitting on the lot for nearly a year. I promise you I'll never have another one of those. People want to buy either a car or a motorcycle. They don't want to buy some Franken-bike three-wheeled motorcycle with a steering wheel instead of handlebars," Bobby explained. "No more novelty vehicles for me."

"Did you lose money to get rid of it?" Mariana was genuinely interested in his business.

"I did not. I thought my buyer would be along someday; I just had to wait for him. So, that's what I did." Bobby was pleased with himself for not turning one lousy business decision into two.

"Good for you for hanging tough," she encouraged. "Hey, did you leave the pizza in your truck?"

That morning, they had agreed that Bobby would pick up pizza for supper on his way home from work. But he hadn't written it down on his notepad, and he'd forgotten it since the morning conversation. Bobby looked stricken and raised his right hand to massage his forehead with his fingers.

"I'm sorry. I forgot the pizza," he lamented.

"Not the end of the world. I'll just call for delivery, and it'll be here in a bit," Mariana reassured. She pulled her cell phone out of her blue jeans pocket and ordered an extra-large pizza – half veggie and half carnivore cravings – with just a few taps on the app.

"I feel terrible," Bobby whimpered, sinking into a chair at the table.

"Dad, it's okay. All taken care of," Mariana soothed. She placed the carrots and hummus in the center of the table and sat down with her father-in-law. "Look, here's an appetizer while we wait!"

While Mariana crunched on a carrot, Bobby retrieved his cell phone from his back pocket. He separated his small pad, fastened by a rubber band, from the phone and looked for the note about pizza, which he already knew wasn't there. When his eyes confirmed it, he muttered a mild expletive under his breath and pushed the pad to the table's edge as far as his reach allowed.

"Forgive yourself. We all forget things because life is busy," Mariana patted the hand still extended toward her.

Bobby looked up at his daughter-in-law, and she read the fear in his furrowed brow and slackened jaw. He said nothing, nor did he need to. Miss Banana reverted to Nurse McBride.

"Hey, let's see your pencil there," she pointed to the golf pencil still rubber-banded to his cell phone.

Bobby moved to hand her the pencil, but she pushed the notepad back to him instead.

"I want you to draw something for me. I want you to draw a clock," she requested.

"What?" Bobby looked confused. "There's a clock right there," he said, turning his body away from her to point at the analog kitchen clock near the door.

"I know. By the way, what time does it say?" she asked.

"It's 6:10."

"That's right. Now turn around and draw me a picture of a clock showing 6:10," Mariana instructed.

She watched him hesitate before setting pencil to paper to fulfill her odd request. When finished, he turned the pad around and pushed it toward her.

"It's perfect, Dad—6:10 on the nose with all the numbers and hands where they belong. The electric cord you drew from the clock to the outlet is a nice touch. I'm giving you extra credit for that." Mariana patted his arm.

"I'm no artist, and it's been a long time since I drew a picture. What did you want this for?" Bobby asked.

"It's a quick test for dementia. That's what you're worried about, isn't it?" Mariana didn't wait for his answer before continuing. "Dad, as long as you can put the numbers and hands in the right places, you're fine. You have regular old run-of-the-mill forgetfulness, like we all have occasionally."

"You can tell that much from my picture?" Bobby's smile returned.

"I sure can!" Mariana got up from her seat, rejoicing with her father-in-law at his relief, and planted another kiss on his cheek.

CHAPTER TWENTY-SEVEN

Christine Williams learned something from her vantage point at a second-floor bedroom window looking down on Cedar Street. Her mailman and the red-haired woman from the green house kitty-corner across the street were involved. She watched them walk hand-in-hand toward Main Street and noted how the woman often glanced up at Will to see his face.

As the couple ambled farther down the street and out of view, Christine smiled at the misty memory of paying the same rapt attention to every word that fell from the lips of her dear Clarkson when they were newly in love. She hurried down the stairs, careful to hold on to the railing, and went to stand before his portrait, which hung above the fireplace in the formal living room.

"I miss you so very much, darling," she said to the forever-young, sandy-haired man in a blue suit and a gold wedding band. His mouth was serious, and his blue eyes were soft.

The portrait was a composite of several favorite pictures Christine had given the rigorously vetted artist she commissioned for the posthumous formal portrait. Although Christine could not recall her husband wearing the exact expression depicted in the finished painting, it was still everything familiar about him. When the picture was delivered and hung in its place of honor two years after Clarkson's death, Christine felt like a bit of him was home again. His presence in the living room helped her sleep better in their lonely bedroom.

Christine steadied herself by placing a hand on the back of one of the twin white sofas after realizing she was winded from rushing down the stairs. After a moment, she sat down and continued her one-way conversation with her deceased husband.

"If only you hadn't left me. If only you'd told me how you were hurting, you and I would be walking down the street and holding hands today. I'm sure we would."

Suddenly self-conscious of the wrinkled hands held primly in her lap, she tucked each under her thighs to hide them. She had aged so many years while Clarkson's hands remained smooth and unblemished in the portrait, as they always would. She wondered if it were possible to meet him again, would he even recognize the old woman she was today as the vibrant girl he'd married long ago? Then again, she hardly recognized herself as that girl.

"Where are we going?" Shelby asked, her hand wrapped securely in Will's as they walked along the sidewalk and through the early evening shadows of trees that lined Cedar Street.

"Nowhere. I mean, we'll end up back at your house, but our journey is more the focus than the destination," Will replied.

"Okay. I'll be journey-focused then," Shelby smiled up at him. "I'm naturally destination-focused – always thinking about where I'm headed. Sometimes, I think my thoughts live more in the future than in the present."

"Me too," Will confessed. "I'm trying to be more present, and I regret not starting sooner." I was always looking ahead to the next thing: getting through college to graduation, getting married, getting through grad school, having children, and getting my doctorate. I'd have been a lot better off if I'd paid more attention to what was happening around me at the moment, but my eyes were always fixed on the horizon ahead of me. Now, to some degree, a man has to look ahead and plan for the future. But I took it too far, which cost me big time."

Shelby understood the cost he referred to was his marriage, and she winced at the reference to his previous wife. Her new love for Will made her feel vulnerable and insecure, though she prayed daily for God's guidance and peace regarding their relationship and its pace.

"Let me ask you a question, Miss Norman. Would you trust me to lead you on a long journey even if you didn't know the destination?"

"Do you want my knee-jerk response or a thoughtful one?" she responded.

"Give me the knee-jerk response!" Will said with a chuckle, anticipating her answer.

"Then, no, I wouldn't," she replied.

The smile vanished from Will's face, and he looked at her. "Changed my mind. Give me the thoughtful answer," his brown eyes pleaded, though his voice was steady.

"Okay, then give me a minute."

Shelby noticed the palm of Will's hand was sweating now, but they walked an entire block in silence before she spoke again.

"I'm going to go out on a limb and assume your question is serious and in the context of marriage because otherwise, it's a fluffy question about playing games. Am I right?" she looked to him for his response.

Will nodded.

"I don't know if you value my opinion about marriage because I've never been married. But I've observed a lot of marriages; I've sinfully played at being married in my past, and now I know what God's word says marriage should be. Will, I know a husband is to be the head of the wife just as Christ is the head of the Church. And just as the Church submits to Christ, I am to follow and submit to my husband. God's word is crystal clear about that. However, although a husband is the head of the wife, he is not her ultimate head. Christ is. So, I would never give the man I married a blank check to lead me on a journey with a sinful destination – or a sinful journey, for that matter – however the metaphor works. Because if I allowed that, not only would I be putting my husband in an idolatrous position above Christ, but I'd be neglecting my responsibility to be a loving helper to him. A loving helper doesn't enable sinful choices that provoke God's displeasure and invite His discipline. I would have to call that out."

When she finished her response, Shelby released a deep breath. She'd given her honest answer but was anxious it wasn't what Will hoped to hear. She could have easily told him she'd follow him unconditionally to the ends of the earth, but if she was going to put her developing faith into practice, she had to start now. So, Shelby told him the truth: she would follow him devotedly, but there was a limit set by God for both of their ultimate good. Although fearful, she would trust God with the consequences for her honesty.

Will stopped them in their tracks. He turned to Shelby and said simply: "That's a woman I can trust."

He took his hand from Shelby's, wiped his sweaty palm on the leg of his jeans, and repositioned her hand through the crook of his arm.

"I love you, Shelby," he confessed for the first time and continued their evening walk.

Chapter Twenty-Eight

"God is good! God is good! God is good!" Mariana raced down the stairs from DeShawn's study and into the kitchen, where her husband and father-in-law were preparing breakfast, waving a paper in her hand.

"That's true, babe. What has He done for us now?" DeShawn asked over his shoulder from his position at the stove where he was cooking his father's omelet.

"Got an email this morning. I have the job at Dr. Buffington's office! Hallelujah!" Mariana exclaimed, hugging herself to her husband's back. "I'll give my two weeks' notice at Louisville General Hospital, and then I'll be working day shifts with no weekends here in Faircourt. Eeeeehhh!" she screeched excitedly.

"It's an answer to prayer," DeShawn agreed, but with solemnity. "We need to thank Him."

DeShawn flipped the omelet onto a plate and handed it to his dad, who was seated at the kitchen table. He returned to his wife, took her hands in his, and bowed his head, saying:

"You have listened and responded to our prayer for a local job for Mariana, and for this, we give You grateful thanks." You have blessed us with Your kindness, and we bless Your name in return. As You have heard our prayer for provision, hear our prayer of thankfulness in Jesus' wonderful name. Amen."

Bobby looked at the intimate scene before him with curiosity and reverence. Of course, he'd seen his son pray every day since he'd moved home because DeShawn always led them in giving thanks before supper. But this prayer was different. Bobby realized he'd witnessed a spontaneous reaction in his son to thank God for an answered prayer. Immediately, he felt the same sensation as last summer when he listened to his neighbors sing the Doxology. It seemed like witnessing praise to God opened a tiny window to heaven for him – alluring and a bit terrifying at the same time.

"Would you like an omelet, babe?" DeShawn asked as he stepped back to the stove.

"No thanks, this one's enough," Bobby answered his son, prompting Mariana to giggle.

"This 'babe' would like one, thanks," Mariana spoke up. "I'm so happy, I might eat two!"

"I've been a patient of Dr. Buffington's for the past ten years or so since old Doc Harvey retired. He's a good GP; probably the best I've ever had. Told me his sister is a cardiologist in the same medical plaza – Elizabeth Reynolds. If my ticker starts to give me trouble, I'll go see her, too," remarked Bobby, proud of his doctor's medical family.

"That so? Why do you like him so much, Dad?" DeShawn asked while whisking eggs in a bowl.

"He's not in a rush like other doctors are. He takes his time and listens to you. Oh, and he's not a pill-pusher. He tells me about natural remedies for things like my blood pressure and cholesterol. That's why I trust him – cause Big Pharma doesn't own him. I know he tells me what's in my best interest, not what's in his wallet's best interest. Not many like that anymore, from what I hear," Bobby explained.

"I'll vouch for that," Mariana agreed. "All the nurses at Lou Gen are familiar with Dr. Buffington by reputation from his patients who've been admitted. That's why I'm excited he's hired me to work in his office. It'll be a much better environment than the corporately run hospital, and the proximity to home is a huge bonus. I'll get back an hour and a half daily commuting time."

DeShawn sprinkled diced peppers, onions, and cheddar cheese over his wife's omelet, expertly folded it, and slid it onto a plate.

"Breakfast is served," he said, handing the plate to his wife, who set it on the table.

Mariana poured herself a glass of orange juice and joined her father-in-law at the bistro set while DeShawn prepared his own omelet. Mariana's eyes widened when he came to the table with it just a few minutes later.

"What in the world? It looks like a pig exploded in your eggs!" she laughed.

"What?" DeShawn asked defensively. "I like ham and sausage. We didn't get a lot of either at KSR. Besides, I made it the same as I made Dad's, and you didn't say anything about his."

"I didn't notice Dad's omelet, but I'm seeing yours alright," she replied, her eyes still staring in disbelief at the plate in front of her husband. "Are there any vegetables in it at all?"

"No, mam. Then there'd be less room for the meat," he answered before shoveling a forkful into his mouth. "Umm, umm."

"It was delicious, son. Real man food for real men," Bobby complimented. Then, wanting to distract Mariana from suggesting healthier, girly-er, omelet-filling alternatives, he added: "There's something else about Dr. Buffington's office you might enjoy. His wife belongs to some flower society. She grows bunches and brings them to her husband's practice all summer. Makes going to the doctor's almost cheerful," he chuckled.

"What a treat that will be, and something to look forward to!" Mariana was pleased. "And speaking of flowers, would either or both of you gentlemen care to accompany me to the garden center after breakfast? They've put out the bright pink petunias I've been waiting for, and you could help me carry the bags of soil and flower boxes to the car."

"I'd be happy to go with you. We could take my truck so your car doesn't get all dirty. But you won't need to buy any flower boxes," Bobby offered.

Mariana cocked her head, and a confused expression replaced her confidence.

"Go check under that tarp on the back porch," Bobby instructed.

Mariana was out the kitchen door as if a starter pistol went off. And when she threw back the tarp, she repeated her earlier refrain: "God is good! God is good! God is good! Thank you too, Dad!"

She came inside carrying a large wooden flower box to show De-Shawn.

"Look at this gorgeous box! And there's another just like it out there. Oh, these must have been expensive – the quality is better than anything you can find at the garden center. I love them!" Mariana gushed and planted a thank-you kiss on her father-in-law's cheek.

"You're very welcome, Miss Banana. They're quality, yes, but expensive, no. Cal Sherman made them for you. All I had to do was get the wood, the sealer, and the brackets. Cal's a real craftsman with a pile of raw materials."

"Thank you, Dad. I guess you've figured out the way to my girl's heart is home decorating," DeShawn chuckled. "Since you're both finished eating, why don't the two of you go on to the garden center? I'll enjoy the rest of my 'exploded-pig' omelet and have the kitchen cleaned up by the time you get home. Then I'm sure we'll be installing flower boxes."

"I'll get my truck keys!" Bobby replied.

"I'll get my purse!" Mariana stood to go.

"I'll get one of those kisses like you gave Dad!" DeShawn placed an index finger on his cheek.

Mariana smiled, bent down, and kissed her husband on his lips. "Oops, I missed!"

Chapter Twenty-Nine

Elodie flattened her back against the pew, enduring the sermon as she had every Mother's Day sermon since her beloved Momma had passed six years ago. She'd been tempted to stay home and skip recognition of the day altogether but for two troubling concerns: appreciation for mothers shouldn't negate the honor due her Father, and being alone in the house while everyone else was at church was not likely to soothe her heartache.

When Elodie lost her Momma, she'd lost her counselor, friend, teacher, cheerleader, and Wheel of Fortune competitor. To this day, she refuses to watch the game show because she knows it wouldn't be the same without her, and Elodie is unwilling for it to be different. Marie once told her: "You don't know how blessed you are to be missing your Momma. It means you had a lifetime of maternal love to be thankful for." But to Elodie, the words only highlighted that what was once whole was now a hole.

So, as Pastor Jefferson preached on the influence of a godly mother in the home, Elodie let her mind wander. It landed on wonderful memories, which produced an awful ache. But at least caring friends surrounded her.

Christine Williams huddled under layers of bedding instead of occupying her front-row seat at Grace Fellowship Church. Mother's Day had become an unofficial day for her to catch up on her rest, as she justified it to herself.

She'd paid her debt to her mother's memory at the cost of her husband's life. And because her husband chose death over life with her, there was no progeny to take her out for an elegant dinner, or to visit for an hour, or to send a simple card. So, she slept fitfully until the day was over.

"Happy Mother's Day, Mom!" Marley exclaimed brightly into her phone.

"Thank you, sweetie. And happy Mother's Day to you, too. I'm sure Ethan made you a masterpiece to add to your collection," Ava responded.

"Indeed, he did. These homemade cards, which extol my virtues as a mom, will be my trophies when he's a teenager and finds fault with all I do or say," Marley laughed.

Her daughter's words found a chink in Ava's armor. "They'll be cold comfort if your child puts distance between you," Ava reacted impulsively and realized she'd put a frown on her firstborn daughter's face. "Aww, honey, I'm sorry. I shouldn't have said that."

"It's okay, Mom. None of us knows what the future holds. My sisters have shown us that. By the way, Marit..."

"No!" Ava cut her off. "Whatever it is, I don't want to know. Because what I know about, I think about. And it's not good for me to waste my life dwelling on things I can't change. So please tell me nothing about Mia or Marit. Nothing is what I can handle."

"Got it, Mom. You shall have 'nothing' for Mother's Day. I can get you 'nothing' for your birthday and Christmas, too," she joked.

"You are my funny one," Ava laughed. "So, do you have any plans for Memorial Day Weekend?" Ava asked, refocusing on the future.

Will was happy to take Shelby hiking through Broad Run Park in Louisville on a sunny Mother's Day afternoon. His boys were, of course, spending the day with their mother and stepfather, and he hoped it would be an excellent opportunity to discover Shelby's thoughts on potentially being a stepmother. He had no way of knowing what he was about to stir up.

They stopped to admire a waterfall along the trail when Will draped an arm around Shelby's shoulder and paid her a sincere compliment. "In my humble opinion, Chase and Lovie are blessed to have you as an aunt. You're very attuned to their personalities and needs and so kind. Even when you step in to correct them, it's never off the handle or harsh. I bet you'd make a good mom or step..." He didn't get to finish before Shelby began to cry. She'd been holding off telling him her darkest sin, and she realized it would come pouring out now without the benefit of choosing her words.

"I was the mother of twin babies until I walked into a clinic and aborted them," she blurted, her eyes flooded, blurring the waterfall beyond. "It was 15 years ago, and I've regretted it every single day since, but there's no way to say my name and the words 'good mom' in the same sentence." She sobbed, unable to look at Will.

Will stood silent for just a moment, comprehending the gravity of Shelby's confession. Then he took her in his arms, holding her tightly and stroking the back of her head as she grieved on his shoulder. And he cried with her. For her.

DeShawn and Mariana drove through the cemetery until Mariana cried: "Over there! There it is!" and pointed out her passenger-side window to a section where a muddy grave was adorned with a single, lifeless floral arrangement. DeShawn turned right and parked the car on the side of the paved pathway.

It had only been two months since her mother had died, and Mariana had not been back to the gravesite since the marker had been placed. It seemed like the thing to do on Mother's Day.

"You came so close to meeting her. She just couldn't hang on any longer," Mariana lamented as they walked to the grave, new grass emerging from haphazard patches of seed.

"Neither could my mother," DeShawn thought. He'd been battling unspoken regrets and sorrow for his mom all day. He feared that if he let them out, they might engulf him.

"The marker looks good. At least everything's spelled right," Mariana noted. She lowered her body and placed a gigantic bouquet of white daisies above the shiny granite, which lay flush to the ground. "There you go, Mommy. I brought your favorite," she spoke to the stone.

"You okay?" DeShawn asked, a little surprised his wife did not seem emotional.

"I am. I'm happy she's not suffering, and I'm positive she's with Jesus." Then she added with a shy grin: "I only talk to her in case she can see me from heaven. I don't know."

Micah sat on his neighbor's porch in the early evening, watching Lovie and Chase play with Mercy in their yard. June bought the children tubes full of soap with wands that produced giant bubbles. When Mercy jumped at the bubbles and popped them, she was showered in liquid, which she immediately tried to shake off. The kids found this delightful and laughed uproariously each time it happened.

"Thank you, June, for your consideration of the kids today," Micah said wearily. "*And thank God this day is almost over,*" he thought and scowled when he reasoned no thanks was due to a God he didn't believe in.

That night, he drained his closet bourbon bottle.

Chapter Thirty

"Are they charging you rent over there yet?" Grant yelled from the house garage to Will, who had stepped onto the back porch of the Norman's house.

"No, but they make me earn my keep," Will chuckled in response to Grant's teasing.

Will visited the Norman house nearly every day. On days he didn't have Sam and Silas, he'd come over to see Shelby and have dinner with the Norman family after he finished his mail route. And now that the weather was warm, they spent a good deal of the evenings outside.

Inspired by her neighbors, Shelby wanted to revive the vegetable garden Dahlia had neglected with the arrival of baby Chase and abandoned when Lovie was born. Will replaced the rotted wood of the twin 8' X 16' raised beds and was about to fill them with wheelbarrows full of soil delivered and dumped by the local mulch and soil company earlier in the day.

"When you get that dirt in the beds, would you like some of our Secret Sauce to mix in? You'll grow vegetables so big, a single carrot could feed a family of five for a week!" Grant exaggerated boldly.

"Oh, yeah? What's in this 'Secret Sauce?' Plutonium?" Will guessed.

"Better. Composted chicken poop! We've already used all we need and have leftovers. And I'll tell you what, those birds don't have an off switch on their production of that stuff."

"Well, I'm not sure..." Will hesitated.

"I'll sweeten the deal for you. I'll bring some over so you don't have to make a trip to the Garage Cave," Grant offered.

"Let me check with the boss – she'll be out in a minute. I'm just the laborer on this project," Will called from Micah's garage, where he retrieved a wheelbarrow and shovel.

Grant pulled the shade sail out of its winter storage in the house garage and unfolded it across the driveway to inspect for damage. Elodie, who kept her vehicle in this garage, said she'd spotted mouse droppings on the floor a week ago. When Grant asked her if they were fresh, she glared at him over the top of her glasses and told him she'd leave that determination up to him.

After finishing clearing away supper leftovers and dishes, the Shermans, the Van Zants, Grant's wife, and Grant were eager to assist with setting up the Chicken Bowl Kiddie Pool. Elodie, who was having a bad day with back pain, shocked everyone when she called Bobby before dinner and asked if he wouldn't mind taking her for another "therapeutic walk" after dinner.

"The shade sail looks to be in good shape. Let me grab the ladder, and Marcus and I will get that put up. Marie, would you and Ava pull out the pool liner? It's in the box marked 'Pool Liner.' June can help you spread it out like I did the sail and check it for rodent damage," Grant took charge.

"What can I do?" Cal wanted to contribute.

"Assuming we can use the liner, you can install the filtration pump," Grant suggested.

While the crew worked on setting up the Chicken Bowl Kiddie Pool, Will wandered over to their backyard with Shelby and exchanged hellos with the ladies and Cal in the driveway before walking around to the stock tank fence enclosure.

"The boss says she'll be happy to take some Secret Sauce off your hands," he announced to Grant, who was standing on the ladder holding an end of the sail.

"Um. Okay. I'll get it for you as soon as I'm done here," Grant replied, remembering his promise.

"No need. I know where it is," Shelby started. "You're busy, and Will could use a break – he's been working so hard. I'll run our wheelbarrow over to the side of the Garage Cave and get it. You don't mind if I cut across your backyard?"

"You are more than welcome to," Grant responded.

"Need a hand, guys?" Will offered while Shelby headed to retrieve the compost.

"Dat's okay. We heard dat you've been working soooo hard," Marcus teased in a voice meant to mimic Shelby's.

"What can I say?" Will grinned and sat down on the grass. "She appreciates my efforts on her behalf."

Marcus and Grant exchanged amused expressions.

"Hey, Marie," Grant hollered to her as she stood, peering over the liner for chewed holes. "Do you appreciate my efforts on your behalf?"

"Every hour of every day, dear," Marie called back flatly without looking up.

"See what you have to look forward to once you have them trained right?" Grant boasted to Will and grinned.

"Marie!" Marcus yelled, refusing to let Grant's comment stand. "Is it true dat Grant has you trained?" he asked, winking at Will.

"Only 95%, to my great shame and embarrassment," she called back again, still focused on her task.

Marcus frowned at Will and then turned to frown again at Grant.

"That's two for two, fellas," Grant laughed.

Grant and Marcus connected the sail's corners and tightened them to their anchors in silence. Then, they took the stock tank from its position leaning against the garage wall, and placed it on the gravel pad.

"Hey, neighbors!" Shelby called when she was halfway across their backyard with the barrow full of compost. "One of your chickens is sleeping. On its side. With its eyes wide open and glazed. The other chickens didn't go near it the whole time I shoveled, and it didn't move."

"Ooo, sounds like we have a dead one," Marie surmised.

"Who's in charge of removing dead chickens from the coop?" Ava looked at the men to identify a candidate.

Marcus, Cal, and Grant all wore grimaces of disgust.

"I'll take care of it," Will volunteered, rising from his patch of grass and heading toward the coop. "I'll need a heavy-duty trash bag to put it in when I get back," he called over his shoulder.

In two minutes, Will strolled across the backyard, holding the dead leghorn upside down by its feet.

"Doesn't he look like a real man?" Shelby marveled as she watched him approach with the carcass.

No one answered her. The men revived their grimaces, and the ladies smiled behind Shelby's back.

"Oh, she's a goner," Ava whispered to Marie.

"No doubt about it," Marie whispered back.

CHAPTER THIRTY-ONE

It was the last day of school for the Faircourt Middle School Falcons, and the long yellow buses lined up in the circle roadway in front of the building waited to make their final runs. Marie, June, Elodie, Grant, and Marcus hurried toward the schoolyard flagpole from their on-street parking spot two blocks away, as best as their frames and infirmities allowed, to pray for the children before the bell rang.

They'd intended to be there an hour earlier, but June began trying to resolve Cal's unpaid medical bills on the phone with an off-shore insurance representative after lunch. Their communication flowed like sludge and made progress painfully slow.

"I'm sorry I made us late," June apologized through ragged breaths.

"Dealing with medical claims is the worst!" Elodie sympathized, trying to ignore sciatic pain as she hustled.

"Is it all straightened out?" Marie wondered if the annoyance she'd felt waiting for June to hang up her phone had been worthwhile."

"Thank the Lord, it is," June gasped, trying to keep up with the others.

In another minute, the frazzled group reached its destination beneath the flag.

"I tink we have ten minutes before da children are dismissed," said Marcus, panting.

"I suggest," Grant gasped, "we pray silently. Too winded."

Heads nodded in agreement as the group formed a small line before the 18' pole and clasped hands to pray. Although Ava had announced the event in the church bulletin, the friends of 306 Cedar Street were the only ones who showed up - minus Cal, who couldn't walk two blocks quickly and would pray from home, and Ava, who was at her job.

Before they approached their Heavenly Father with petitions for the children inside the middle school and the elementary school next door, each friend focused on calming their breathing and hurried spirits. They were serious about their duty to intercede for the youngsters they were familiar with and the larger number they didn't have contact with. No one wanted to barge into the throne room of grace carelessly or irreverently.

As they settled, each one prayed for the schoolchildren and the challenges they might encounter over the summer, including the lack of parental supervision from working parents, hunger from missed lunches provided at school, the anxiety of those going on to high school, and fears of school friendships growing apart over the long weeks. They knew Chase and Lovie were concerned about the latter two issues for themselves. And what concerned their young neighbors concerned their senior friends as well.

Standing at the end of the row, Elodie shifted her weight uneasily from one foot to the other, trying to align her painful lower back. In desperation, she dropped June's hand and lowered herself to the ground until she lay prostrate with her face cradled in hands buried in the fragrant grass. In this posture, she refocused on her prayers, oblivious to the sound of the dismissal bell and the heavy footfalls of excited middle schoolers pouring from the building.

Ryan Wiggins and Trevor Allman, middle school big-shots and basketball team members, were the first kids out the door. When they spotted Chase Norman's neighbors praying at the flagpole, they hung back until Chase exited.

"Hey, Norman! Your creepy neighbors are bringing their religion onto school property. That's not allowed. Why don't you tell 'em they should go home and clean their dentures?" Trevor, laughing, incited his former friend and teammate.

"Yeah! They should change their Depends while they're at it," Ryan guffawed and gave Chase a parting slug on his upper arm before running toward his bus.

Trevor followed on Ryan's heels, sprinting toward the school bus across the grass, passing close to those praying. Too close. Elodie, still lying prone on the ground, received Trevor's heavily planted foot across her lower back as he ran over her. Nobody would have testified it was intentional if he hadn't laughed mercilessly and shouted over his shoulder as he continued running: "Somebody left their trash on the ground."

Elodie didn't make a sound or move a muscle. Still praying with closed eyes, her companions didn't realize what had happened.

"Miss Elodie! Miss Elodie! Are you alright?" Chase shouted as he ran to her side.

The friends' eyes flew open, and June let out a gasp as she connected Chase's words to the motionless body lying on the ground next to her. June fell to her knees beside her friend just as Chase arrived, tossing his backpack to the ground and kneeling opposite June. Marie, Grant, and Marcus moved to hover over June's shoulder.

"I can't feel anything," Elodie spoke into the grass.

"I'm calling an ambulance right now!" Marie reacted, pulling her cell phone from her trouser front pocket.

"Don't!" Elodie commanded sharply. She took a deep breath, and then, ever so slowly, vertebra by vertebra, she moved to sit up.

"I don't tink dat's a good idea, El," Marcus expressed concern and lowered himself to put a hand on her shoulder, gently impeding further progress.

Elodie submitted and explained, "I can't feel anything, but I can move everything. And what I can't feel is the pain. I'm not in pain anymore!"

"Are you sure?" Grant was skeptical.

Elodie turned her head and glared at him over the rims of her glasses. "Is there someone else you think would know better than me?" she shot back and completed repositioning until she sat on her backside. "Come here and let me get a hold of you and Marcus. You boys can help me stand up."

Grant and Marcus exchanged doubtful expressions, but neither was willing to challenge Elodie's instructions. They moved to either side of her and helped her to her feet.

"Now, stand back a minute," she ordered.

Each man took two tiny side steps, and Elodie tested her range of motion. She shook her arms about, lifted each knee in the air, and then carefully twisted her waist back and forth.

"That little hooligan fixed my back!" Elodie exclaimed in amazement.

Chase looked toward the buses and saw Trevor in the back window of one pulling away from the school. He was still laughing and flashed an obscene hand gesture.

Chase turned back toward his neighbors and remarked: "He's like Joseph's horrible brothers in the Bible. But what he meant for evil, God used for good!"

"Out of the mouths of babes," Marie observed, shaking her head.

Chapter Thirty-Two

"How's the back doing, El?" Ava asked as she plopped on the couch for Thursday Meeting, tucking a foot under her bottom. She'd heard from Marcus about Elodie's maliciously delivered healing when she returned home from her job at Grace Fellowship late that afternoon.

"I am fine as a frog's hair split three ways!" came the chipper response.

Elodie was giddy from the afternoon's event at the flagpole and the unexpected, merciful relief from months of pain—something she wasn't even praying for when it happened. At supper, everyone noticed she sat up straighter and was more participative in the mealtime conversation than she'd been in many weeks. She'd even changed into her favorite color-block flowy skirt. Her countenance brightened in every way.

"I am rejoicing with you, my friend," June cheered.

"There's nothing like feeling good when you're used to feeling bad," Cal remarked knowingly.

"You might not want to let the word out that your back is better," Marie coyly suggested.

Elodie turned and looked at her, confused.

"If Bobby hears you're not in need of therapeutic walks anymore, then you'll have to confess you simply enjoy promenading through the neighborhood on the arm of a handsome man if you want it to continue," Marie needled with a grin. Everyone chuckled except Grant.

Elodie scowled and responded: "You should promenade yourself to a lake and jump in it!"

Inwardly, Elodie conceded Marie had a point she hadn't considered. She enjoyed an occasional walk with the neighbor she used to detest for more than its rehabilitative benefit. She discovered that she and Bobby 'got on,' as her late mother used to phrase it. During the few walks they'd taken together, they'd discussed cooking, sports teams, Faircourt, and a bit of their childhoods. The one thing they did not discuss was faith – hers and his lack thereof.

Without revealing specifics of Garage Cave conversations, Marcus had hinted to Elodie that he was navigating the fallow ground of Bobby's spiritual condition in their Friday game nights. She didn't want to risk undoing any progress. At least not yet. Elodie respected Marcus was plowing this field, but she also knew a good farmer didn't spend the entire growing season planting seeds because the Reaper would come for His harvest unannounced. Nobody is guaranteed tomorrow. What Elodie could do was water Marcus' efforts with prayers for Bobby's salvation. And she did.

"What do you think, dear? Would you like to drive me to the lake so El can be rid of me?" Marie asked her husband.

He offered no response.

"Grant, are you under the weather?"" Cal inquired, calling out Grant's lack of engagement.

Grant shook his head upon hearing his name. "What? I'm sorry, was somebody talking to me?"

"I asked if you were OK. You're not paying any attention to us," Cal accused.

"Yeah, sorry," Grant apologized again.

"Is someting wrong?" Marcus asked.

Grant sighed and leaned forward in his chair before answering. "Maybe it's not 'wrong,' but I don't understand something. Why are some people blessed for doing the right thing and other people punished for doing the right thing?"

"For example..." Marcus replied, wanting to draw out more of Grant's thoughts.

"For example, Elodie was obedient to pray publicly for the kids at school, and God rewarded her with miraculous relief from her back pain. But when I was obedient in witnessing to Joe Jacobs on the job, I got fired," Grant responded with a hint of complaint in his tone.

"Maybe she's more spiritual than you are," Cal blurted. For this, he received a light jab from his wife's elbow in his side.

"This is not the time for sarcasm or joking!" June whispered her correction.

"I can't help it. You understand my mouth runs ahead of my brain," Cal pouted in a returned whisper.

"Are you positive losing your job at the country club was a punishment, Grant?" Ava asked.

"Sure seems like it," Grant responded quickly, leaning back into his chair.

"I bet it does," Ava sympathized. "But you know feelings aren't a reliable source of truth. We have to trust God. Losing your job certainly couldn't be punishment because God doesn't punish obedience. He rewards it. It might be that taking you out of a hostile environment is God's protection, or you'll receive your reward in eternity for enduring persecution for Christ's sake. We don't know which of these it may be or if it's both. But what I can tell you for sure is your disappointment isn't wasted because God is accomplishing something in you through it. And second, Elodie is no more blessed for her obedience than you are. You just can't see yours yet. But it's there. Trust Him."

Marcus listened attentively to his wife's counsel and tenderly squeezed her hand. He understood – all of them understood – the faith she expressed in God's goodness despite contrary circumstances came from the crucible of her own testing fire.

"I'll say one ting more because I'm sure you'll take it like a man," Marcus added. "Who told you dat you could escape suffering as a child of God? It certainly wasn't Jesus. He said:

Remember the word that I said to you: 'A servant is not greater than his master.' If they persecuted me, they will also persecute you. If they keep my word, they will also keep yours. John 15:20

Grant nodded his head in acknowledgment and then responded: "I know Jesus warned about that, but in the heat of battle, I forget it. I need it tattooed on my body somewhere."

"How 'bout on the inside of your eyelids where you'll see it?" Elodie suggested mischievously, not intending to be helpful.

Grant leaned over to Marie and whispered, "There's no way that woman is more spiritual than anyone in this room."

For this, he too received a light jab from his wife's elbow in his side.

Chapter Thirty-Three

"Will!" Cal shouted in surprise at the sight of him walking through the open doors of the Garage Cave.

"I'm afraid so. Bobby asked me whether I would sub for him tonight. He says he's about to drown in a river of snot from some kind of virus," Will explained as he handed Cal a bag of honey-mustard pretzel pieces.

Grant's eyes lit up at the sight of the coveted snack. He rushed to put a bowl on the card table, indicating Cal should not delay making the honey-mustard manna available to transport his tastebuds to paradise.

"Settle down, Grant. You're as bad as Mercy, who acts like she'll never see another meal," Cal rebuked, nodding toward the dog, who was sniffing around the contents of the Garage Cave.

"No doubt Grant's happier to see my snack than me," Will baited him.

"Did you figure that out on your own, or did someone to tell you?" Grant taunted in return. He sat at the table, waiting for the bowl to be filled.

"Have a seat," Marcus waved his hand at Will. "So, you say Bobby's sick? Dat explains why Elodie sent a casserole dish of her chicken and rice curry to da McBride's house. She made dat a few times when she visited the parsonage and one of da girls was ill. She said da curry could be tasted when noting else could. I should've guessed someone was sick over dere," he reasoned.

Cal shook his head and grinned. "That girl has come a long way. Remember how hateful El Camino used to be to Bobby?" He finally opened the bag of pretzel pieces, dumped them in the bowl, and sat in the remaining chair.

Grant dipped his hand in the bowl and removed a fistful while Marcus dumped the dominoes out of their box and began turning them face down.

"Speaking of coming a long way..." Will hesitated and began helping Marcus turn the dominoes over. "I'm planning to ask Shelby Norman to marry me."

Grant's hand loosened its grip on its bounty, and a few pretzel pieces fell to the concrete floor. Mercy was upon them in a flash.

"You've only been dating for a week!" Cal exclaimed.

"Five months," Will corrected.

"Well, that's probably a week in dog years," Cal muttered.

Marcus determined to be more constructive in his reaction to Will's information. "Why are you telling us before you tell Shelby?" he asked.

"I don't think a proposal will be the shock to her that it is to you. She knows I love her. But I'm telling you because I'd like to hear your thoughts. As you're aware, this wouldn't be my first rodeo, but there's a lot of wisdom and experience around this table, and I'd be a fool not to avail myself of it," Will admitted.

"What do your boys think of the idea?" Grant asked, his first concern being how his twin sons might have reacted to his remarriage if he'd been in Will's situation.

"I'm not consulting them on this decision," Will was blunt. "Obviously, they know I've been dating Shelby, but they don't get a say in this."

Grant lifted his bushy eyebrows. "Are you serious? This will have an enormous impact on their lives."

"You think I should?" Will wavered, and an expression of self-doubt appeared.

"I do!" Cal advised.

"Perhaps we should hear Will's reasoning," Marcus suggested, inviting Will to explain.

Will raked his fingers through his dark hair and sat back in his chair. "I'm afraid if I give my boys a hint of influence in my relationship with Shelby before we're married, they'll try to exploit that influence after we're married. Wouldn't I be setting Shelby up for a power struggle with Sam and Silas if I cracked that door open now?"

"Good point. I hadn't considered that," Cal admitted, wiping pretzel salt from his fingers onto his overalls.

"Me either," Grant agreed sheepishly. "It's a bold move."

"I tink it's a wise move," Marcus affirmed. "Do you have peace from God about dis?" he asked.

A wide grin spread across Will's face, crinkling the corners of his brown eyes. "I really do. She's as beautiful on the inside as on the outside - humble, curious, and fun. She's honest about her failures, has great motherly instincts, and makes an outrageous meatloaf. And although she's a new believer, she sincerely desires to grow. In fact, her spiritual youth makes me think about God in fresh ways, which has invigorated my growth," he gushed and paused before continuing.

"I've prayed and asked God to do whatever it takes to keep me from making a mistake. Neither my boys nor I want to live through another divorce. But there's been nothing but peace in my heart and no roadblocks. All I see is a green light. Do any of you see a yellow or red one?" Will asked.

"Do you know her well enough? As mentioned, you've only been dating a week in dog years," Cal reiterated his initial comment.

"I suspected the length of our relationship might come up," Will smiled. "I know the most important things about Shelby. Will there be surprises down the road? I'm sure there will be. And that's a two-way street. Along with sex, I'm saving my pre-caffeine irritability in the mornings for marriage," he chuckled. "The important thing is that we're committed to Christ first and then to each other no matter what rolls out of bed in the morning."

"I saved my flashes of youthful temper until after marriage," Cal confessed. "Didn't want to scare June-bug off."

"I never pulled up my shirt, stuck out my belly, and danced in front of Marie before we were married. Ha! I do that all the time to her now. Then again, I didn't have this when we were first married," Grant said, patting his small Buddha belly.

"I could have lived my whole life without knowing that, Grant. Now I can't stop visualizing it," Will complained.

"Ha ha! Too bad," Grant laughed in Will's face. "We're going to miss having Shelby next door," Marcus steered the conversation along.

"About that. Maybe the gray house across the street from Micah's hasn't been rented yet because God is saving it for us. Who knows? I called the number on the sign and left a message that I'm interested in it," Will informed them, grinning.

CHAPTER THIRTY-FOUR

Will, DeShawn, and Jonathan paraded through the doors of Henry's Jewelers in Louisville like men on a mission, fanning out in search of the case with engagement rings.

"Jackpot!" Will exclaimed as he came upon it.

His friends rejoined him to scrutinize the glittering quarry under the glass.

A middle-aged sales clerk, clutching a keyring filled with mechanisms to unlock the jewelry cases, pursed her lips and approached the men, trying to ascertain who among the group was already wearing wedding rings and could be ignored.

"Someone getting married?" she asked in a husky voice that gave her away as a pack-a-day smoker.

"This guy - who looks like the last man in the world any woman would agree to wed," Jonathan answered, pointing a finger over Will's head.

"We don't even know if she'll agree, to be honest," DeShawn ragged, piling on.

Jonathan lowered his voice as if divulging sensitive and confidential information. "There's a lot of wishful thinking between his ears," he whispered.

Will rolled his eyes at his companions and turned back to the clerk. "I'm looking for an engagement ring for the woman I'm going to propose to. I brought my friends to be helpful, and you can see how that's turning out. My name is Will, and these are DeShawn and Jonathan. Their wives don't let them out of the house much, understandably so.

The pant-suited clerk remained stone-faced. She preferred selling diamond rings to men who brought in their brides-to-be, women who possessed a dozen pictures on their phones of rings they saw online, and who inevitably did eighty percent of the sales job for her.

"What's your budget?" she asked pointedly, focusing on Will.

"My budget is embarrassingly modest. Do you have something like a 'scratch and dent' section you could show me?" Will asked sheepishly.

The clerk blinked, shook her head, and furrowed her penciled eyebrows.

DeShawn jumped in to bolster his new friend. "Hey, brother! My wife doesn't even have a diamond, just a plain gold wedding band she had to pay for herself."

"Kesha's got a small diamond, and that was because we didn't have kids yet. After four of 'em, my wallet hasn't seen a fifty-dollar bill in years." Jonathan chimed in.

The clerk's furrow deepened as she envisioned her commission dwindling.

"What can I get for a thousand dollars?" Will asked, stretching his limit to the max.

"Natural or lab-created?" she asked impatiently.

"Huh?" Will didn't understand the question.

"Natural, mined diamonds cost more. Lab-created diamonds are chemically identical but less than half the price because they're manufactured," the clerk explained in a more relaxed tone, scrounging some sympathy for the customer with shallow pockets.

Will turned to his friends. "What do you think? Do women care if they're chemically identical?"

"Nah, man. It's still a diamond. Go big or go home," DeShawn advised.

"She's going to show everyone she knows that ring, probably people she doesn't know. No one could tell the difference, right?" Jonathan looked at the clerk for an answer.

"Not without a jeweler's loop or a nitrogen test," she educated the men.

"I don't think Shelby will be hung up about what kind of diamond she gets since I'm the real prize in this deal," Will reasoned to his friends with a grin. "Okay! Let's see the lab-created rings," he decided.

In five minutes, Will selected a three-quarter carat, oval-shaped, lab-created diamond solitaire set in yellow gold. He remembered Shelby always wore yellow gold.

"What ring size does your girlfriend wear?" the clerk asked before ringing up the sale.

"I have no idea," Will admitted. "Can I return it to be resized if it doesn't fit her? I want to take it with me so I can propose with the ring."

"That'll be fine. All our rings come in size seven, and we size up or down from there. You can bring it back to be resized at no charge if it doesn't fit her."

"Can he bring it back for a refund if she turns him down?" DeShawn joked.

"He can do that too," the clerk answered seriously. "You've got 30 days, just like the online retailers."

Will handed the woman his credit card, and she took the ring to the register on the other side of the store to process the sale.

"You guys don't really think Shelby might turn me down, do you?" Will asked when the clerk was out of earshot, his confidence bruised.

Jonathan and DeShawn exchanged eye contact and wordlessly agreed to reverse course to the best of their ability.

"Every other woman in the world would probably hate you, but you're perfect for Shelby," Jonathan responded.

"You two go together like ham and biscuits," DeShawn agreed.

"So yeah, if I had to bet, I'd say she'd be willing to settle for you," Jonathan reinforced.

Accepting their comments as the most encouragement he could expect, Will challenged DeShawn: "Ham and biscuits? Don't you mean peas and carrots?"

"Peas and carrots might get along, but nobody eats 'em except old people. Everybody likes a ham biscuit. They're relevant. Keep up, man," DeShawn chided.

"Great. Now I want a ham biscuit and coffee," Jonathan whined and leaned against a counter.

"When we're done here and if you behave, we can stop at The Donut Hole on the way home. Why do I sound like I'm talking to Silas?" Will said, shaking his head.

"She didn't need to dig into your finances like that, man," DeShawn, changing the subject, sympathized with Will.

"She kind of did. And actually, she helped me out. I wasn't aware there was such a thing as lab-created diamonds. Been a few decades since I bought the last one," Will admitted.

"I'd like to get a nice diamond for Mariana, but she supports me right now. Besides, she just started the new job with Dr. Buffington, and it's a pay cut from her hospital salary. I gotta figure something out," DeShawn lamented.

The clerk returned with a small gold bag and a receipt, handing both to Will.

"Best wishes. I hope it lasts forever," she said with a hint of cynicism.

"That makes two of us!" Will responded.

CHAPTER THIRTY-FIVE

"Look out, Calorie!" Elodie barged out the kitchen door in her bathing suit, a towel wrapped around her waist, as Cal tried to enter.

He took two steps backward to give her leeway, not expecting Ava and June, also in bathing attire, rushing behind in Elodie's wake.

"'Scuse us!" Ava pleaded as she bumped into Cal, who had attempted to advance.

"Hey! Is that an ice cream truck?" June emerged, winked at her husband, and shouted after the women, who halted in the driveway to listen for the musical vehicle.

June scampered past them, opened the enclosure gate, and plopped into the Chicken Bowl Kiddie Pool.

"The chunky girl's not the rotten egg this time!" June shouted to the victims of her deception, who were still listening in vain for the nonexistent ice cream truck.

Ava got the jump on Elodie and was next in the pool.

"The first shall be last, El!" Ava taunted.

Now shamefully identified as the putrid ovum, Elodie sulked into the enclosure to join her friends in the stock tank.

Cal shook his head at the grown women's shenanigans and disappeared into the house without comment.

"Well, June! What a stone-cold liar you turned out to be," Ava indicted with a laugh and a splash of water in June's direction.

"Don't think of it as a lie. Think of it as disinformation," June smiled wryly.

"I think of a lie as a lie," Elodie grumbled, pulling her towel off and tossing it on a yellow-painted Adirondack chair. "I don't play that game of callin' sins mistakes or puttin' nonsensical made-up words on 'em. If it was a sin a hundred years ago, it's a sin today." She lifted each leg over the stock tank pool's rim and sank into the cool water. The skirt of her bathing suit – leopard print on a hot pink background – floated around her.

June's eyes grew large, and the corners of her mouth turned down.

"You're right, Elodie. Words matter. I'm sorry I lied to you and Ava, and I apologize. I got caught up in the competition, and the spirit of Marie possessed me." June was contrite.

Ava rolled her eyes at Elodie and took up for June. "She didn't say there was an ice cream truck; she *asked* if there was one – and we stopped to listen. You're just being a spiritual diva and trying to make June feel bad because you were gullible, and now you bear the stench of sulfur."

Elodie ignored Ava's rebuke and instead turned toward June. "Is she correct? Did I make you feel bad?"

"Yes, I'm sorry. I feel terrible," June apologized again.

"Ha! Good!" El laughed and sent another splash of water June's way.

"As you can see, June, Elodie is better at dishing it out than taking it. Over the decades, I've learned how to spot when she's dishing. I'll give you pointers so your learning curve isn't as protracted as mine was," Ava consoled. "And by the way, speaking of Marie, where did she disappear?"

It was Marie's idea for the women to take an after-dinner dip in the Chicken Bowl Kiddie Pool. She should have already been in the pool since she had a 10-minute head start on her friends, who had to put away canning equipment and strawberry preserves from their afternoon project. But while Marie was retrieving a white-with-navy-polka-dots bathing suit from her dresser drawer, a flash of activity outside caught her eye. She moved to the window and saw Christine Williams weeding her side yard rose garden. Marie tossed the bathing suit on her bed and headed downstairs.

The pocket doors of the living room were closed, and Marie could hear Uncle Joe's gravelly voice at Petticoat Junction wafting from behind them. She decided it would be a quick visit across the street and wouldn't disturb the men's entertainment or the ladies' working in the kitchen. Marie headed out the front door.

Christine stopped working when she noticed Marie crossing Cedar Street, approaching her. She placed a gloved hand on her hip while waiting for her neighbor to cross the sidewalk and strip of lawn.

"I came to admire up close what I've been admiring from afar. Your roses are in their glory! Do you mind?" Marie nodded at the closed picket gate, requesting permission to enter.

"You may come in," Christine answered formally.

Marie opened the latched gate and stepped through. "Your garden is the showpiece of the neighborhood. Do you have a favorite?" Marie asked, interested.

"If I did, I wouldn't tell it. Not after what happened last year," Christine snapped protectively.

"Fair enough," Marie answered, unfazed by her tone. "How about if I tell you my favorite?" She scanned the garden and took a few steps toward a blooming bush that climbed an arbor near the back of the house. "That one. Definitely that one!"

"Joseph's Coat," Christine identified the variety, a multi-colored mixture of warm hues. "Not one of my prize-winning tea roses, but it's cheerful and undemanding."

"Cheerful," Marie repeated, "is an excellent description. I like it because with all of those colors melting through it, it defies a succinct description. It's not a pink, yellow, or orange rose – it's all of them. It's complicated, like people are."

"And do you like complicated people as well?" Christine probed.

"Hmm," Marie stalled, giving herself a few seconds to produce a thoughtful answer to Christine's direct and personal question. "I suppose, like the Joseph's Coat, you might not want your life's garden dominated by them, but they are the most interesting by far."

Believing she'd been subtly complimented, Christine allowed a smile to cross her face. This mild expression of delight was a trophy to Marie. She was making progress in befriending her challenging neighbor.

Filled with optimism, Marie offhandedly gestured to the empty gray house next door. "I hope whoever moves in next door to you will also be cheerful but uncomplicated," she mused.

"I try to vet my tenants carefully, but there have been a string of disappointments over the last several years. I'm in no hurry this time," Christine replied, the terseness returning to her tone. And turning abruptly to face the McBride house, she added: "But I can assure you of one thing, they will not be ex-convicts!"

"She owns the gray house!" Marie processed the information.

Chapter Thirty-Six

Grant beamed as Joe Jacobs entered the room just before the lesson began.

"Joe!" Grant rose from his seat and extended his hand to greet him. "Glad to have you join us this morning. I want you to meet our teacher."

He waved Will over and introduced them.

"I see a wedding band," Will commented to Joe. "Do you have family with you today?"

"My wife, Allison, was befriended at the Welcome Center by a woman named Shelby, who took her to a women's class. And the Pastor's wife herded my kids to the children's area," Joe explained.

"Will, you know Shelby, don't you?" Grant teased.

Will blushed and evaded the question by responding, "I think it's time for us to start."

Marcus moved himself over one chair so Joe could sit next to Grant. Will passed out his lesson sheet and instructed the men to open their Bibles to Romans 13, calling on Grant to read the first four verses of the chapter.

*Let every person be subject to the governing authorities. For there is no authority except from God, and those that exist have been **instituted by God**. Therefore whoever resists the authorities resists what **God has appointed**, and those who resist will incur judgment. For rulers are not a terror to good conduct, but to bad. Would you have no fear of the one who is* *in authority? Then do what is good, and you will receive his approval, for **he is God's servant** for your good. But if you do wrong, be afraid, for he does not bear the sword in vain. For **he is the servant of God**, an avenger who carries out God's wrath on the wrongdoer.*

"The way ancient writers highlighted important points was by repeating them. What point do you see stressed in this text through repetition?" Will began his lesson with a question for the class.

"God is sovereign over governments and their governors!" David Cowman, the funeral home director, shouted out.

"You didn't raise your hand," Lefty Schneider, a church deacon, chastised with a smirk.

"It's okay, Lefty," Will assured. "We don't run this class like a grade school. And David is correct – Paul is emphasizing that God establishes all governments, and every ruler is appointed by His favor. But he's only talking about good governments and rulers, right? God's not responsible for the bad ones, is He?"

Joe Jacobs sat straighter in his chair, suddenly interested in where this lesson was going. He'd never been to a Sunday School class and assumed it would be a pre-sermon lecture. He was not expecting an interactive exercise on a subject he was keenly drawn to.

With no answer to Will's question forthcoming, Marcus jumped in. "If da text does not specifically exclude da bad ones, why would we take da liberty to exclude dem?"

"Valid point, Marcus," Will commented. "And in case we wonder if this is an isolated claim – that God appoints all governmental leaders – I point you to the list of verses in your handout that make the same point. The most significant of these is John 19:11, in which Jesus tells Pilate he would have no authority over him (Jesus) unless it had been given to him (Pilate) from above. And in that verse, we also have the answer to whether God is sovereign over bad governments. He is!"

"Are you saying God brought Hitler to power?" Lefty was incredulous.

"Hitler, Hitler, Hitler. Why does everyone always bring up Hitler?" Cal mumbled, but loudly and clearly enough to be heard by all.

"I think what you want to resolve, Lefty, is whether God takes responsibility for raising up Hitler to accomplish His purposes, not what Will has to say," Tom Farmer, the church's part-time maintenance man, interjected defensively. "Unless you have other scripture to cite, what's in front of us is clear. He is King of Kings and Lord of Lords – all of 'em."

"Let's imagine ourselves as citizens living under Hitler for a moment," Will pivoted.

"Oh, brother," Cal muttered and lowered his head.

Grant shot his friend a look that wasn't friendly. "Go on, Will," he encouraged.

"Okay, never mind Hitler. Let's say our government insists we call good what God has declared evil or face serious consequences. Do you submit to that as our text would indicate?" Will challenged.

Grant raised his hand and began speaking. "When a high priest told Peter to stop preaching the gospel, he said he must obey God rather than men. Oh, wait, that was a religious and not a civil authority – never mind."

"I don't know that we need to disregard that example, Grant," David countered. "It shows that principles of authority exist, but over all is the ultimate lordship of Christ. Wives don't submit to husbands who would lead them into sin, nor should citizens submit to any kind of ruler who would lead them into sin."

"That's right. When a law was passed in Babylon that said prayers to God were forbidden, Daniel disobeyed. And when the midwives were told to kill Jewish baby boys, they disobeyed, too," Tom recalled.

"So, if we can't obey laws contrary to God's laws, what can we do?" Will pressed.

"I guess we pray for courage!" Cal engaged with positivity.

"Anything else?" Will prodded.

The room was silent for a moment as the men thought.

"We should also pray that God's will be done on earth as it is in heaven," Lefty suggested.

"Amen!" shouted Tom.

"How do ya'll feel about trying to do more than pray God's will be done on earth? Can Christians be politically active?" Joe Jacobs blurted, unable to contain his curiosity.

For the next 40 minutes, the men engaged in a vibrant discussion of the historical influences of Christians on culture, the relationship between the church and the state, and current governmental policies on family issues. Joe Jacobs was an enthusiastic participant, adding his expertise on pertinent points of law to the discourse.

When the class was over, Joe approached Will with an outstretched hand.

"I think I'm going to like Sunday School. That was a stimulating discussion!" Joe complimented Will. "If I didn't know better, I'd suspect you planned that lesson in Romans just for my benefit."

"I may not have known you'd be here today, but God did," Will smiled, shaking Joe's hand firmly.

Chapter Thirty-Seven

"Oh, we're going inside the establishment this evening, are we?" Shelby asked in amazement as Will held Latte Da's door open for her.

"Yup! Throwing caution to the wind and hoping the memory of my vomit fountain in the men's room has been forgotten. It's been six months, so I should be good," Will reasoned, his mood upbeat.

The cafe was tranquil for a Sunday evening. But the weather was warm, and the big-draw annual Faircourt First Responders Charity Softball Game: Police Station vs Firehouse was underway at the high school ball field. Will led them to a small table by the window.

"This is where we sat on our first date," Shelby recalled. "Only wasn't there an electric fireplace here?" She pointed to a space between the tables.

"I don't think I was here long enough to remember that detail," Will grinned. "Why don't you save our special seats here, and I'll get us something to drink. What can I get for you?"

"Since we're reminiscing, how 'bout a Coconut Snowball?" she requested, her green eyes shining.

"I can ask if they make Snowballs in May. But if they don't, do you have a backup for me?"

"Mocha Latte, skim milk."

"Got it!"

Will walked up to the counter and recognized the pink-haired barista with the nose piercing and string of musical notes tattooed down the side of her neck. How could he not? Only this time, he also noticed a name tag: Five.

"Fee-vay?" Will guessed the random word had an exotic pronunciation.

"No, it's five – like the number. Good try, though, Peppermint Tea-guy," she answered.

"Oh. You remember me," Will's shoulders slumped.

"Sure do!" Five smiled mischievously. "What can I get you?

Remembering his mission, Will confided in the barista. "Is there any way on this planet that you could make me two Coconut Snowballs? It was the special you had between Thanksgiving and Christmas last year. If I had a thousand dollars, that's what I'd be willing to pay for it, but I just spent my last grand on a ring I'm about to give that lady over there."

"I got you, Lover," Five chuckled.

Will reached for his wallet, and Five raised her hand, palm up, telling him to stop.

"There's no charge considering the occasion. But I can't promise I'm not going to watch you propose. Actually, I can promise I will. It's a slow night."

"Fair deal," Will smiled, then waited at the counter while she made the coffees.

In a few minutes, Five handed the drinks to Will.

"Wish me luck!" he said under his breath.

"Nah. You don't need it," she encouraged with a grin.

With a confident stride, Will walked back to the table, and Shelby, noting his footsteps, looked away from the kids riding bikes down Main Street and up at Will.

"Success! Two Coconut Snowballs!" he cheered, holding them aloft.

Shelby beamed, delighted, and Will was overcome. She looked gorgeous wearing ankle-length blue jeans and a cream-colored button-front silk blouse. Her hair was tied up in a messy bun; loose tendrils framed her freckled face and dangled across golden hoop earrings.

Will silently petitioned God's favor on his pursuit, placed the drinks on the table, and sat opposite the woman he admired and adored.

"What are your plans with the boys next weekend?" Shelby asked, picking up her coffee.

"Don't want to talk about that right now," Will answered while stealthily removing the diamond ring from his front pocket, hiding it in his hand.

"Okay, then. You pick the topic of conversation," Shelby demurred.

"I thought we'd talk about us," he began, capturing her undivided attention. "Shelby, I love you, but I've realized it's not enough. It's not enough to love you without the certainty you'll be in my life every day that I have left on this earth. You know I don't have a lot of material wealth to offer you, but everything I have or am is yours if you'll have me."

Will slid from his chair to his knee and asked, "Will you marry me, Shelby?"

"No! I can't believe this is happening. But, yes! Yes, I'll marry you! Tomorrow?" she responded jubilantly.

Will produced the ring, and Shelby held out her hand to receive it. After he slipped it on her finger, she placed a soft kiss on his mouth.

Five and her co-worker, a high school girl named Audrey, clapped their hands to support the lady's acceptance of the guy who seemed to visit Latte Da to create a commotion. A couple at a table across the cafe joined in their applause as Shelby glowed with joy.

"I would marry you tomorrow, except that's not enough notice to gather our family and friends. I want to marry you in front of God and everyone we know. Besides, I still have to find a roof to keep over your pretty head," Will explained.

A slight frown crossed Shelby's face at the thought of moving away from her niece and nephew and the Cedar Street neighborhood she loved. She brushed the loss away to focus on what she was gaining.

"Okay. But promise me it won't be a long engagement. What about a wedding at the end of summer? How about Labor Day weekend?" Shelby requested, her eyes pleading.

"Absolutely! No long engagement. Labor Day weekend sounds good to me," Will agreed.

"You can get off your knee now," Shelby giggled and then released a deep sigh.

"Is my face still smiling? I feel like I'll never stop," she asked as Will reclaimed his seat.

"Still smiling," Will confirmed, returning a broad smile of his own.

"I never thought this would happen for me – my own husband and my own home. I'll be 44 by the time we get married if I don't die from euphoria first," Shelby calculated. "And if that wasn't blessing enough, it's all happening with the finest, most godly man I've ever known. Will, I'll be so proud to be your wife no matter what material wealth you have or haven't. It's not important to me. You know that, right?"

"Well, I'd hoped, but I'm relieved to hear you say it," Will held her hand across the table. "So, is there anyone you'd like to tell that we're going to be married?" he teased.

"Let's go tell everyone!" Shelby exclaimed, jumping up.

They grabbed the untouched Coconut Snowballs and headed toward the door.

"Congratulations, Mr. and Mrs. Peppermint Tea!" Five called after them.

"Not only did she remember me, she remembered what I tried to order before giving me that horrid chai tea," Will explained to Shelby.

"She can call us whatever she wants as long as it's got that 'Mr. and Mrs.' in front of it. I love the sound of it," Shelby gushed.

Chapter Thirty-Eight

"I think you're going to want to see this." Ava poked her head into Pastor Jefferson's office after a single knock to announce her intrusion.

"What is it?" he asked, looking up from his computer screen and his half-finished sermon.

"It's the reason this church will henceforth be known as Williams Fellowship Church," Ava answered cryptically.

"Huh?" Jonathan answered, cocking his head in puzzlement.

"I'm telling you, you're going to want to see it," Ava repeated and turned to go.

Jonathan rose from his chair and followed her through the vestibule. They walked out the front doors and joined Tom Farmer on the left side of the church lawn. There, the three of them gawked, awe-struck, at the sight of a boom truck lifting an enormous unpolished granite rock from a flatbed semi-truck parked on the roadside. The light gray rock was ten feet wide at its base, eight feet tall at the highest point on the right side, and 16 inches thick. It was roughly chiseled along the sides and across the top, where it tapered to six feet tall on its left side. And across its smooth front, in 12-inch carved letters coated black inside, it read: WILLIAMS.

"Looks like the new headstone for Christine Williams' husband has arrived," Ava remarked with droll understatement.

"I've seen municipal war memorials smaller than that," Tom commented, leaving his mouth agape.

"Space satellites won't have any trouble reading the name," Jonathan added flatly.

"Even though the grave is in the back corner of the cemetery, people will be able to read that monument driving down the street," Ava assured the astonished men.

"With cataracts and sunglasses!" Jonathan added. After pausing, he wondered, "Hey, doesn't something like that have to sit on a base?"

"Already in place. They must have installed it Monday on our day off," Tom said, pointing across the small cemetery to a large, thick slab of polished granite lying on the ground.

The tiny group of church employees continued to watch the unloading of the massive stone.

"I can tell you one thing. If another tree falls on the Williams' headstone, it won't be the headstone that breaks," Tom asserted.

"It's so big, it's ridiculous!" exclaimed Ava.

"Would you like to be the one to tell Mrs. Williams that?" Jonathan offered.

"That task is above my pay grade," Ava laughed.

"It's above all of ours. Anyway, I'm afraid there's nothing we can do about this. Mrs. Williams would point out that there's nothing in our bylaws regulating the size of headstones in our cemetery, and she'd be right. We're just going to have to live with this giant meteor she's bombed us with," Jonathan shrugged and walked back to his sermon preparation.

"Can you imagine what something like that must cost?" Tom wondered, shaking his head.

"In dollars or audacity? Christine Williams doesn't lack either," Ava chirped before returning to her office.

"When you said 'it wouldn't be modest,' you were underselling it," Marie chuckled as she approached Christine Williams, who stood admiring her new monument in the evening light.

"Probably. But as they say, under promise and over deliver," Christine responded, not taking her eyes off the rock.

From their vantage point, standing 15 feet in front of the monument, Marie read the information carved in the base: Clarkson Dean Williams, May 10, 1946 - December 1, 1978, and Christine E. H. Williams, July 31, 1947 - . On either side of their names was a cluster of engraved roses.

"What would your husband say about it if he could see it?" Marie asked.

Christine chuckled before she answered. "He'd say it's the second set of stones he had that were bigger than his daddy's."

"Father/son relationships can be complicated," Marie nodded, unfazed by the unbelieving woman's crass reply. "My Grant has butted heads with our boys from time to time."

"Clarkson and his father did not agree on a single thing, and nothing Clark did was ever good enough for that man. I think that's why he got close to my father." Christine astonished herself with this new insight and regretted sharing it. She braced for whatever bothersome follow-up question her neighbor might ask in response.

"Men need at least one other man in their life to be close to – to sharpen their masculinity," Marie remarked.

Christine was disarmed by Marie's refusal to pry and made another candid confession: "I didn't understand that as a young wife."

"If I had understood, as a young wife, everything I've figured out about men now, I might have spared myself some drama," Marie empathized without realizing how relevant her comment was to Christine.

"What do you think your friends will say about the monument when they see it on Sunday?" Christine asked, eager to change the subject.

"Oh, they've already stopped by to look. Drove here before supper when they heard about it," Marie admitted.

"And their comments?" Christine prodded.

"They've never seen anything quite like it," Marie answered tactfully.

"How diplomatic of them. Now, what did they actually say?

"Well, one called it the Williams Whale. Another said the monument could have its own ZIP code. And someone suggested a betting pool on how long before it was vandalized with spray paint."

Christine gasped in shock. "You don't think that would happen, do you? Who would dare?"

"No, no! Calm down. I made all that up because you shouldn't reject a polite answer to scour for an impolite one," Marie dared to chastise the older woman.

Christine turned to glare at Marie, who wore a confident, contagious smile that melted Christine's hostile impulse.

"You're not intimidated by me, are you? I find that equally annoying and amusing," Christine admitted, allowing a faint smile to appear.

"Come on, I'll walk you home," Marie offered. "And if you're determined to find out what the wagging tongues of Faircourt have to say about your monument, you can look online."

And to Marie's surprise, Christine accepted her offer and turned to walk with her.

CHAPTER THIRTY-NINE

"Where's Grant?" Ava asked Marie, the last to enter the living room for Thursday Meeting.

"He's mowing because it's supposed to rain for the next four days, and he claims to know this meeting will be dominated by a discussion of Shelby's wedding," Marie answered.

Cal and Marcus exchanged expressions of alarm.

"I could rake da clippings behind Grant!" Marcus offered, forgetting the mower had a bagger.

"I could...ah...ah...make sure he doesn't run out of gas," Cal suggested lamely.

"Oh, go ahead, you two," Ava laughed. "Grant's not wrong. What could be more pressing to discuss than Shelby and Will's wedding?"

The men ran out of the living room as if murder hornets chased them.

"Since the guys bailed on us, how 'bout we have Women's Thursday Meeting upstairs on Elodie's bed," Marie suggested.

"Last one there..." Ava began.

"Oh, no, you don't! I'm not comin' out on the short end of that race again," Elodie objected. "We're too old for that game. Everybody just proceed nice and orderly to my room."

Five minutes later, the women settled themselves on Elodie's king-size bed. June and Elodie sat with their backs against the wall where a headboard would have been if Elodie had owned one. Ava and Marie draped themselves across the bed, lying opposite one another and facing June and El. A cool breeze from an open window blew across the room, signaling the expected rain.

"So, the only things we know about this weddin' are the names of the bride and groom and the date, right?" Elodie stated.

"Shelby did say she wanted us all to be involved, but we don't know what that means exactly," Marie added.

"It means work!" exclaimed Ava.

"I don't mind helping," June offered. "I haven't been to a wedding in years, and I just love them. The air drips romance, and everyone sets aside their cares for a few hours to celebrate and think optimistically about the future."

"Let's see, I've not been to a wedding since..." Elodie checked her memory.

"Marit and Robby's was a year and a half ago," Ava reminded, frowning.

"I remember your and Marcus' wedding like it was yesterday!" Marie jumped in to swing the discussion away from unpleasant territory.

"Who could forget it?" Elodie chimed in. "August 3rd in the year of hell's furnace A.D."

Ava and Marie shook their heads as smiles formed with the memory.

"You should have been there, June. It would have changed your thinkin' about weddin's. They got married outdoors on the hottest blazin' day of the decade at three in the afternoon. Have Ava show you the pictures! Everyone looks like they were sprayed with a firehose. We were soakin' wet with perspiration – literally drippin'. It was disgustin'."

Now, Ava and Marie began to laugh.

"It's true," Ava said, wiping a laughter tear.

"And the pastor's wife tried to be helpful," Marie began and interrupted herself with a snort. "She grabbed a container of baby powder from the nursery."

"Oh! That's right!" Elodie joined in the laughter.

"She told us to put some on our hairlines and the back of our necks to absorb the sweat and cool our skin – the guys too!" Marie started explaining again.

"It made smears of white paste on everyone! You can also see that in the pictures, especially on Elodie and Marcus' dark skin. Whenever I look at my wedding pictures, I can smell body odor and baby powder," Ava said, daubing at tears of laughter on the outside corners of her eyes.

June wrinkled up her face and shook her head, imagining it.

"But at least everyone at my wedding was sober," Ava grinned.

Marie and Elodie stopped laughing, and June looked puzzled.

"I got married for the first time at the age of 18," Marie explained to June. "My father insisted on having an open bar, and since he was paying for it, we didn't object. I had no clue I'd live to regret it. My father got roaring drunk at the reception and kept repeating, 'I paid for that.' The food, my dress, the photographer, cake, flowers, the band – he pointed to everything and shouted, 'I paid for that.' It was mortifying." Marie felt the shame anew and looked away from her friends.

"Your dad, what a character," Elodie sympathized, being deliberately vague.

"Marie, I'm so sorry for bringing that up. After all these years, I thought maybe it was time to laugh about it. But I can see it'll never be funny, and it was stupid of me. Please forgive me," Ava apologized from her heart.

"I forgive you," Marie responded and squeezed Ava's hand. "Anyway, I learned from that mistake, and we had no open bar when Grant and I got married. Of course, there was no Daddy either because he wouldn't come," Marie explained to June.

"How 'bout your weddin' June? Any stories?" Elodie prodded.

"Not like Ava or Marie have. Our wedding was tiny. There were about 20 family members and friends, and we got married at Cal's parents' house because it was larger than my parents' tiny parsonage. It was early October, so the weather wasn't too hot or cold. Nothing exciting about it at all," June recalled. "Cal did get his wallet stolen on our honeymoon, though. That wasn't fun at all."

Ava, Elodie, and Marie all groaned in sympathy.

"I wish I'd known all of you as young brides," June lamented. "You too, Elodie, as a younger single woman."

Marie and Ava looked to Elodie and offered a wordless invitation to share her secret.

"I was married for exactly 52 hours," Elodie looked at June and confessed.

June's eyes grew wide despite her best effort to hide her surprise.

"I was duped by a good-looking, slick-talking man with a smile that made all the ladies come runnin' to him. He said he chose me, and I believed him because that's what I wanted to believe. We married at the courthouse and had no money for a honeymoon. He just moved into my apartment. Two days later, he was stabbed to death in the bed of another woman by her jealous husband. And that was that," Elodie explained. "As far as I'm concerned, I've never been truly married."

"How awful," June exhaled the breath she'd held while Elodie shared her story.

"Still think of weddin's as all romance and optimism after hearing our stories?" Elodie asked, looking over the rim of her glasses at June.

"I understand not everyone gets a happily ever after, and I'm so sorry for you and Marie. But I'll always hope and pray that every new bride will be so blessed," June answered sincerely.

Chapter Forty

Mariana restocked the examination rooms with supplies before the doctor's office closed for the weekend, humming as she worked. She looked forward to the long Memorial Day weekend and getting together with the Cedar Street neighbors.

"Hey, hope you enjoy the weekend," Dr. Buffington wandered into the room Mariana was working in to say goodbye.

He was in his early sixties, clean-shaven, with a full head of white hair he claimed to have acquired prematurely in his thirties. He had gentle blue-gray eyes and deep smile lines, which combined to inspire trust in his patients.

"Thank you, Dr. Buffington. And you as well," Mariana responded cheerily.

"Do you have any plans?" he asked in a light, interested tone

"Just a cookout with our neighbors on Monday. Other than that, I'll be catching up on household chores and errands."

"One of your neighbors is Christine Williams," the doctor stated instead of asking.

"Yes," Mariana closed a cupboard and turned to face her employer, suddenly wary.

"I've known Christine Williams for 30 years – since opening my Faircourt practice. She used to do some advertising mailers for me when she still owned the printing company, and she's in the local flower society with my wife, Rita. I know she's a bearcat when she doesn't like someone, and she doesn't like you. She made accusations and put a bug in Rita's ear to convince me to fire you," the doctor explained.

Mariana gasped, afraid of losing the new job she loved. She rubbed clammy hands against her blue scrubs uniform.

"You have nothing to worry about, Mariana," Dr. Buffington assured. "Rita and I are not her puppets, and I don't appreciate her trying to butt into our business. The only reason I'm telling you this is so you know who your enemies are. I don't much care for folks who smile to your face and try to stab you in the back."

"She doesn't bother to smile to our faces. She snarls," Mariana corrected. "I don't know what accusations she made, but if she said my husband was recently released from prison, that's true. He served 20 years. I'm sorry I didn't disclose that during my interview."

"No, no! It wasn't necessary. I was interviewing you for a job, not your husband. But I'll confess something. I wondered if you were related to my patient, Bobby McBride, so I compared the address on your application with my patient files and put it together. I knew you were DeShawn's wife before I offered you this job."

Mariana released the tension that had gathered in her shoulders and sighed in relief.

"How did Ms. Williams even figure out I worked here? She must have spies everywhere!"

"She overheard Rita telling another Flower Society member we had a new nurse in the office, and your name was mentioned positively during that conversation. Christine approached my wife afterward to warn her you should be replaced immediately," Dr. Buffington explained.

"She made a scene about us at our church, too," Mariana lowered her head.

"I hate to hear that, Mariana. Rest assured your position is secure, and she can't touch you here. But watch your back, because she's used to getting her way. I know this is distressing to hear, but you can't protect yourself if you don't realize you need it."

"Thank you for telling me, Dr. Buffington. We're doing our best to steer clear of her."

"Son, that was delicious! Your fried chicken is as good as Miss Elodie's. But don't tell her I said so. If you do, I'll deny it," Bobby laughed, pushing away the empty dinner plate.

DeShawn did not respond to his father's compliment, concentrating instead on his wife's sullen expression. He noticed it when they sat down to eat, but he didn't want to quiz her if she was simply tired.

"Babe, you alright? You've been unusually quiet throughout supper. Tough day at work?" he inquired.

Bobby regretted he hadn't noticed his daughter-in-law's demeanor and riveted his attention on her.

"The job was fine," Mariana sighed, putting her fork beside her half-eaten plate of food. "But Dr. Buffington told me Christine Williams tried to get me fired from it."

"What?" DeShawn exclaimed, astonished.

"That hateful witch!" Bobby jumped up from his seat.

"It's okay, Dad," Mariana tried to calm him before his blood pressure skyrocketed. "My job is safe. The doctor didn't like her trying to meddle in his practice, and he only told me about her attempt so I would be careful of her, that's all."

"What did you ever do to her?" Bobby demanded. "Nothing!"

"It's because of me, Dad," DeShawn admitted dejectedly.

"That woman is about to get a visit!" Bobby pushed his chair into the table and took a few steps toward the front door.

"No! No! No! Dad, please don't. You'll make it worse for us," De-Shawn pleaded.

That stopped Bobby in his tracks. He didn't want to add to the young couple's troubles. He turned around and sat back down with his little family at the table.

"So, you're just going to turn the other cheek? After this, you'll be out of cheeks," Bobby grumbled.

DeShawn folded his hands on the tabletop, mirroring the composure gathering internally.

"Dad, you need to know I will not hesitate to defend my wife if she's genuinely in harm's way. There's no question. But this situation doesn't call for it."

He looked to Mariana to gauge her agreement, and she responded, "That's right."

"We're not going to seek revenge because that doesn't honor the Lord or demonstrate we trust Him to be our defender. Yes, we're going to turn the other cheek, but we'll do more than that. Mariana and I will bless those who curse us. We'll pray for them and seek their good. That's our plan with Mrs. Williams," DeShawn stated while Mariana nodded her endorsement.

"I don't know how you do that," Bobby retorted with a shrug of his shoulders.

"Neither do I," DeShawn responded honestly. "Except by God's help and strength. Any man can go off on whoever's hurt them. But I'm trying to be a different man, Dad. I'm trying to be a God-fearing, God-pleasing man. He knows that, and He'll help me."

"See? That!" Mariana held her hands toward DeShawn as if showing off a prize while looking Bobby in the eye. "That's why I married your son," she beamed proudly.

"Sexy has changed since I was a young man," Bobby shook his head, not entirely understanding what Mariana found so attractive about being God-oriented.

"No, it hasn't, Dad. It's just not our ultimate priority," DeShawn grinned at his wife, pleased with her compliment. He understood it well, and it was the same reason he loved Mariana from the depths of his heart.

CHAPTER FORTY-ONE

The backyard of 306 Cedar Street was brimming with friends and neighbors enjoying the holiday break from their routines. Seven residents of the house, three McBrides, four Normans, Will and his two boys, and six Jeffersons gathered for food and lawn games on Memorial Day. However, the threat of heavy clouds releasing loads of rain caused them to wisely move the food indoors.

The men had organized themselves into four corn hole teams and were conducting what started as an all-in-fun tournament. It grew increasingly cutthroat, with trash-talking and whispered strategies among the participants.

"It's a good ting we have da indwelling Holy Spirit to restrain our tongues," Marcus observed wryly.

"Do you think there will be competitive games in heaven?" Cal polled the collective group.

"If there are, you'll be a sanctified loser there," Will ribbed.

"And you'll be humble, Will!" DeShawn defended Cal, grinning at him.

The water balloons and Dollar Town squirt guns attracted the children to the Chicken Bowl Kiddie Pool enclosure. At the moment, a garden hose was draped over the fence, refilling the water that had been splashed out. Although most of the kids were blue-lipped from the cold water and dropping air temperature, it didn't inhibit their enthusiasm to soak one another.

"Has there ever been a real chicken in the Chicken Bowl Kiddie Pool?" Silas asked, eyeing the coop of feathered birds across the yard.

"Not yet!" Chase answered with a gleam in his eye.

"Let's go get one!" Kayne Jefferson encouraged the older boys.

"You guys better not, 'cause you'll get in trouble," Lovie, the only girl, cautioned. "Besides, I don't want to play in chicken poop water!"

"True," Chase reconsidered. "They poop everywhere!"

In the kitchen and dining room, the women gathered condiments, set buns on platters, and prepped lettuce, onions, and tomatoes for the hamburgers and hotdogs. Besides these picnic staples, Mariana brought Barbeque Chicken Pasta Salad, DeShawn brought his homemade blueberry lemon cake and chocolate raspberry cake, Bobby brought two party-size bags of potato chips, Will brought two boxes of bomb pops for the kids and six 2-liter bottles of soda, Shelby brought baked bean casserole and homemade chocolate chip cookies, and Kesha Jefferson brought an enormous fruit salad in a hollowed-out watermelon carved with a handle shaped like a flowing ribbon. In sum, it was a veritable summer feast.

"Kesha, your fruit salad looks like an artistic labor of love. How did you find the time with four boys under your roof?" Maric wondered.

"I got Jonathan to take them all to the park this morning to run off some energy, although you couldn't tell it by looking at them now," Kesha answered. She glanced out the kitchen window to count four brown heads near the stock tank before she continued. "Then I put my praise music on the Bluetooth speaker and had some church while I chopped fruit," she laughed.

"We kind of had that this mornin' when we were makin' hamburger patties, only it was June playin' the piano in the livin' room," Elodie recalled.

Just then, an ear-splitting clap of thunder jolted everyone into action.

The men abandoned their corn hole tournament, dropping beanbags and hustling children out of the stock tank enclosure and into the house. The ladies ushered them all inside, instructing children to leave the water balloons and guns they carried outside the kitchen door. Shelby and Sam, Will's oldest son, who had been having a little tête-à-tête on the front porch glider, scurried in the front door.

"Ha!" Ava exclaimed when they gathered in the kitchen. "We didn't have to ring a dinner bell to get everyone inside. The Lord did it for us at just the right time!"

"Aaaagh!" Christine shrieked at the deafening sound. Alone in the substantial house meant to accommodate a family, she was immersed in the weather reporting channel and expected the rainstorm they said could turn violent. Still, the thunderclap startled her and shook her nerves.

Christine hated summer storms. It was the only time she disliked living alone. Over the years, she'd done everything possible to mitigate vulnerabilities. Twenty years ago, she installed a lightning rod to channel any strike safely to the ground. Ten years later, she removed a majestic oak tree behind her house because, in the remote chance the wind uprooted the entire tree, it could crush the roof. Five years ago, she discovered a loose post in her picket fence and had the whole thing inspected and sturdily reinforced. She didn't want a strong wind shooting pickets like missiles through her windows. Just last year, when she'd heard about looting after a storm in another city, she had a whole-house generator installed behind her house so she would always have lights.

Christine turned off her television, grabbed her cell phone from the kitchen counter, and headed for the security of her unfinished basement, where she kept a folding cot in a cleared corner. She pulled her sweater tightly around her, laid down on her side, and tucked an arm under her head. Without a pillow or blanket, she'd wait out the storm that would be upon Cedar Street, curled up on the cot.

It wasn't long before the rain started and the wind picked up, hurling sideways pellet drops against the low basement window above her head. Though it was hours before sunset, the basement was practically dark. A vivid flash of lightning followed the next crack of thunder, dispelling the darkness momentarily.

On and on, waves of cracking thunder and serrated swords of electricity rolled over Christine's head. She attempted to drown out the clamor by placing her hands over her ears. Every explosion elicited a spasm of muscle tension in her shoulders and abdomen, and in her distress, she cursed her beloved Clarkson for leaving her alone.

Although it felt like an hour, the fast-moving storm passed over the neighborhood in less than ten minutes, leaving no significant damage. When all was quiet outside, Christine remained curled up on the cot, too exhausted to do anything but let liquid stress run from her eyes and weakly wish she had a companion to get through life's storms.

Chapter Forty-Two

Lovie walked through the open door of her Aunt Shelby's bedroom and vaulted onto the queen-size bed. She rolled onto her stomach, propped her elbows, and placed her hands on either side of her jaw.

"Whatcha doin'?" She asked Shelby, who stood in front of the open bi-fold doors of her closet.

"I'm trying to decide what to wear to church tomorrow," Shelby answered, biting a fingernail. "Say! If I bought us matching summer dresses, would you come to church next week with me as my mini-me?" Shelby recalled how much Lovie had delighted in her new dress for Easter service. Maybe she could entice her precious niece to attend church on an ordinary Sunday with 'dress ministry.'

"Aunt Shelby, I'm too old for matching dresses. That ship has sailed," Lovie answered flatly.

"Ha!" Shelby laughed. "You heard your dad use that expression last night when Chase asked him if he'd want to try being a professional golfer. And you used it correctly!"

Lovie beamed, pleased with herself, and recognized an opportunity. She sat upright on the bed, cross-legged, and continued, adding honey to her voice, "But, I would wear any dress you wanted me to if I was in your wedding."

"Oh, you would?" Shelby chuckled and abandoned her wardrobe inspection. She moved to the bed and stretched out next to Lovie.

"Yes! I'm probably too young to be your maid of honor, though I'm willing if needed. And I'm definitely too old to be a flower girl. But I could be a junior bridesmaid. When Lena's mother remarried, Lena was a junior bridesmaid," Lovie reasoned, trying her best to be persuasive.

"A junior bridesmaid, huh?" Shelby mulled.

"Uh-huh. Come on!" Lovie grabbed Shelby's hand and pulled her off the bed toward the door.

"Where are we going?"

"The neighbor ladies are on their front porch drinking sweet tea. I just came from there. They can give you advice," Lovie appealed. She had a good feeling the ladies would advocate for her.

Shelby smiled and humored her niece, knowing she was working an angle. She was okay with it. Besides, Shelby enjoyed interacting with the ladies' next door. They might even have some helpful suggestions for her.

"I'm baaack!" Lovie called to the friends still seated on their front porch.

"Long time no see," Elodie teased her.

"I brought Aunt Shelby so you could help her decide on a junior bridesmaid," Lovie stated, making a hopeful face with teeth clenched loosely to express her preferred outcome.

Shelby stood behind her niece and winked at the older women.

"Oh, a junior bridesmaid position is up for consideration?" Marie played along. "That's a big decision dependent on a variety of factors. Why don't you ladies come up on the porch so we can delve into this?"

Lovie and Shelby seated themselves on the porch floor, their backs resting against the two center pillars.

"How large is your bridal party, Shelby? Perhaps it's big enough, and you should be cutting and not adding attendants," Ava queried with feigned seriousness.

"Well, Kesha Jefferson is going to be my matron-of-honor, and Mariana McBride will be a bridesmaid. That's it so far. But Will is having

Jonathan as his best man and Sam and Silas as groomsmen, so it's a little lopsided."

"Interesting," Marie nodded.

"See? You need me!" Lovie exclaimed.

"Now, wait a minute," June interrupted, scrambling for an objection. "Have you decided on a color scheme? It might spoil your pictures if it doesn't suit Lovie's skin tone."

Lovie shot June a look of consternation for potentially sabotaging her campaign.

"That is yet to be decided," Shelby answered.

"There's no more cheerful color combination on God's green earth than pink and yellow!" Marie interjected, forgetting the charade they were playing with the child and trying to be helpful.

"I don't think Will is a big fan of pink," Shelby advised, trying to be gentle with her dismissal of the suggestion.

"Since you're getting married on Labor Day, how about red, white, and blue?" June recommended.

"It's also the unofficial end of summer and beginning of autumn," Ava contributed. "You might try cranberry and orange!'"

Shelby wrinkled her nose, dismissing those suggestions as well.

"Periwinkle blue and lilac purple," Elodie threw out her proposal without elaboration.

"It's been her bedroom color scheme since Elodie was a teenager a hundred years ago," Marie explained to Shelby with a dismissive eye roll.

"I love it!" Shelby exclaimed. "It's calm and refined. Not too girly. I think Will would agree."

"You'll have to excuse her. Marie's not familiar with 'calm and refined.'" Elodie gloated.

Marie stuck her tongue out at her friend in response.

"I look good in both blue and purple!" Lovie aimed to refocus the discussion.

"I guess that settles it then," Shelby wanted to put her out of her misery. "Lovie, would you consider being my junior bridesmaid? You don't have to give me an answer right away. You can think about it over the next week or so."

"I'll do it!" Lovie shouted to establish the agreement without delay. "Can I get my hair done fancy?" She was on to her next goal.

"Well, we can't have it looking like this, can we?" Shelby teased as she reached over and flipped a straggly lock of Lovie's blonde hair.

"I call this a productive porch meeting – two important decisions made!" Ava cheered.

"Only a hundred more to go," Shelby exhaled, tipping her head against the pillar.

"You're getting married at Grace Fellowship, I presume?" June inquired.

"Yup. That's a done deal," Shelby answered.

"And your reception?" Marie raised a curious eyebrow.

"Still up in the air. It won't be a huge affair – between 50 and 70 people. But we'd rather not have the reception in the fellowship hall. We're thinking of something outdoorsy since the weather will be warm. The local park pavilion is an option, and Will's going to call Monday to see if it's available on Labor Day."

The ladies looked among themselves, doubtful. Then, Ava's countenance brightened as an idea emerged.

CHAPTER FORTY-THREE

By the gracious invitation of longtime members Earl and Edith Eggleston, Grace Fellowship Church was having an old-fashioned potluck picnic and baptism service at the Eggleston farm pond.

The social committee planned to provide the tables and instructed everyone to bring their own folding chairs. They organized a sign-up list to ensure an appropriate ratio of entrees, salads, and desserts. They also planned with forethought to bring a few white baptism gowns and towels for those following the ordinance.

What the social committee did not plan for were the clouds of biting mosquitoes and the breeze that carried the odor of Eggleston's pigsty across the buffet line.

"I think I've lost my appetite," Marie lamented as she tried to cover her nose with a handkerchief and serve herself from the table fare.

"If you breathe through your mouth, the smell isn't too bad," Elodie instructed, standing behind her.

"Ooooh! Got a bug in my mouth!" June exclaimed.

"Well, keep your teeth clenched when you mouth-breathe," Elodie elaborated.

"I have a bug. In my mouth!" June repeated with revulsion. She stepped out of the buffet line and began spitting at the ground.

"Darlin', we're doing the seed-spittin' contest after dinner, not before," Cal tried to correct his wife's behavior from further down the line.

"Bug!" June snapped at him.

"We're having a bug-spittin' contest after dinner?" he looked puzzled.

June turned away and focused on the task at hand. After several more attempts to dislodge the insect, she threw up her hands and confessed: "I must have swallowed it."

"Let's find a table upwind," Ava suggested after she filled her plate with salads.

"There are no tables upwind," Grant whispered behind her. "I already checked."

"We're going to make da best of dis," Marcus encouraged in a low voice.

"Look! A mosquito is dining on me. Right there on my arm! I'm carrying him to our table, and his belly is filling as I watch," Ava remarked, amazed and horrified at once. Carrying her plate in one hand and a cup of watery lemonade in the other, she had no choice but to allow the insect to bite her.

By the time the friends seated themselves at a section of the tables, which had been arranged end-to-end to form one enormously long dinner table, most of the children were finished eating. They seemed oblivious to the environmental irritants and happily scampered around the farm.

The Egglestons were not prepared for this. The children chased the pair of nesting ducks from their pond-side abode. They threw all manner of food scraps into the pigsty, including forbidden hamburgers and chicken bones. And the kiddos helped themselves to ripe blueberries from the few bushes Mrs. Eggleston planned to harvest for canning.

"Pastor Jefferson!" Earl Eggleston whispered over Jonathan's shoulder as he finished his supper. "Can we get the baptisms moving along? These kids are wreaking havoc!"

Jonathan looked around to locate his kids, but he did not see them. He wiped his mouth and rose to comply with the request.

"Kesha, can you round up the kids and tell them it's time for the baptism service? Corral them near the pond, please," he instructed.

It took another 15 minutes for the children to settle on the grass around the pond. The adults positioned their chairs in a semicircle behind the children, and the four baptismal candidates donned white robes and formed a line at the water's edge.

"Have you been baptized?" Chase, about to witness his first baptism, whispered to Silas.

"Yup, just last year. But not in a pond or anything cool like this. I got baptized at the church by my dad," Silas whispered back.

"Your dad?" Chase's eyes widened. "But he's not the pastor!"

"Yeah, I don't know the rules, but Pastor Jefferson said it was okay, and my dad wanted to do it. Anyway, he did it just like Pastor does. You'll see." Silas slapped a mosquito biting his bare leg.

Pastor Jefferson, barefoot and wearing black shorts and a t-shirt, waded into the pond, trying to banish concern about the presence of snapping turtles in the water. He beckoned the first candidate to follow him. Shelby Norman, clad in a white baptismal gown, heeded her pastor's instruction.

Chase's jaw dropped in stunned surprise. His Aunt Shelby hadn't told him she was getting baptized. In fact, she had told no one but Will.

"Church, this is Shelby Norman. Shelby came to faith last year through the faithful witness of a neighbor and now seeks to follow Christ in obedience by being baptized and joining our fellowship," Jonathan spoke to the congregation assembled at the pond.

The ladies of 306 Cedar Street exchanged expressions of surprise and delight.

"Shelby, have you repented of your sin and placed your faith solely and completely in Jesus Christ, who, by his perfect life, death on the cross, and resurrection, secured your salvation from God's holy judgment?" Jonathan asked.

"I have," responded Shelby.

"Based on your profession of faith, I baptize you, my sister, in the name of the Father, Son, and Holy Spirit," Jonathan pronounced.

He covered Shelby's nose and mouth with a handkerchief and lowered her backward into the murky pond water until she was fully submerged, proclaiming: "Buried in the likeness of His death." And helping her upright again: "Raised to walk in the newness of life."

Pastor Jefferson then turned to the assembled congregation and asked: "Based on Shelby's testimony of faith and her obedience to follow the Lord in the ordinance of baptism, do you accept her into the membership of Grace Fellowship Church? All those in favor, please signify by raising your hand."

As best as Jonathan could tell, every voting member present raised their hand. He patted her on the back and signaled the next candidate to join him in the pond as Shelby waded out. Then, Jonathan repeated the baptismal procedure with 44-year-old attorney Joe Jacobs, 11-year-old Janie Helms, and 10-year-old Evan Fletcher.

"Evan Fletcher is a little punk!" Chase whispered to Silas. "How is he getting baptized?"

"Baptism isn't about us being good enough," Silas whispered back. "It's about Jesus' work on our behalf being good enough. Evan is a baby Christian just starting out on his journey of sanctification. If you think about it, there's still a lot of 'punk' left in us, too."

Chase couldn't disagree with that. It had been a long time since he'd hit Lovie, but he still wanted to once in a while when she got on his last nerve. He'd also like to knock a tooth or two from Trevor Allman's nasty smirk, and he still looked side-eyed at Christine Williams when he saw her at church. The more he thought about it, Chase had to admit he had as much punk in him as Evan Fletcher.

After the baptisms concluded, Mr. Eggleston dismissed everyone to the buffet line again since the entrees and salads had been replaced with cakes and fruit. Will, Chase, and the neighbors waited for Shelby to return from the Eggleston farmhouse, where the baptized could dry off and change clothes.

"Why didn't you tell us you were getting baptized?" Marie asked when Shelby appeared at last.

"I didn't want to draw attention to myself for that. Besides, I knew you'd all be here regardless," Shelby admitted shyly, still fluffing damp locks of hair.

"I could have gotten baptized with you," Chase groaned at the missed opportunity.

"Well, you need to talk with your dad about that," Shelby reminded.

Chase lowered his head and walked away as the others congratulated and encouraged his aunt. *"Talking to Dad is easier said than done,"* he thought. It had occurred to him recently that his father spent more time alone in his bedroom, giving Lovie's care over to his sister in the evenings. Chase sensed his dad pulling away from them, and he didn't know why. But he knew it hurt.

Chapter Forty-Four

"Did you have a pleasant stroll around the neighborhood?" Bobby asked DeShawn and Mariana as they walked in the kitchen door.

"We did," Mariana began. "We thought we would get to know Grant Renniger a bit because he was starting his walk just as we passed his house, but he ditched us after a few minutes. He said he forgot something at home and hurried back the way we came like his hair was on fire."

Bobby chuckled, understanding his neighbor's hurry to get to his bathroom.

"We got to say hello to the ladies on their porch on our way home, though," DeShawn added. "They're some sweet saints."

"Oh, the ladies are out?" Bobby asked, raising an eyebrow.

"Better get moving if you want to ask Miss Elodie to walk with you before you have to bring her home when the streetlights come on," DeShawn teased his father.

Bobby grinned at his son and headed out the front door so the women would see him approaching sooner than if he came up the side of their house. He figured it would seem more casual and less likely to surprise them. As he stepped onto his porch, Bobby realized he would still have to walk around the neighborhood if Elodie declined his invitation. He didn't want it to appear that getting fresh air and exercise wasn't worth doing if Elodie didn't join him. It wasn't, but he didn't want it to appear that way and embarrass himself.

"Good evening, ladies," Bobby said, pretending to tip an invisible cap on his head.

"Hello, Bobby," June was the first to reply. "It's a pretty evening for walking. I'd walk myself if I weren't so comfy enjoying the evening from my chair here."

"Well, you stay comfy then. What about you, Miss Elodie? Would you like to take a therapeutic walk for your back?" Bobby asked, unaware Elodie's back was perfectly healed.

Elodie looked sheepishly at Marie before answering, "Why not?" as if she had nothing better to do. She rose from her chair, fluffed her tiered white summer skirt, and met Bobby at the end of the walkway from the house to the sidewalk. Together, they headed down Cedar Street at a leisurely pace.

"I hope you've not been in too much pain today," Bobby said sympathetically.

Elodie wondered if any of the guys had brought up her healing at Garage Cave game night. She'd like to keep up the pretense of accepting walking invitations purely for the exercise value but knew she had to tell the truth. She'd be mortified if Bobby learned her back had improved, and she got caught in a pretense acting like it hadn't. More importantly, she'd be ashamed to be dishonest before her omnipresent Savior.

"Not a bit. In fact, in a strange circumstance only God could orchestrate, my back has been healed," Elodie answered forthrightly.

"You don't say! I've never known anyone with back trouble to get permanent relief without going under the knife. Good for you." Bobby congratulated her.

"I was tryin' to doctor myself with pain relievers, hot and cold packs, rest, and soakin' in the Epsom salts. But in the back of my mind, I was gearin' myself up for the possibility it might take surgery to fix what I had goin' on. In my wildest dreams, I never would have imagined that some hooligan kid trying to hurt me would end up being what God used to heal me," Elodie confessed.

"Who tried to hurt you?" Bobby demanded with a scowl.

"Doesn't matter who. God got the last laugh on him. But I was prayin' at the middle school for the kid's summer recess, and my back was achin', so I just laid out in the grass to pray," Elodie explained matter-of-factly.

"You laid out in the grass?" Bobby grimaced. His mind recalled Ava laid out on her backyard grass when she was grieving her daughters, and he wondered if his neighbor ladies were into some goofy religious practices.

"It sounds weird, I know," Elodie admitted. "But I don't care. Sometimes, when I pray to God in my room, I lie out on the floor because some prayers just call for it – like when you don't know what to do with yourself about somethin'. God sees. He knows.

Anyway, this kid steps on my back, laughin' and hollerin' about there bein' trash on the ground. But as soon as his foot left me, I knew I didn't feel any pain. I admit now I feared he'd paralyzed me, so I wiggled my feet right away and realized I was okay. Since then, I've been pain-free thanks to God puttin' that foot exactly where it needed to be."

"Maybe the kid thought you were drunk and passed out," Bobby blurted.

Elodie stopped in her tracks and glared at him over the rim of her glasses before a wry smile crept into the corners of her mouth.

"Well, I didn't think of that. But we're not teachin' our children it's okay to step on the sobriety-impaired now, are we?" she replied defensively.

Bobby stopped a step ahead and looked back at Elodie. "We shouldn't be, but who knows what goes on in classrooms these days," he answered, shaking his head.

The two neighbors continued to walk in silence for the next block until Bobby said what he'd been pondering: "You and I are a lot alike in some ways. But in other ways…" He left his sentence unfinished.

"In other ways, we're different," Elodie completed the thought.

"We both like big band music and dancing!" Bobby scrambled to focus on their common ground. "And corn pudding. Your friends are becoming my friends. We both like sports and suspense novels."

"But, we're different where it's most important to be the same – in our faith in God," Elodie spoke candidly.

"Yeah," Bobby admitted dejectedly before rising to challenge her. "But why does that have to be the most important thing?"

Elodie considered her answer before she gave it. She added some transparency and vulnerability to her honest conversation.

"A long time ago, I married and didn't make it the most important thing. That marriage lasted a weekend, and I'll not make the same mistake again."

"Elodie, I'm so sorry," Bobby responded, uncertain if he was sympathizing with her hurt or apologizing for being faithless. He had several questions but chose not to pry. If she ever wanted to, she would tell him the details. But now, at least, he understood where she was coming from.

"You know," he began again after walking a bit more. "When you said you pray laid out on the floor when you're not sure what else to do with yourself? And you said God sees you, and he knows everything? I could almost want your faith just to have that."

"*Almost,*" Elodie considered the word in her mind, "*is just not close enough.*"

Chapter Forty-Five

S helby ran to the front door when she heard the mail drop from the slot and hit the floor. It was her daily habit to fling open the door and blow Will a kiss as he continued on his route. But today, instead of being several paces down the walkway, he stood at the door.

"I have fabulous news, and I have horrible news. Which would you like first?" Will asked as soon as the door opened.

"Um, I guess the horrible news first so that the fabulous news will take the sting out," Shelby answered quickly, knowing Will had little time to chat.

"I'm not sure that'll work. I need to tell the fabulous news first so the horrible news makes sense," Will bargained.

"Okay," Shelby laughed. "Whatever."

"I've rented us the gray house!" he turned and pointed across the street. "You'll get to stay in this neighborhood and won't have to move from your family but 30 yards. The landlord will even hold it for us until August 1st because they believe we'll be good, quality tenants, and that's important to them in the long term. It'll give us a month to move our stuff in and get all set up before the wedding."

"No way!" Shelby squealed with delight. "Can we afford it?"

"Yes. The rent is reasonable," Will assured.

"This is more than I ever hoped for, Will," she stepped across the threshold and hugged her fiancé's neck.

"I told you it was fabulous news," he grinned. "But are you ready for the horrible bit?"

"Go ahead. I can't imagine what could burst my happiness now."

"Christine Williams owns the house. She's our landlord," Will groaned.

"I don't care!" Shelby responded chipperly. "We're going to be living in a house in this neighborhood, which was never a possibility in my imagination. We'll be the perfect tenants for Mrs. Williams, and we won't give her anything to complain about. How bad could it be?"

"You have the best possible attitude, Babe. She knows we'll be the next tenants and is pleased enough to hold the house for us for several weeks. That's getting off to a good start, right?"

"Absolutely! Oh, Will, this is the best news ever. Thank you for doing this!"

"I knew you'd be excited and pleased," Will shared in her happiness. "Gotta go now. We'll talk after work." He turned and started down the porch steps.

"You forgot something!" Shelby called after him. And when he turned toward her, she blew him his daily kiss.

Come over after supper. We have a proposition.

Shelby read Marie's text message; her curiosity piqued. At 6:30 PM, she headed to her neighbors' house and found the ladies waiting for her on their front porch.

"Good evening, girls!" Shelby greeted them playfully. "Have you been hatching a scheme?"

"We might be," answered Ava.

"Did you have any luck reservin' the pavilion at the park for Labor Day?" Elodie asked.

"No. Will said the lady at the Parks Department laughed when he asked. She said it's rented two years in advance for summer holidays," Shelby answered dejectedly, hand massaging her right temple.

"That's what we figured," June responded.

"So, here's what we'd like to offer: Instead of renting the pavilion and hiring a caterer, what if you rented one of those large white tents and had the reception on our corner lot lawn? We'd gift you the catering. You said about 70 people at most, right? We could manage that," Marie suggested.

"Tell me you're serious!" Shelby demanded, hands on hips, daring them not to be serious.

"Serious as a nun with a ruler," Elodie grinned.

"I don't know what to say. That sounds perfect!" Shelby stepped back onto the walkway, trying to picture the tent on the back side of the magnolia tree.

"An outdoor reception in the beautiful yard of the beautiful home of my beautiful friends. Will and I were at a loss for what to do, and you've saved the day. Thank you so much for your generosity. Don't mind me. I have to sit," she said, returning to the porch and lowering herself onto the steps.

"God has poured out His blessings on Will and me today. Besides providing the venue for a reception, I found out today who will be renting the gray house across the street." Shelby paused for dramatic effect, giving the ladies a few seconds of curious anticipation. "Us! We'll just be across the street from Micah, the kids, you all, and the McBrides. I didn't even think to ask God for that because it was too much."

A look of concern appeared on Marie's face. "Do you know who owns the house?" she tried to sound casual.

"Our landlady is Christine Williams," Shelby answered merrily. "She's holding it for us until August 1st."

"What?" June wondered if she'd misheard.

"Christine Williams owns the gray house?" Ava asked, needing it repeated to process the information.

"She mentioned it to me a few weeks ago," Marie volunteered.

"And she's holding it – not collecting rent on it – until August 1st?" Ava asked, trying to reconcile the kind gesture with the person responsible for it. "We're talking about the same woman who called the police to shut down Chase and Lovie's lemonade stand and who slapped Pastor Jefferson's face? That Christine Williams?"

"Maybe she had one of those personality-alterin' mini-strokes," Elodie guessed.

"Or, maybe God's working on her heart like we should all be praying for," Marie felt suddenly protective of the difficult neighbor she was getting to know.

"I didn't think she had a heart," Elodie muttered.

"Shelby, we all rejoice with you for the blessings God has given you today," June redirected the conversation. "How about we thank Him for His goodness?"

As a new Christian, Shelby was caught off guard by the suggestion. Did June mean to pray right there on the porch? She sat frozen as the women rose from their seats and encircled her, clasping hands. And then June prayed.

"Heavenly Father, only one of ten lepers healed by Jesus returned to give Him thanks. We want to be like that one – quick to recognize Your hand of blessing and quick to express our gratitude. Thank you for providing housing for Will and Shelby above and beyond what they hoped for. Thank You for reminding us all of Proverbs 21:1, which says a king's heart is a stream of water in Your hand, and You turn it wherever You will. So, too, You have turned the heart of our difficult neighbor to display Your kindness. Truly, nothing is too hard for You!

We also thank You for the joy of being part of Your provision for Will and Shelby's reception. May their celebration dinner with family and friends give us all a little longing for The Marriage Supper Of The Lamb in our eternal home.

Lord, as You often hear our prayers for Your help and rescue, now hear our prayer of grateful thanksgiving for Your loving kindness. For blessing us, we bless the name of Jesus in Whose name we pray. Amen."

Chapter Forty-Six

"Good morning, Calcium," Elodie greeted her breakfast partner as she entered the kitchen, tightening the belt of her purple chenille robe. "It sounds quiet in the house for a Saturday mornin'. Usually everyone but your wife is putterin' around by now."

"Marie and June are the only ones here besides you and me. Grant left to scope out another golf course, and the Van Zants took off with overnight bags about 20 minutes ago," Cal shared.

"Overnight bags? Where'd they go?" Elodie quizzed.

"Marcus said Marley called them last night and invited them to spend Father's Day weekend at their house. It was all last minute."

"That was smart of Marley to ask them at the last minute and not give them too much time to stress about it. It'll be a little hard for them since this will be the first they've ventured to Bloomington since leavin'," Elodie reasoned. "Sure hope they have a good time with Marley's family. Say, what'd you eat for breakfast?"

"Bran Flakes," Cal responded with a grimace. He ate them only to please June.

"Ugh. I can't do that," Elodie walked over to the pantry to explore its other options.

"Good morning, Cal, Elodie," Marie acknowledged her friends. She wore a soft grey summer sweater and wide-leg dark blue jeans. Her salt and pepper hair pulled into a messy bun on top of her head.

"Marie, how'd you like to go to Latte Da for breakfast with me? I'm cravin' one of those lemon-poppyseed muffins Ava brought home from there once. Remember how good those were?" Elodie coaxed.

"Sounds like a plan to me. But you're not going in your bathrobe," Marie stipulated.

"You think you needed to say that?" Elodie griped. She gave Marie a playful poke in her ribs as she passed her on her way toward the staircase.

"I remember how good those muffins were," Cal pouted to Marie.

"You want to come with?" Marie offered with a genuine smile.

"Are you going to make me change my clothes?" Cal wanted to know.

"Those are your Saturday white t-shirt and overalls, correct? You haven't gone crazy and put on your Wednesday set, have you?" Marie teased.

Cal gave her a puzzled look, wondering if she seriously thought he had overalls for designated days.

"Never mind. Go ask Sleeping Beauty if she'll let you out in public with El and me," Marie instructed.

Cal rose from his seat to seek his wife's approval to accompany Marie and Elodie to Latte Da. In five minutes, both Elodie and Cal were back in the kitchen.

"Junie says I have to bring her home a muffin. Don't let me forget it," Cal said, putting a baseball cap over his thin white hair.

"I thought you had breakfast," Elodie reacted to the news Cal would join the ladies.

"I thought so, too. Turns out it was just my pre-breakfast appetizer," Cal grinned jovially. "I'll get my truck and drive you ladies in redneck style. Meet me out front."

"Oh, joy," Elodie deadpanned.

Cal hoisted himself into the driver's seat of his white F-150 and turned the key in the ignition. Glancing in his left side mirror, he noticed Micah's van parked at an unusual angle in the driveway next door. Moreover,

Micah seemed to be slumped over the steering wheel.

Cal jerked the key from the ignition and raced as quickly as he could manage over to Micah. He rapped his knuckle on the driver's side window.

"Micah! You okay, buddy?" he shouted.

Micah roused himself and, after clumsily attempting to open the electric window while the vehicle was off, opened the door.

"Can I help you?" Micah slurred, spewing a cloud of noxious alcohol breath under Cal's nose.

"You alright there, Micah?" Cal braced himself in case his neighbor tumbled out of his seat. Instantly, he wished Grant, an experienced father of men Micah's age, was nearby to handle the situation in his place.

"Never better!" Micah responded too quickly. Then, taking stock of his situation, he explained. "Had a late night and didn't want to disturb the family coming inside. Took a nap out here. What time is it?"

"It's 7:35," Cal informed after consulting his watch.

"Okay, they'll still be sleeping. I'll go get some coffee at the gas station." Micah reached for the van keys on the dashboard.

"Can I see those?" Cal asked, holding his hand out to receive them.

Micah looked at Cal suspiciously but handed them over as requested.

"You'll find these in your mailbox later this afternoon. You're in no shape to drive," Cal insisted, stepping away from the vehicle.

"I'm a grown man!" Micah growled, eyebrows knit fiercely together.

"So am I," Cal answered, standing his ground and squaring off with his angered neighbor. "You don't want me to take your keys away, and I don't want to do it. But I care about you, son, and I'm not about to let you hurt yourself or your family. I'll do everything in my power to prevent it. Now, you don't have to prove to me you're a grown man, but if you need to prove it to yourself by knocking me down for these keys, help yourself. I won't give them back without a fight."

After a tense moment of indecision, Micah spat: "You're a miserable old man!"

He pulled his van door shut, remaining inside.

Cal put Micah's key ring in his pocket as he returned to his truck. *"I've been called worse,"* he shrugged as he walked.

"What took you so long? Did you have to hand-crank the engine on this thing to get it started?" Marie ridiculed, opening the passenger door.

"I said hello to Micah out back," Cal answered.

The ladies asked nothing about their conversational exchange, and Cal didn't offer any details. Instead, the women poked at one another, trying to get the other to take the seat next to Cal.

"Come on, heifers! Load yourselves in the truck!" Cal commanded the dawdling ladies, who looked at each other in astonishment at his cheeky remark.

Cal's encounter with Micah had released a dab of testosterone, and he was feeling it.

Chapter Forty-Seven

Even though he showered, shaved, and dressed for church, Grant felt tired as he entered the kitchen for tea and breakfast. The previous day's golf outing had drained him after being away from it since last fall. He could tell he'd lost some stamina in those long months.

"Happy Father's Day!" Marie, Elodie, June, and Cal greeted him from their seats at the kitchen table.

"I'm Father to none of you. But, thanks," Grant smiled, still pleased to be acknowledged.

"Well, it's Father's Day, and you're the only one here it applies to. So, there you are," Elodie commented bruskly.

"I've made your tea and bought you the raspberry/cream cheese Danish you like. Come sit!" Marie instructed.

"There's one piece left!" Grant noted with dismay.

"We thought you'd be pleased to share it with those making a big deal over you for nothing we've benefited from. Besides, it's a middle piece. Marie made sure we saved you that," Cal justified.

Grant chuckled and shook his head as he took his seat. "I do love the middle piece, and I appreciate your kindness." He bowed his head and gave private thanks before biting into his Danish.

"I wonder if Chase will be joining us for church today or staying home with his dad," June wondered aloud.

Cal shifted uneasily in his chair at the mention of Micah. He had said nothing, even to June, about the drama in the Norman driveway yesterday, but he figured he should give the household a heads up that a potential estrangement – a Lovie-lied-on-Grant 2.0 situation – was brewing. He picked up a spoon and began needlessly stirring the quarter cup of coffee remaining in his mug.

"I have to tell you guys something," he began, riveting everyone's attention. "Micah and I almost came to blows in his driveway yesterday morning."

"What!" June exclaimed.

"Why?" Marie prompted for details. She fiddled with her chain bracelet in nervous anticipation of the answer.

"I took his van keys from him and told him he'd have to fight me for them. Thought he was going to try it for half a second," Cal explained.

"Have you completely lost your God-given sense?" Elodie demanded.

"He was drunk," Cal supplied the critical detail.

His friends released a collective groan, "Ooooh."

"I jumped to a conclusion. My bad," Elodie recanted her terse criticism.

"You did the right thing," June commended her husband.

"I was wishing you were there instead of me. Your boys are around Micah's age," Cal made direct eye contact with Grant. "I've got no fathering experience."

"Wrong!" Marie interjected. "You might have been able to say that before yesterday, but you were a father to Micah by showing the man some tough love when he needed it."

"Yeah, buddy. You stepped up for him like any good dad would," Grant encouraged.

June beamed with pride at her husband, and he basked in it for a moment before remembering something.

"He called me a 'miserable old man,'" Cal recalled.

"You're the least miserable old man I know, even though you've had every reason to be!" June declared.

"Miserable old man, miserable old man, M.O.M," Marie thought aloud. "You weren't a father to Micah. You were a mom!" she laughed, and the others joined her.

***

Micah watched for Cal's truck to return from church with the vigilance of a Marine sentry at the picture window of his living room. He was supposed to be taking Lovie and Chase to visit Dahlia's dad for Father's Day but felt he couldn't go until he'd spoken to Cal. Otherwise, it would continue to preoccupy his thoughts and ruin his sleep as it had last night.

Five minutes after noon, Cal's white truck pulled into the driveway next door, and Micah was relieved to see that he was alone. As he hurried out of his kitchen door onto the back porch, he figured Miss June must be walking home with the others.

"Cal! Hey, Cal!" Micah called out.

Cal stood at the end of his truck's tailgate and waited as Micah crossed the narrow grass strip separating their driveways. *"He's giving me a head's up that he's coming, so this isn't an ambush. Wonder if he wants to apologize,"* was all that Cal had time to process.

"Cal, I feel terrible about what happened yesterday," Micah confessed when he reached his neighbor and stood before him. "I hope you understand I wasn't myself."

Cal recognized he wasn't apologizing, so he didn't throw out cheap forgiveness. Instead, he asked: "Who were you?"

"I don't know," Micah answered, shifting his gaze to his feet. "I went out Friday night, and I guess I had too much to drink."

"And then you drove yourself home. That was foolish, Micah."

"I knooow," Micah whined. He wanted to smooth things over without a lecture.

"Well, who gets to raise Chase and Lovie if you kill yourself or if you go to prison because you kill someone else? You know, just so we don't have to wonder. Will they become Shelby's responsibility because you can't handle yours?" Cal spoke his mind.

His words found their mark, and Micah slumped against Cal's truck and exhaled heavily.

"I messed up, Cal. I'm messing up. I feel like I've fallen into a black hole, and all I want to do is pull the lid over it."

"Then we'd better go back to figuring out who will raise your kids. You want to pull the lid over your hole? You can do that. But Chase and Lovie need you now, so you should wait until they are grown. Your other option is to climb out of that hole. You've a hard hand to play, Micah, being their mother and father. But it's your hand, and you have a lot of people around to love you and help you. Not every single parent has that.

"I just want..." Micah began and stopped.

"What do you want, son?" Cal asked with tenderness.

"I want to be happy again. I'm miserable," Micah admitted, fighting hard not to be swept away with visible sorrow.

If Micah had faith in Christ, Cal would have consoled him with the deep comforts of God's promises toward His children. As it was, all he knew to do was step toward Micah and embrace him in a man-hug as a demonstration of his concern and affection. Micah received the gesture and they stood embracing until Cal chided: "Guess there's more than one miserable old man around here."

"I apologize for that," Micah chuckled, stepping back.

"I forgive you. You know, the acronym for 'miserable old man' is M.O.M., so you might have subconsciously been thinking of me as a parental figure," Cal suggested without revealing the source of that tidbit.

"I'm sure that's what was happening in my addle-brained state," Micah agreed, eager to latch onto the kinder version of his ugly words that Cal graciously offered.

"I'm not going to lecture you..."

"Too late!" Micah cut him off with a grin.

"Okay. To my lecture, I will simply add: You won't find the happiness you're looking for in a bottle. It didn't work Friday night, did it?"

"It did not. Nor in any time before that. It deadens the pain, though," Micah answered honestly.

"I understand. But 'dead' is not the goal, right? In any sense of the word," Cal exhorted.

"Right," Micah confirmed and extended his hand for a handshake.

Cal turned toward his nightstand to turn off the light and noticed the blue envelope. He opened it and withdrew a card with a picture of an older man, his arm draped across the shoulder of a younger man, and the printed words: Happy Father's Day. Inside was the handwritten message: You don't have to have a biological child to be a father. We're delighted to witness what a wonderful one you've been to Micah these past few days. Happy Father's Day, Cal! Love, Grant & Marie.

It was the first Father's Day card he'd ever received. Unable to speak, he handed the card to June. After she read it, she smiled at Cal and brushed a tear from his cheek.

Chapter Forty-Eight

"What do you think of a periwinkle and lilac color scheme for our wedding?" Shelby asked Will. They were sitting on the back porch steps of the Norman house, watching Lovie draw pictures with sidewalk chalk on the driveway.

"Oh yeah, that's fine," Will answered flatly.

Shelby side-hugged him and gushed, "Oh, thank you! Nobody's ever had a pumpkin and puce color scheme. We'll be so original!"

"What? Pumpkin and what?" Will turned to Shelby, now giving her his full attention.

"I can tell when you're not listening to me," Shelby laughed.

"Did I agree to something I wasn't paying attention to?"

"You agreed to a periwinkle and lilac color scheme for our wedding. Miss Elodie suggested it, and I like it."

Will considered the combination. "I like it too, and I stand by my previous agreement."

"What were you thinking about when you weren't listening to me?" Shelby quizzed.

"I was watching Lovie draw that car. Sam used to draw them the same way when he was little – every time, like a VW bug. So, I was thinking about Sam and that he only has two years of high school left. I don't know where the time went. It flew by," Will reflected, rubbing a hand over his short, dark hair.

Before Shelby had a response, he shook off his nostalgic mood and said: "Speaking of cars, I have something in mine for you. Be right back!"

He jogged to his car, parked on the road in front of the house, and retrieved the item. Returning to the back porch, he held it out to Shelby.

"A book?" Shelby stated the obvious.

"It's a devotional book. There's one page for every day of the year, and they're kind of like guided tours through Bible passages. I read a page of this and the related Bible passage every morning before I pray and start my day. If we had the same book and you're agreeable, sometimes we could talk about what we read," Will explained.

Shelby examined the front and back covers and leafed through several pages.

"That's a great idea, Will. Thank you. I have notes in my Bible, but this looks like something different, perhaps more application than explanation."

"That's a good way to put it," Will acknowledged before adding: "I wanted to make sure that while we're planning our wedding, we don't forget to plan our marriage. I want to be intentional about ensuring we develop the spiritual aspect of our marriage and not just wing it."

"What you just said makes me doubly attracted to you than I was before you said it," Shelby chuckled.

"Really? What might happen if I repeated it?" Will asked mischievously.

Shelby smiled but ignored the question. "You are so different from any other boyfriend I've ever had. None of them ever talked about the spiritual aspect of a relationship or even understood one should exist. Then again, neither did I. I trudged through a lot of lonely years wishing for a husband, but you were worth the wait, Will," she sighed and laid her head on his shoulder.

"I want to make sure you still feel that way in 25 years!"

They were silent before Shelby shouted to Lovie: "Lov! Do you have any blue, purple, and green chalk left?"

"Yup, I do!" Lovie shouted back.

"Then draw me a junior bridesmaid bouquet with those colors," Shelby suggested to keep her niece occupied.

"Okay. I will!" Lovie answered and got to work on a chalk-free section of the driveway. The solar flood lamp on the garage peak was tripped on by the fading evening light.

Shelby flipped through the book in her hand again and wondered aloud: "Spiritual growth seems like a painfully slow process. Was it slow for you at first, or were you always like you are now?"

"How am I now?" Will asked, amused. The corners of his eyes crinkled.

"You know everything, and you make it look easy."

"Well, looks are deceiving. Maybe I know a lot about the Bible because I studied it full-time for ten years. Should have picked up something after all that, right? But just because someone has head knowledge doesn't mean they find putting it into practice easier than anyone else. I struggle with my sinful nature, and I have an Enemy the same as you and everybody else. In fact, just this morning, I couldn't seem to pray above the top of my head. I was scatterbrained and antsy, and I couldn't figure out what was happening with me. Was my restlessness and inability to focus in prayer the fault of my fallen nature or an attack of the Enemy? I had zero discernment."

"Does it matter?" Shelby asked innocently.

Will cocked his head and tried to form an answer. While he hesitated, Shelby continued.

"You would not believe how often that same thing happens to me. It's embarrassing. But it never occurred to me I needed to figure out if the problem was inside or outside. I just ask Jesus to help me through it, and before I know it, the flow is restored."

"Pray until you can pray," Will quoted under his breath.

"What?" Shelby requested repetition.

"Pray until you can pray. It's a quote from a famous English minister, Charles Spurgeon. It's basically what you do. You pray until you can pray – with God's help," Will informed.

"Pretty much," Shelby agreed.

"And there's your perfect example of head knowledge losing out to application! I might be able to cite a quote from a Victorian-era preacher. But there you are, organically putting the principle into timely practice while I'm floundering over the source of my trouble."

"Hmm!" Shelby muttered in surprise, raising her eyebrows.

"Miss Norman, God is so good to me in providing you for a wife. I can see your fresh perspective will be an invaluable aid to my spiritual growth. I'm a blessed man," Will confessed.

"Since we're engaged, you might start calling me by my first name," Shelby giggled. "Try it out!"

"Shelby," Will whispered.

"You are killing me, man! Now, I'm quadruple attracted to you!" Shelby gushed.

"Well, I better go home before I say something else that makes you fling yourself at me!" Will laughed heartily, delighted by her admiration.

He gave Shelby a quick kiss goodbye and walked toward his car. On his way past Lovie, he tousled her hair and admired her bouquet sketch.

"I hope we can find flowers as pretty for our junior bridesmaid," Will complimented.

"If you're lucky," Lovie answered with overflowing confidence and a grin.

CHAPTER FORTY-NINE

"What are you doin' in here, little man?" DeShawn asked, surprised to see the neighbor boy who attended his church standing inside his garage on a Saturday afternoon.

"I'm not stealing anything!" Chase, startled, defended himself.

"Okay. But I didn't ask what you weren't doing. I asked what you were doing," DeShawn reiterated, moving a few steps closer to the boy.

"Your garage door was open, and I wanted to see if Mr. McBride still had his bicycle built for two. I helped him clean out a bunch of junk last summer, and I was hoping he didn't get rid of it, too. I see he's hung it up on the wall now. And for your information, I'm not a 'little man.' I'll be starting high school in August."

"My bad," DeShawn reversed course. "So, why are you interested in the bike, Freshman?"

"I thought if the bike was still here, I'd ask your dad if he was going to ride it in the Faircourt Bike Parade like he did last year. If not, I was going to ask if Silas and I could borrow it. There's no sense in a guy risking his pride for a favor if there's no chance in the first place."

"My dad rode Blue Beauty in the Faircourt Bike Parade last year?" DeShawn, distracted by the information, asked with wide-eyed surprise. "Who rode with him? Miss Elodie?"

"You've got to be kidding. She didn't like him last year. At all. Mrs. Renniger rode with him," Chase explained.

DeShawn leaned against the tailgate of his dad's S10, which Bobby had parked in the garage, now that the junk had been removed and there was room for it again. He wasn't surprised his father held on to Blue Beauty, but he was stunned to hear his father had ridden the bike with anyone else since his mom had died. He assumed his dad kept the bike as a memorial to her as he'd kept the green enamel stove for him, unused until last Thanksgiving at his urging.

DeShawn refocused on his conversation with the boy.

"We've walked to church with the same Cedar Street pack, but I don't think you and I have ever spoken. I'm DeShawn," he said, extending his hand.

"I'm Chase," he responded, shaking DeShawn's hand. "And we have spoken. It was the day you tried to talk to Mrs. Williams."

"Oh, yeah. I think I tried to forget the whole episode. Sorry," DeShawn apologized and changed the subject. "Your dad doesn't go to church with you, does he?"

"Neither does yours!" Chase shot back.

"True. I guess that's something we have in common, huh?"

Chase, tired and hot, joined DeShawn in leaning against the tailgate.

"I wish my dad was saved," Chase lamented. He wiped away beads of summer sweat from his hairline.

"Do you do more than wish?" DeShawn challenged.

"I...er...I... I'm not sure what you mean," Chase stammered, confused by the question.

"Do you talk to your dad about the Lord? Are you telling him how important he is to you? Do you pray for the Lord to draw your dad to Himself in repentance and faith?"

Chase didn't want to be disloyal to his father, but a brewing resentment was taking hold of his heart that needed release. "I don't even see a lot of my dad. On weekdays, we have supper, and then he watches television in his room. On the weekends, he's there, but it's like he's not there. I want to tell him I want to get baptized, but it won't go over good. No, I don't pray for him like I should."

"*Whoa!*" DeShawn thought to himself, realizing he'd walked into a domestic minefield when he'd only meant to encourage the boy to be proactive in his witness.

"When I was about your age, I drifted apart from my dad. A lot of that was on me because my friends became more important than my parents. But like you say, sometimes it's the dad who grows distant. In either case, I'm not sayin' it's a good thing, but it's pretty common as boys grow into young men," DeShawn sympathized as completely as he could.

Chase remained silent.

"When I was a boy, I didn't understand my father. I sure didn't want the same things he wanted. He used to want me to come to his car lot and help with the detailing. I hated that place and those chores. Sometimes, I hated him. I wanted to be off running with my boys when he wanted me to learn how to work and take pride in it. It's funny – he wanted better for me than I wanted for myself. I couldn't understand that then." DeShawn acknowledged, open and transparent.

"How come you don't work now?" Chase asked boldly. "Your father and wife go to work, but you're here every day."

"Oh, now you're up in my business, Freshman!" DeShawn balked, staring at the child.

"It was okay when you were up in mine!" Chase, unintimidated, scoffed.

"Yeah, that's fair. Well, I plan to go to seminary part-time, about when you're off to high school. But I need a job, you're right. Why don't I get one? I guess I'm scared."

"You? Scared? Little old Mrs. Williams over there is scared of you!" Chase pointed to Christine, trimming hosta blooms in her Tamarack Street side yard.

"Mrs. Williams is scared of what she doesn't know. I guess that's my problem, too. I went to jail when I was 18 years old and then to prison. That's not much older than you are now."

"Four years," Chase informed him.

"I've never had a job. So much has changed. And people fear me – there's that. It's a lot. I just wish it were all different."

"Do you do more than wish?" Chase tossed the man's challenge back at him with an impish grin.

"Aww, you got me, man!" DeShawn reached over and playfully squeezed Chase's upper arm.

"Does your dad still need help at his car lot? Seems like that would be a good place to start," Chase suggested as he rubbed his arm, pretending it hurt.

DeShawn thought for a moment. It had seemed the obvious solution from the beginning. His father even suggested it when he learned his son would get out of prison. But DeShawn resisted because every memory of his father's business had been loathsome. It was the job of last resort. Mariana hadn't pushed the idea because she knew how he felt. For these past few months, His father and wife let him get by as he remained stuck in anxiety and indecision.

But DeShawn now realized his memories were, as he'd just verbalized to Chase, those of a kid who didn't appreciate his father's wanting more for him than he wanted for himself. They were the memories of a foolish kid who, like so many others, didn't want to learn to work and take pride in it. He wondered: Could God mean to bring him back to the place he ran from earlier just as He'd commanded Jacob to return to Bethel, where he'd run from his brother Esau? It dawned on DeShawn that he had the opportunity to make a different decision at the same place he'd made a bad one.

"Maybe I'll take your advice. Seems sound," DeShawn smiled at Chase. "So, would you like me to ask my father about borrowing the bike?"

"Sure!"

"Be right back, then." And DeShawn was off and into the house.

While he waited for the man to return, Chase watched Christine Williams working in her yard. *"Should I be praying for her, too?"* he wondered, shuddering with aversion.

"I've got bad news, Freshman. My wife said she beat you to it and asked Dad last week if she could ride it with him in the Bike Parade. So, it's spoken for this year. But, if you want to try it out and take Blue Beauty for a spin with me now, Dad said that'd be fine with him."

"Let's go!" Chase agreed, rubbing his palms on his khaki shorts.

"You want the front or back seat?" DeShawn offered the choice as he hoisted the bike from its wall rack.

"I want to say 'front,' but I've never ridden one before and don't want to put us in a ditch," Chase confessed.

"Okay, you get front next time, and I get it this time," DeShawn agreed.

They took off across Cedar Street and down Tamarack, past Christine Williams working in her yard. After they passed, she turned to watch them. She saw Chase pedaling in the rear seat and holding his hands high in the air as DeShawn steered them. And she heard them both laughing with glee.

Chapter Fifty

The Rennigers knew no one had claimed the guest room for the long 4th of July weekend, so they were confident springing G-Lu as a surprise holiday guest on the household. Grant drove to Champaign Thursday morning to pick her up and brought her back to Faircourt just in time for Thursday Meeting. Only Ava was suspicious when she found Marie removing the dust cover from the bed and polishing the furniture in the spare room. But she dared not question her friend about a potential guest lest she be recruited in the preparations. Ava had her own project to tend to. She'd let the garden weeding get ahead of her, and she vowed to remedy it by the end of the day.

G-Lu was warmly welcomed when she entered the house with Grant just as the house assembled in the living room. Everyone stood, in turn, to embrace their petite visitor before Cal grabbed a chair from the dining room and sat in it, forfeiting his comfortable spot on the end of the couch for the senior Mrs. Renniger. Even Mercy took to the newcomer, planting herself at G-Lu's feet after giving them the once-over with her nose.

Marcus ran the meeting, as he usually did, taking time to explain to their guest all the events going on over the next few days. Tomorrow, the actual holiday, was the annual Faircourt Bike Parade. Without bikes or access to the six-passenger golf cart Grant secured last year, none of the household members would take part this year. But all of them except for

Marcus and Cal, who would be tending the smoker, would walk downtown to watch to support those friends and neighbors who participated. These included Bobby and Mariana McBride, Micah, Chase and Lovie, Shelby and Will, and the Jefferson Family.

G-Lu asked if Christine Williams participated in the community event. After the household's tittering laughter subsided, G-Lu said she thought it a shame Mrs. Williams stayed so much to herself. She also bluffed that if she'd had advance notice of the parade, she would have packed her helmet and roller skates. The nearly 95-year-old's comment raised eyebrows, but no one challenged her. It could be that she was serious.

After the bike parade, neighbors on the left (Normans) and right (McBrides) would join the household for a brisket cookout, lawn games, optional Chicken Bowl Kiddie Pool dip, and a combined fireworks display. The day would start early and end late.

Saturday wouldn't be as full, but Shelby Norman's bridal shower was in the afternoon. It was to be held in the fellowship hall of Grace Fellowship Church and hosted by matron-of-honor Kesha Jefferson. June, Elodie, Ava, and Marie planned to attend, and they assured G-Lu she was welcome to join them. She politely declined, insisting she'd be wiped out from the previous day's activities and needed to catch her breath. Besides, she informed them that July 5th was her birthday and that she'd like to treat them all to an ice cream cake after supper. And that was, of course, the reason Grant brought her home for the long weekend. A 95th birthday was a milestone birthday that called for a celebration with family and friends.

Sunday's plans were pretty standard, though standard meant an entire morning of Sunday School and Worship Service. G-Lu said she looked forward to hearing her daughter-in-law teach the Senior Women's Sunday School class – the position she wrangled, as a first-time visitor, for Marie by nominating her for the job. Marie, feeling feisty, told her mother-in-law she could look forward to droning instruction on the duties of the Kohathites, Gershonites, and Merarites as detailed in Numbers chapter 4. She remembered G-Lu quipping years ago that the Book of Numbers gave her spiritual hives.

After Marcus outlined the weekend's activities to catch G-Lu up to speed, he told her about Shelby and Will's end-of-summer nuptials and the ladies' commitment to hold and cater the event on their property. Marcus' intention for this Thursday Meeting was to clarify his, Grant's, and Cal's expected participation. The couple had asked Marcus to officiate the ceremony since Pastor Jefferson was Will's best man, but beyond that, the guys knew it was too much to hope they'd be asked to stay out of the way.

They were right. The guys had no formal responsibilities. Still, the women said they'd appreciate their help to supply ladders and tools for putting up decorations, removing said decorations after the event, and cleaning up the tables afterward. The rental company would install and remove major items such as the tent, tables and chairs, and portable dance floor. Marcus, Grant, and Cal understood that as 'helpers,' they would be at the beck and call of the women to do whatever was needed and agreed to it – for one day. One significant day.

At the end of her holiday stay, G-Lu wished she'd asked her son for an electric fan as she tried to fall asleep in the pink guest room bed on Sunday night. The air conditioner was struggling against the heat. Then again, G-Lu always slept poorly the night before traveling.

Even though it took under four hours to return to Pleasant Pond Retirement Village, remaining seated for more than 90 minutes proved challenging due to her lower back and knees becoming rigid and sore, requiring breaks to walk and extend. And though she didn't mention it to Grant or Marie, the flight of steps to the guest room was also getting to be a bit much for her. On top of a poor night's sleep, all this would make G-Lu think twice about accepting future invitations to Faircourt, except she couldn't imagine declining time with her family. Now that she had turned 95, she wondered how much time they had left on this side of eternity.

She reflected on the past few days and felt satisfied and fulfilled in her time spent here. On the 4th of July, she managed to kick a little water around in the Chicken Bowl Kiddie Pool, to the delight of Lovie and the horror of Grant. She owed the tiny adventure to the playful encouragement and physical help of muscular DeShawn McBride, who lifted her in and out of the stock tank and held her carefully while she took a few turns in the water, cooling her feet and reminiscing about the old cement stock tank on her grandfather's farm.

Later that evening, G-Lu spent time with the bride-to-be, Shelby, who sought her out to glean marital wisdom. She told the younger woman to love God more than Will, to make a pie when they argued so she'd be anticipating and prepared with a peace offering when it was over, and to pick up socks and underwear from the floor without critical comment or else regret not doing so if Will were suddenly taken from her. All three things G-Lu pronounced with unwavering certainty born of experience.

June made the ice cream cake G-Lu intended to buy, and it was, as everyone agreed, one hundred times better than the store-bought, flash-frozen bricks. Mercifully, there were just two candles on the cake, in the shapes of a nine and a five, and G-Lu easily blew them out. Instead of a wish, she asked her Savior to give her courage and grace to face the increasing trials of aging – a request she now incorporated into her daily prayers.

G-Lu sat attentively through Marie's Sunday School on the tiny but powerful book of Jude and afterward gave her an unabashed commendation: "Best lesson I've ever heard on Jude. Engaging discussion questions. I was impressed, Marie." She thought Marie would never close her slackened jaw until she stammered, "Thank you!" G-Lu thought she might try another compliment on her next visit and finally drifted off to sleep.

Chapter Fifty-One

"*This is surreal,*" DeShawn thought as he sat in the passenger seat of his father's little red truck, riding to McBride Motor Mart for his first day of work at the family business he'd sworn he'd never involve himself in. Although he felt peace knowing it was what he was supposed to do now, the sights and sounds of the place he remembered as a teenager flashed through his mind, stirring up memories.

He worked in the blue powder-coated metal building at the back of the lot with the detailing crew. He'd hated operating the industrial vacuum, which forced him to contort his already enormous frame into cars in awkward, uncomfortable positions for four-to-six-hour shifts. However, as the only teenage employee, he was stuck with the least desirable job. He resented the older men he worked alongside, men in their late 20s and 30s, who gave him grief – sometimes physical abuse - for his advantages as the boss's son, as if he enjoyed mysterious perks and prestige they did not. He was also envious that his best friend, Jonathan, got to hang out at the drugstore, flirting with Kesha Hendricks and drinking colas instead of working for his dad, a plumber.

Things would be different now. Most notably, he'd work in the smaller sales office building in the middle of the lot and have his own private space. He would occupy his auntie's former office since she had retired entirely and sold her half of the business to Bobby. DeShawn would manage the uncomplicated detailing side of the company, as she had, but would also learn the dealer's side of auto sales from his dad.

As they approached the car lot, the first thing DeShawn noticed was the change in signage. In place of the hand-lettered wooden sign in neon orange, which required annual touch-ups and ropes of plastic, multi-colored flags crisscrossing the lot that he remembered, there was an interior lighted sign mounted between two 20' poles strategically positioned on the corner of the property. On either side, it had a giant monogram of the letter 'M' in an elegant block font. Centered below the monogram were the words 'McBride Motor Mart,' all in navy blue on a background of light gray. Each vehicle on the lot had a 15" pom-pom of silver and navy attached to the top left corner of the windshield.

"Dad, the place looks great! Classy." DeShawn complimented his father.

"The credit for that goes to your aunt. She insisted we 'rebrand' as she called it, about six or seven years ago. Yeah, she did a good job," Bobby beamed with pride.

When the men walked through the sales office door, DeShawn noted a mixture of familiarity and strangeness. The small building contained just four rooms and a small bathroom. Bobby followed his son as he reacquainted himself with them.

DeShawn's new office was at the front of the building, to the right of the entrance. Once DeShawn politely asked his father for a job at the Motor Mart, Bobby called in a contractor to make the space a blank canvas for his son. The contractor had stripped the space of furnishings, repainted it a clean but not stark white, and re-carpeted it.

"I thought you'd like to pick out your new office furniture. Get what you like so you'll be comfortable," Bobby offered. "I have a catalog on my desk."

"Okay. Sure, Dad," DeShawn smiled.

Past DeShawn's office on the right was a breakroom with a small refrigerator, sink, coffee maker, and a dinette set with four chairs. They replaced the old fridge with one that made ice, and added a large microwave to the amenities, but the wooden dinette set was as DeShawn remembered it, wonky pedestal base and all.

Across the narrow hall was a storage room with a row of tan filing cabinets, which looked the same as it had 20 years ago, except DeShawn remembered the tops of the cabinets covered with copy paper boxes. However, they were gone now, cleared away by Auntie before she retired. Carved into this room was the tiny bathroom with just a toilet and sink. Tan ceramic tile replaced the worn linoleum ten years ago when yellow jackets burrowed a hole through the floor from underneath.

The last room was Bobby's office, right across the hall from De-Shawn's, where it had always been. Bobby sat in his chair, but DeShawn remained standing, looking around, taking it in. His eyes fell on two pictures perched on the credenza behind his father. One was an old picture of DeShawn's family when he was still a teenager. In coordinated outfits in blue and white were Bobby, Julia, DeShawn, and Clair - everyone smiling, unaware of the grief that awaited less than two years from that day.

The other picture showed two preteen girls with natural black hair floating above their shoulders, one wearing a frilly white blouse and the other a bold, multi-colored sweater.

"Clair's girls?" DeShawn nodded at them.

"Yes. And they're as different as they dress. Fendi's in the white, and Prada is in the colors. That picture's a few years old. They're bigger now - teens. Prada will give her mother a run for her money, no doubt about it. She does things her own way. That girl's a mess!" Bobby informed, chuckling and shaking his head.

DeShawn continued scanning the office, deciding this room could have been a time capsule. The room was just as he remembered, except for the picture of his sister's daughters, whom he'd never met. At last, he sat in one of the two chairs in front of his father's desk. A memory flashed before his eyes of his teen self, putting his feet up on the desk and his dad swatting them off with a sharp reprimand.

"Your office still looks the same. Still got stacks of papers spilling out of your organizing boxes," he observed with a laugh.

"Well, that's going to be the first thing I'll need your help with. I kind of fly by the seat of my pants around here, and that's not a system I'd like anyone to inherit," Bobby responded, knowing full well the 'anyone' inheriting the system was standing across from him. "But before we dig into the nitty-gritty, why don't I make a pot of coffee for us? I got you a new mug for your first day. Be right back!"

While his father puttered in the breakroom, DeShawn grabbed a stack of papers from the desk to make a start on their organization. He sorted through copies of credit applications, title transfers, and proof of insurance cards, matching the paperwork to its common transaction. As he worked, a small paper fluttered to the floor. DeShawn reached for it and saw a check made out to McBride Motor Mart for $5,700. The date on the check was fifteen months prior, so it could not be cashed.

"Holy cow!" DeShawn thought. *"Somebody never paid for their car!"*

He tucked the check back in its appropriate pile and continued sorting until his father appeared with two mugs of coffee. Bobby took a sip from one of them, a navy mug with 'BOSS' in chunky white letters. He set the other on the edge of the desk near his son. It was an identical mug, but in dark gray.

"Thanks, Dad. That's nice," DeShawn grinned, reaching for the coffee. "Hey, let me ask you something," he tried to sound casual. "Have you ever not cashed a customer's check because they were in a tough spot, maybe?"

Bobby laughed. "That sounds like something you would do, but not me. And if you ever want to do that, we'll have to discuss it. You can't run a business giving the store away."

"Roger that," DeShawn answered, taking a sip from the steaming mug as he tried to decide what to do about the uncashed check. He wondered, *"If there's one, are there more?"*

"Looks like you started without me. You got a plan?" Bobby asked.

"Nope. Just looking to see what you have here. I'm going to do whatever you tell me to do," DeShawn responded, deciding to spare his father embarrassment.

"I'm going to do whatever you tell me to do," Bobby repeated, teasing. "Where was that phrase in your vocabulary in high school?"

DeShawn shrugged his shoulders with a smile, and Bobby grabbed another pile of papers.

"Guess we might as well get started on these. I just sort of set things down as I collected them. They all need to be separated into transactions and filed," Bobby explained.

He taught DeShawn the purchase process from an inventory and customer perspective and was amazed at how rapidly DeShawn learned.

Father and son worked through the day, clearing the stacks on Bobby's desk and credenza, intermittently attending to potential customers on the lot. They also ordered furniture for DeShawn's office from the local Office Supply, which promised delivery in two days.

"It was a good first day," Bobby affectionately slapped his son on the shoulder as they walked to his truck.

"It was a good day," DeShawn agreed. "I learned a lot I didn't know." *"And something I didn't want to know,"* he thought.

Chapter Fifty-Two

It was Will's weekend with his boys, and after church service, Shelby, Sam, and Silas sat with him at one of Latte Da's sidewalk tables to enjoy lunch under a blue sky embellished with gigantic lolling clouds. It was a tad cooler than usual for a July afternoon, and the outside tables were popular.

While they waited for Five, their familiar pink-haired waitress, to bring their sandwich orders, Shelby asked: "Good sermon today, right, guys?"

Sam and Silas muttered their weak agreement.

Will looked at Shelby and rolled his eyes to signal his disappointment with them.

"I have $5 for anyone but Shelby who can tell me what Pastor Jefferson's text was," Will challenged to see if the boys had been listening at all.

"Ooh! It was Matthew 6! Part of Jesus' Sermon on the Mount. Pay up, Dad!" Silas shouted excitedly, extending his palm toward Will.

"So it was," Will admitted, reaching for his wallet to pay his debt.

"Got any other questions?" Silas asked eagerly.

"Um, that's it for now," Will answered, placing the five-dollar bill in his son's hand.

In another few minutes, Five placed their orders in front of them, making sure everyone got what they wanted and had what they needed.

"She looks like a freak," Sam commented a little too loudly as soon as Five had turned her back.

They all noted Five had turned around with a scowl on her face. She'd heard him.

"That was unkind!" Shelby reprimanded, under her breath.

"And you're not my mother!" Sam shouted back at Shelby, grabbing the attention of every nearby table patron.

"Jessica is your mother," Will jumped in. "I know that, you know that, and Shelby knows that. So, there'll be no further need to point out who your mother is and who is not. We're all clear on the subject. Got it?"

Now it was Sam's turn to scowl. "You're taking her side over your flesh and blood?" he kept up his teenage attitude and volume.

Will removed the napkin from his lap and placed it on the table. He was aware that Sam had attracted an audience for their drama, but he intended to nip this disrespect toward Shelby in the bud.

"I am. And here's something you should know: I always will. Shelby is going to be my second wife, but that does not make her second best. I will treat her with the respect and devoted love you would have expected me to give your mother. Even though your mother and I are not together, I'm still responsible for being an example to you of how a husband treats his wife. She must always come before the children. I won't abandon that responsibility or any others just because you don't like it. And another thing, if you or your brother ever try to make me choose between you and Shelby, I promise you will not be happy with how that works out for you. Have I made myself clear?"

As Sam sat in stunned silence, a man sitting at an adjacent table rose to his feet and began clapping his hands. The woman he dined with followed his example, and soon, the occupants of another nearby table followed suit. Will's speech to his son was getting a public standing ovation.

It was too much for Sam to swallow. He leaped up from the table, his paper napkin flying, and hurried away.

Silas sat mouth agape, anticipating what his father would do next.

Will waited a moment, letting Sam get out of sight. Then he gulped his iced tea, stood, and gathered his sandwich in his napkin.

"He's headed to his mom's house. I'm going to get in the car and hang back – follow him to make sure he gets there. It's only three miles. The walk will be good for him – let him cool off. Can you walk back to your house with Silas after you both finish here? I'll pick him up after a while. I'm sorry, Shelby," Will apologized.

"No need to be sorry at all," Shelby smiled up at him, pleased at how he'd handled himself and proud of what he'd said.

Will crossed the street and drove off in his car to not quite catch up to Sam. He thought he should call his ex-wife and warn her about the angry boy who would be on her doorstep in less than thirty minutes.

Jessica answered the phone, suspicious and anticipating a problem. Will never called her when he had the boys. She softened after she'd listened to him explain the situation and express his regret that it all played out publicly.

"I'm sorry that happened. But to tell you the truth, I'm not surprised. Sam's played that card a few times with Rick and me and gotten away with it. Rick's son does it, too, and it's caused plenty of problems. So, good for you for putting your foot down. I wish we had," Jessica confessed.

"I appreciate that," Will responded. "I'm following him to your house, but he doesn't know it. The walk should help settle his temper, but I'd like to take him back to my place once he reaches yours. The boys are scheduled to be with me until 8 PM, and I think he needs to learn that running away from his problems won't solve them. Besides, Silas is watching all of this play out. I think he can learn from his brother's mistakes without repeating them. What do you think?"

"I agree. We weren't expecting the boys to be home, so we planned to have dinner at some friends' house this evening. I'll back you up he must return to your place until eight."

"Thanks. That'll help a lot," Will answered sincerely. "See you soon."

"Hey, Will," Jessica had something more to say before they hung up.

"Yeah?"

"I just want to say I'm glad you called to let me know what happened with Sam and to get us on the same page. I'm sorry I haven't been as cooperative when it comes to co-parenting, and I hope this will be the start of a new chapter of teamwork between us for our boys' sake."

"Thanks, Jess. I hope so, too," Will agreed and hung up. He smiled and offered a casual prayer of acknowledgment and thanks.

"That was quite the hat trick You pulled off from one drama: Sam's going to learn a lesson, Shelby's proud of me, and Jessica wants to play nice. Thanks, God!"

Chapter Fifty-Three

"Grant, you're sitting out Garage Cave tomorrow night, and Marcus is going to call Micah and ask him to sub for you," Cal instructed during Thursday Meeting.

This was news to both Grant and Marcus.

"I'm good wit dat. I need a break from dis one," Marcus agreed, pointing a thumb at Grant.

"What did I do?" Grant whined.

"Nothing. I just haven't seen Micah in a while, and I'd like to check on him to see how he's doing. The card table seats four, so you have to go," Cal explained.

"Why don't you boot Bobby?" Grant pressed, knowing it wasn't an option to exclude a neighbor.

"I'll sit out, and Grant can go. Dat would still give me a break from him," Marcus offered.

"No!" Cal reacted. "No offense, Grant, but I might need professional help with Micah."

Grant turned to Marie. "I could still have a Friday night snack, right?" he asked.

"Could I stop you?" Marie returned his gaze, looking through her eyelashes.

"Wild horses couldn't stop him," Elodie chuckled.

"Okay then," Grant nodded to Cal, satisfied he would not be deprived of his accustomed refreshment. "What's my ailment?"

"Huh?" Cal was confused.

"Why are you going to tell Micah I need a sub? Do I need to develop a limp or a cough?" Grant queried.

"No, we don't do devious. I'll tell him Elodie was on your last nerve, and you planned an early night. It's plausible, and it might actually happen between now and den." Marcus looked over the rim of his own glasses at Elodie, who was already doing the same to him.

"That's true," Marie laughed, and the Shermans and Van Zants nodded in agreement.

"Snacks have arrived!" Micah announced as he sauntered into the Garage Cave like he didn't mind the light rain that dampened his shirt on the short walk over.

"Oreos, Chips-A-Hoy, and a gallon of 1 percent milk. Not much notice to ask Shelby for her homemade cookies," Micah reasoned.

"No problem at all," Bobby assured him, grabbing red plastic cups from the stack on Cal's workbench.

"How's things going at the car lot, Bobby?" Cal was being careful not to pounce on Micah. He busied himself in opening the cookie packages.

"Going real good. DeShawn's just finished his second week, and he's doing fine. Smart boy – catching on real quick," Bobby beamed with pride. "The home cooking has taken a hit, though, now that he's not home during the week to do that. But we're all getting by."

"I'm happy for you, Bobby. I know you're glad to have him working with you. It's important to be proud of your son," Micah said, his voice trailing off.

Marcus noted a hint of disappointment. "I've never had a son, but I bet dat's true. I'm sure you're proud of Chase. He's growing into a solid young man," he commented.

"He wants to be baptized," Micah responded dully.

"That's great!" Bobby, an unexpected ally in the matter, affirmed.

Cal and Marcus exchanged surprised glances. Both remembered when Bobby bemoaned that DeShawn's religious faith created a wedge of separation between them. Something changed.

"I let him go down this path of choosing his own beliefs, but he's disappearing farther and farther down the horizon. From where I stand, it doesn't look 'great,'" Micah bemoaned.

"No, no, I get it. That was me and my boy, too," Bobby empathized. "But now I've lived with it awhile and seen some things. His faith has made him a good husband to Mariana and a wonderful son to me. He's a good man. Truthfully, he's a better man than I am, and I'm proud of that. Don't you want better for your son – as a person, where it matters?"

"Of course, I want good things for my son!" Micah responded, yelling.

"No, I'm not talking about 'things' – possessions and stuff. I mean, don't you want him to be a better man than you are?" Bobby clarified.

Micah sat back in his chair before answering. "You won't be offended if I say something?" he sought permission to be honest.

"We say it straight in the Garage Cave," Bobby assured, dunking an Oreo in his cup and popping the entire thing in his mouth.

"Your thinking seems backward to me. Aren't men supposed to be the role models and examples for their sons to look up to?" Micah argued.

Bobby swallowed his mouthful and answered. "That's alright. But I think you're missing a word in that question: average. Aren't average men supposed to be the role models and examples? Yes, they are, and I don't want to be the average man. I'm not scared to let my son soar past me. Not anymore."

Micah seemed lost for words, so Cal spit out a few that had gathered on his tongue. "My father would have stepped on my body to keep himself above me. I was never good enough, let alone better than."

Micah and Marcus remained silent.

"That's too bad," Bobby responded, feeling someone should acknowledge Cal's vulnerable statement.

The men sat quietly, watching the rain fall as they consumed most of the cookies and half of the milk.

"Maybe we should make these men's discussion nights instead of game nights. We hardly touch the games anymore," Marcus commented.

"I like the discussion. It's good for me when I'm here," Micah spoke up at last.

"It's good for me, too. Makes me think and use my brain," agreed Bobby.

"I never win at games anyway," nodded Cal.

"Grant might have a cow," Marcus reflected.

As if their male DNA encoded them to react simultaneously, all the guys bellowed, "Mooooo!""

CHAPTER FIFTY-FOUR

"You know, this has double-date vibes written all over it," Mariana needled her husband.

"You think so?" DeShawn disagreed but wanted to hear his wife's thoughts.

They were preparing a light summer supper to be shared on their front porch with Bobby and Miss Elodie. Mariana blended a cold strawberry/cantaloupe soup, and DeShawn mixed a curried pasta salad with chicken.

DeShawn had brought a card table and chairs from the attic the previous week and put them on the front porch. He and Marianna had been having coffee and Bible reading at it every morning before work. It was Bobby's idea to have supper on it Saturday night and to invite Elodie to occupy the fourth chair as if it would go to waste.

"I don't know. I'm confused," Mariana explained. "He insists they're just friends, but his actions indicate he wants to be more than friends," she responded, pouring the soup into a pitcher.

"Actually, I asked him about it last night after you'd gone to bed."

"You did?"

"Yeah. He told me they'll only be friends because he won't pretend to be something he's not – in this case, a man of faith – and Miss Elodie wouldn't want it any other way. But he says that being friends with her reminds him how to be a man, and he likes that. And it's enough for him.

I told him, that made sense to me."

"Well, okay then. It pains me he isn't a believer, but I have to give him credit for not pretending. He's honest with us and with Miss Elodie, and I respect that."

"So do I," DeShawn acknowledged, finished with the pasta salad.

Together, they carried the food out to the porch, where the table was covered with a white tablecloth Bobby had purchased new this morning and set with dishes. Waiting for Bobby to bring Miss Elodie over was all that was left.

While they waited, Mariana dead-headed spent blossoms from the pink petunias in her flower boxes, tossing them behind the bushes below.

"Find any more un-cashed checks at the office?" she asked as she worked.

"Ugh! No. But the more I learn and the more I see of his files – or the random stacks of papers that pass for files - the worse it gets. He's got two cars on the lot without clear titles, so we can't sell them unless we pay off the liens. And there are several contracts that don't have all the stipulations attached yet. How hard is it for someone to provide proof of insurance? Dad should have had them weeks ago. And I'm not positive yet, but I think he sold a BMW last month to someone who had stolen an identity. It's probably in a crate on its way overseas by now. But Dad admitted he knows he's not as sharp as he used to be, even though he can still draw a clock, whatever that means."

Mariana smiled sympathetically. "He knows that being able to draw a clock passes a cognitive test, but yes, he is getting forgetful with age. Aren't you glad you're there to sort all this out for him? Are you telling him about the problems now?"

"I am glad. There didn't seem to be any sense in telling Dad about the check he didn't cash – water under the bridge, though I can't imagine how his bookkeeper missed it, and that's another issue to address. I tried to find the buyer, but they vanished into thin air. Anyway, I had to tell him about the title issues and the BMW because he's over my shoulder a lot, but the stips I can handle and get those contract files complete. Hey, here they come!" DeShawn shut down the discussion.

"Hey, girl! Aren't your pretty pink flowers looking good?" Elodie greeted Mariana as she ambled up the walkway on Bobby's arm, the skirt of her mint A-line dress trailing on a warm breeze.

"Thank you. They're petunias," Mariana shared.

"I wouldn't know a petunia from a pansy. Flowers are Marie's department," Elodie admitted. "But I know pretty when I see it!"

"You and me both, Miss Elodie!" DeShawn grinned, squeezing his wife with a muscular arm shown to advantage in a fitted blue t-shirt.

"Looks like Miss Banana has everything all set for us," Bobby observed, pulling a chair for Elodie at the table.

"All you have to do is enjoy," DeShawn beamed, flashing a wide smile identical to his father's.

When they all were arranged around the table, DeShawn gave thanks to God for his family, the friendship of Miss Elodie, and delicious food – taking none for granted. And for the next forty minutes, silverware and conversation rose and fell. Once the chilled fruit soup and salad were a memory, DeShawn announced: "I hope you all have saved a little room for Chocolate-Covered Cherry Cake."

"I'll make room!" Elodie insisted, fluffing the skirt of her dress with no waistband. "I used to make that cake back in the day."

"So did my Julia," Bobby remembered.

Mariana noted the slight furrowing of her husband's eyebrows at the mention of his mother's name. Bobby saw it too, and not for the first time. It had bothered him that DeShawn had refused to go with him to the Faircourt Memorial Cemetery to see his mother's resting place near the Majestic Oak and to honor her on Mother's Day. And there was always this sudden tension in the air whenever he mentioned his wife's name in front of his son. Julia's name was a landmine for DeShawn, and

Bobby accidentally tripped it from time to time.

Elodie looked from DeShawn's furrowed brow to Mariana's sad expression of concern for him to Bobby's release of a pensive sigh. She tiptoed into the mother territory she had explored with Chase last summer, trusting it would go easier with an adult.

"DeShawn," she spoke softly, "tell me about your Mom."

DeShawn looked down at his empty plate, and his chin quivered.

Mariana nodded to Elodie, a simple sign indicating her approval of the request. Bobby kept his eyes fixed on his boy. They waited until he could speak.

"She was everything a mom should be – loving, patient, and forgiving. When she walked into a room, a peaceful calm followed her. The simplicity of her soul was beautiful. I'm ashamed to say I took advantage of her gentleness when I was an idiot teenager. Thought I was a big man getting away with everything I could – disrespectful to her when Dad wasn't home. The biggest regret of my life is that I hurt her terribly – telling myself I was protecting her when I was really protecting my pride by not letting her see me in prison. And then she got sick and died, and it was too late. I can restart every part of my life – family, job, friends, church, community – but I can never restart my relationship with my mom. The ache of living with that is a prison I'll never be freed from."

DeShawn turned to his father and looked him in the eye. "Dad, I couldn't go to the cemetery with you because I can't face her. I'm not sure if I'll ever be able to do that. Just understand it's not because I'm mad at her or you. I'm mad at myself." And then he lowered his gaze again.

"Son, I can try to put myself in your place and feel what you feel, but it's not in my power to fix this for you as much as I wish I were able. But here's what I can tell you: your mom loved you with all her heart and never stopped. And I believe if she could whisper to you from beyond, she'd tell you she still loves you and wants you to be happy and free. She wouldn't want you in a prison of your own making for her sake," Bobby assured.

He scooted his chair closer to his son and leaned over to embrace him. DeShawn wept on his father's shoulder, releasing shame, guilt, and sorrow.

"Thank you," Mariana mouthed to Elodie.

Chapter Fifty-Five

"Hiya, Calcutta!" Elodie chirped, expecting to see her breakfast buddy at the kitchen table.

"He's not here," answered Ava from Cal's usual chair, Mercy sitting at her feet. "He drove June to a dawn o'clock colonoscopy appointment at Louisville General."

"Oh, fun for her," Elodie grimaced.

"Necessary evil for all of us. But the worst part is behind her," Ava sympathized with her absent friend.

"You're up early for breakfast," Elodie noted.

"Yeah, I need to get out to the garden before it gets too hot. We've got corn and cucumbers ready to be picked and processed," Ava downed the last of her coffee.

"Need some help?"

"Sure!"

"Okay, I'll let Marie know when she comes down," Elodie laughed.

"I should have known!" Ava rolled her eyes in scorn.

"Just kiddin', don't get your knickers in a twist, girl. Let me just have a little coffee and a bagel. Then, I'll change into garden clothes and be out to help. I'll be 15 minutes, tops," Elodie offered.

"Okay. That will give me time to gather some produce baskets from the garage and pull a few weeds. Mercy needs to be let out, too," Ava agreed as she rinsed out her mug at the sink and put it in the dishwasher.

"Come on, Mercy! Let's go outside and mind your business. Then, you can visit the chickens while I weed," Ava encouraged the dog, who bounded out the kitchen door at the invitation.

True to her word, Elodie appeared at the garden within 15 minutes to help pick veggies.

While Ava gathered Silver Queen corn in three bushel baskets, Elodie worked in an adjacent quadrant, picking English and pickling cucumbers. When they finished, they stopped to rest and admire their bountiful harvest.

Suddenly, Ava thought to look around for Mercy. She wasn't in sight.

"I don't see Mercy, do you?" Ava asked anxiously.

Without waiting for Elodie's answer, she began calling: "Mercy! Mercy, girl! Mercy, time to come home!"

Mercy completed her morning toilet and checked out the pecking birds in the chicken coop's run. She gave them a series of non-serious growls to encourage a burst of wing-flapping, but having grown used to this treatment, the chickens ignored and disappointed the doodle dog.

There wouldn't have been anything else for Mercy to do but return to Ava and sniff about a pile of freshly pulled weeds if she hadn't spotted a flash of movement. The McBride cat, Rover, was crossing Tamarack Street heading toward the Garage Cave. Mercy and Rover had encountered one another, and the old cat did not appreciate the exuberance of the young dog – a position Mercy delighted to exploit.

She took off running toward Rover, who about-faced and hightailed it back to his yard and into the protective branches of a maple tree on the far side of the house. Mercy circled the tree several times. She'd lost sight of the spry feline but not the scent. No problem, she could wait.

Mercy sat down at the tree's base, forcing Rover to stay put. She would have kept him treed for much longer, but her siege was cut short by a boy with a toy gun who shot a rubber-tipped foam dart at her backside from the backyard of Bobby's neighbor. Forgetting Rover up the tree, Mercy launched herself into aimless action. Out of sight of her own house, which might have helped her bearings, she threaded between houses on Tamarack Street. Her only goal was to lose the boy with the dart gun.

The lazy kid never gave chase, but Mercy, unaware, didn't stop running until she was tired. She shimmied through a fence compromised by two missing pickets and dropped by the front door of a small plastic playhouse in a backyard also containing a toddler swing set and a sandbox. There, she took a panting rest and laid her head between her outstretched front paws.

Mercy lifted her head when a young woman, engrossed in a phone call on her cell, opened the back porch door and let out her dog. The woman closed the door, knowing her black Labrador would be safely contained in the yard. He spotted Mercy and made a beeline for her.

Mercy jumped to her feet and then froze submissively as the dominant dog sniffed around her, familiarizing himself with her scent. Apparently, he liked what he smelled.

With Elodie and Ava in the back seat and Marie riding shotgun, Grant drove his Camry around their Faircourt neighborhood looking for Mercy, calling her name out the window. They were so focused on their mission that Marie was startled when Grant's cell phone rang in its dashboard holder.

"Hello?" she answered and then listened to a young woman's voice on the other end. As she listened, she turned to the others and mouthed: "She's found!"

"Thank you so much for calling and letting us know you have her. We've been looking frantically, and we'll be right over!" Marie assured the woman.

"849 Ash Street," Marie instructed Grant.

"Ash Street!" Ava exclaimed. "She's had herself a big adventure on her little legs. That's several streets away."

The group arrived at the address and loaded Mercy into the back seat between Ava and Elodie. The dog refused to look at any of them, keeping her head down.

"You'd think we were the ones who ran away from her!" Elodie observed indignantly.

"Guess we can't trust her. We'll have to keep her on a leash from now on when she goes out," Grant suggested.

"It's at times like this that I wish dogs could talk. Wouldn't you like to hear what she had to say about why she's being so shy suddenly?" Marie wondered aloud. When no one answered, she concluded, "Well, I would."

Chapter Fifty-Six

From her vantage point in a redecorated second-floor guest room window, which had never welcomed a single guest in the fifty-two years she'd lived there, Christine Williams watched Chase and the McBride felon ride down Tamarack Street on the bicycle built for two. Again.

"It's a dereliction of parental duty to allow one's child such an alarming association!" Christine fumed. She marched downstairs to retrieve the cell phone she'd left in her office.

Sitting at the writing desk, she hesitated a moment. For the first time, she considered what someone else might think of her intervention, specifically Marie and her housemates. Christine noted there seemed to be quite a bit of friendly interaction among the residents of the house across the street and their neighbors on either side.

"But the child isn't safe. Nobody is actually safe," Christine shook off her doubts. She pressed her brother's contact button, leaving a detailed message regarding her expectations for action.

***

Steering from the front seat, Chase guided Blue Beauty and his passenger west down Tamarack Street, taking a right on Poplar and then a left down Sycamore, past Grace Fellowship Church, and then a mile beyond to the place he was drawn: Faircourt Memorial Cemetery.

Chase had not been back to his mother's burial plot since the day of her funeral and, for some time, was an emotional jumble of curiosity, longing, and pain that he couldn't talk to his father about. Anyone, really. This Saturday afternoon ride with DeShawn created an opportunity to wander there, as if by happenstance, so that he didn't have to ask permission or make it into a big to-do by confessing his need to be close to his mother again.

Chase guided the bike under the arched entrance, which supported an old wisteria vine that was now out of bloom. He steered along the wide pathways to the landmark he remembered being directly across from his mother's grave.

"Going to stop for a minute at the bench up here," Chase shouted back to DeShawn as he reversed his feet to initiate breaking. DeShawn coordinated his efforts to bring the bike to a halt.

When they reached the spot, Chase jumped off the bike, hurried to his mom's headstone, and bent and kissed it lightly. It was enough for now to have found her.

"Your mom?" DeShawn guessed when Chase returned to the bike.

Chase nodded, choked up but dry-eyed.

"Okay, then. Now let's find mine 'cause I've never been. Dad said she's near the Majestic Oak in the center of the cemetery," DeShawn requested impulsively.

Chase brightened at the prospect of helping his friend navigate his identical maternal quest and found his voice.

"I know where that is! We passed it coming here," Chase informed and hopped back on the front seat.

They parked the bike at the base of the oak tree in the center of the cemetery and went in opposite directions to search for the name 'Julia McBride' on surrounding headstones. When DeShawn spotted it, he let Chase continue to look, keeping the moment to himself.

Unprepared for this unplanned encounter, DeShawn wasn't sure what to do or say. So, he began by following Chase's example. Bending over the weathered headstone that bore his mother's name, he gently kissed it. Then he stepped back to whisper a few words that flowed from his heart: "I love you, Momma, and I'm so sorry I hurt you. I didn't deserve you. But God is making me a better man. I'll take care of Dad, and I hope you'll be proud of me when we meet again. Momma, how I hope we meet again."

Chase, not having any luck finding the McBride headstone, looked over and saw DeShawn standing still before a marker. He walked back to the bicycle to wait for him there. When DeShawn returned, he broke into a wide grin. More of his burden of guilt and shame for neglecting to visit his mother lifted from his heart. He'd faced her at last and made progress.

"This was a good idea, Freshman," DeShawn acknowledged as he climbed onto the back seat.

"To tell you the truth, I was only thinking of myself. I didn't realize your mom was here, too," Chase confessed.

"And to tell you the truth, I was a little wigged out when you pulled up in here. I forgot your mom was here because I was only thinking about mine. I never thought I could do this," DeShawn admitted.

"Maybe we can visit our moms together again sometime," Chase turned to look back at his friend and suggested hopefully.

"Maybe," DeShawn answered, adding, "It's hard."

"Yeah, but like you said, it's good, too. It's a good hard," Chase reminded.

"A good hard," DeShawn repeated the phrase. "Freshman, you are always calling me out and giving me something to think about!"

Chase laughed and motioned that it was time to push off. He retraced their route through Faircourt but increased their pace down the streets to create more airflow around them. They were panting from exertion when they finally crossed Cedar Street and wheeled into the McBride driveway.

Marcus, wearing tan shorts and a white golf shirt, exited his van across the street in the Garage Cave driveway and waved to the duo, who returned his friendly gesture.

"It's a blazing hot afternoon for exercise," Marcus commented, walking toward the young men across the street for a check-in chat.

"It makes it harder, but it's a good hard, right, Freshman?" DeShawn answered, then turned to wink at his riding partner.

Marcus smiled at the budding camaraderie evident between his neighbors. "After supper, we'll be cooling our legs in da Chicken Bowl Kiddie Pool. If you're curious about how many we can cram in dere, you're welcome to join us wit your families," Marcus invited.

"Thanks, Marcus, but I got a date with the Mrs. tonight. We're going to the big city to see a musical performance I'm told I better enjoy for the price Mariana paid for the tickets," DeShawn chuckled.

"Lovie and I are free. We might come if Dad says we can," Chase responded.

"Bring your dad if he's not busy," Marcus urged.

Chase sighed, and his shoulders slumped. "He's not busy, but he's not coming either." After a moment, he added: "I always pray now he'll get saved, like DeShawn told me."

"Dat's someting God has graciously given him – a praying son. But while you're waiting on God to draw your dad to Himself and change him from da inside out, don't live your life focused only on what your dad is not. Love him as he is. Let me tell you someting, ya? Over my years as a pastor, I've known a few women married to unbelieving men. Of course, dey wanted dere husbands to be saved, but dey always spoke of dem like dey were da best men on two legs. No complaining, no comparing to men in da church, none of dat. Dere husbands were not godly, but dos women were, and dere example was inspiring. So, your dads may not be godly, but you can be inspiring examples of godly sons regardless," Marcus pointedly shifted to encourage both sons of unsaved men sitting on Blue Beauty.

"What do you say, Freshman? Challenge accepted?" DeShawn asked.

"Challenge accepted," Chase responded half-heartedly.

Chase was certain nobody else knew his father was drinking regularly to the point of being drunk. But he knew it and felt embarrassed.

Chapter Fifty-Seven

"It was a bad idea to go dress shopping after dinner," Marie lamented, trying to suck in the distended abdomen taunting her in the dressing room mirror. "This silver silk across my gut looks like I'm wearing the Chicago Bean."

"I was hoping to lose weight before I had to buy a dress," June whined over the partition separating her cubical from Marie's. "And this floral is a mistake. Someone's going to sit on me and search for the recliner lever."

"The wedding's in less than a month. We couldn't put this off any longer," Ava reminded her friends in a muffled voice as she pulled an emerald crepe dress over her red hair in the dressing room across the narrow hall. "Do I really need another green dress? I'm in a rut, but the color is a safe choice."

"I weigh the same as I did when I graduated from college. Not sayin' it's an ideal weight, but I'm consistent and don't have any notions about being anythin' else," Elodie stated matter-of-factly from the space beside Ava.

"What are you trying on, El?" Marie asked.

"I've got a lacy turquoise blouse and flowy, wide-leg pants in a navy and turquoise Indian print. Best thing about these britches? They've got an elastic waist that could fit another person inside while I'm wearin' them," Elodie boasted.

"That sounds perfect for a wedding we're catering. Hey! What if we all bought the same outfit? It could be like our crew uniform," June hollered her suggestion to make sure everyone heard it.

"I promise if you all buy this outfit, I won't," Elodie threatened.

"Okay! Okay. But flowy pants is a great idea instead of dresses," June backed down.

"Isn't it? I don't know why you all are trying to look like the mother-of-the-bride when we have work to do," Elodie challenged.

"You have a point," Ava agreed. "Would you mind if we looked for pants outfits in other colors, or have you claimed that entire fashion category?"

Elodie chuckled and responded: "I'll allow it."

"June, are you going to be able to get out of that dress by yourself, or will you start screaming for help like you did at Big Mart last Christmas?" Marie teased.

"I'm already out of it, but thanks for your concern. I have a question, though: What are these body parts called that look like puffy pillows below your shoulder blades? Is there a name for them?" June inquired, seeking anyone's answer.

"Back fat!" Elodie hollered across the hallway in response.

June sighed. "I know what they're made of. I just thought they had an identifying name."

"How about back bunions?" Marie suggested with a giggle.

"I've always wondered what this little flap of droopy skin under your chin is called," Ava diverted, inspecting hers with an index finger in her dressing room mirror.

"That's a turkey waddle, and I've got that, too," June lamented.

"No matter how much I diet and exercise, this tummy pouch is here to stay," Marie complained, patting hers.

"And I have that! I'm three for three," June whined.

Conspicuous in its absence was Elodie's grievance about herself.

"So," Ava prodded, "what do you have going on that you'll admit to,

El?"

After consideration, Elodie answered, "Well, I've got a touch of blotchiness in my skin here and there, and I've always been what they call big-boned."

"What do you know? I don't have either of those!" June rejoiced, now fully dressed and exiting her cubicle.

"Why do we care?" Marie asked, with the silver dress slung over her arm, joining June in the hallway. "Do you imagine Grant, Cal, and Marcus discuss and bemoan their aging bodies?"

"Maybe not to each other, but I know Cal misses the man he was," June replied candidly.

"That's why we care, Marie. We miss the women we used to be," Ava concluded, closing her dressing room door on the way out.

"I don't want to care anymore," responded Marie. "I don't mean that in the sense that I want to just throw my hands up in the air and not take care of myself. But I don't want to look in the mirror and hate my middle for the rest of my life."

"I don't care! I threw my hands up in the air a long time ago," Elodie claimed, joining the ladies in the hall. "That's why I needed a minute to remember my flaws. When I look in the mirror, I see myself and am comfortable with that – even the flaws."

"That's a blessing, Elodie. I've never been comfortable with my body," June confessed.

"Does Cal complain?" Elodie questioned.

A shy smile crossed June's face. "No."

"Come here, girls," Ava encouraged. She directed them to line up with her in front of the triple mirror at the end of the dressing area hallway.

There they stood – arms woven behind one another's waists – facing themselves in the truth-telling mirror.

"I think the aging process is meant to remind us that our bodies are decaying and there's not much we can do about it. So, we'd better look

Elsewhere for our confidence and contentment," Ava proposed.

"*Charm is deceitful, and beauty is vain, but a woman who fears the LORD is to be praised,*" quoted Marie.

"Proverbs 31:30," June recited the familiar reference, frowning at her reflection.

"We all know it, but a thousand voices from culture and media tell us otherwise. And they don't whisper their message; they yell it at us," Ava acknowledged.

"Then we need to be louder, at least, to each other. Ava, thank you for demonstrating your fear of the LORD by encouraging us not to look at who we are, but to Whose we are," Marie commended her friend, catching Ava's eyes in the mirror.

"You're welcome. That means more to me than ten shallow compliments from anyone else," Ava smiled, crinkling the corners of her blue eyes.

"I'm going to need you girls to help me remember Bible truth when I'm tempted to self-pity over earthly standards of beauty," June requested, her eyes filling. "I can't look in this mirror and say I'm content, and I can't even imagine what that would be like. I've hated my body since junior high school."

"We'll help you," Elodie agreed, squeezing June around the back of her waist.

"Let's go find our comfy wedding pants outfits!" Marie suggested, dropping her arm from Ava's back.

"I'm all set. Gonna sit myself on this bench while you all go huntin'," Elodie stated. She looked back in the mirror when her friends had gone and stuck her tongue out at it - for June.

Chapter Fifty-Eight

Bobby stood at his office window, watching his son work with a customer on the lot, unaware his face beamed with delight. DeShawn was immersed with the thin, middle-aged woman and her teenage son, making gestures with his hands to visually assist his explanation of the vehicle's features. The woman nodded in comprehension at intervals, and the teen smiled. These were good signs for making a sale.

Bobby mused about the difference in his circumstances, comparing last year on this day to today. Last year, he was doubtful he'd ever see his son again, believing he had six more years to serve in prison. But now, not only had he reestablished a connection with him, but they'd also built a deepening relationship living under the same roof – with a daughter-in-law Bobby loved added in the mix. And now, here was DeShawn, managing the family business as if he'd been doing so for years and not weeks.

Bobby also had to acknowledge that the houseful of friends who moved in across the street had prodded from his reclusive social habits in the past year. They'd made him their friend, too, and broadened his interactions with other neighbors as they broadened their own. He even had a special friend, Elodie, for walks and talks.

Bobby had so much to be thankful for, and he knew it. At nearly 71 years old, Bobby McBride felt reborn into the world of happy people. The only thing that could improve it was if DeShawn could reconcile with his sister, Claire. But Bobby understood nobody got everything they wanted.

Curious to hear his son's sales pitch to the woman and her son, Bobby unlatched the sliding window and cracked it open an inch.

"This model has all the recommended safety features that will help put you at ease when James is driving himself. Besides lane-keeping assist and lane-departure warning, it also has automatic high beams and blind-spot monitoring," DeShawn explained.

"James, why don't you sit inside the car and see what you think of the interior?" the woman directed her son, who happily obliged.

She turned toward DeShawn and confided with a worried frown: "It's certainly loaded with all the bells and whistles. And it would be good to know my son has something safe and reliable to drive. The only question is: can I afford it?"

"Mrs. Daniels, we work closely with Faircourt Savings Bank down the street. They have the best interest rates for car loans in town," DeShawn assured her.

"I...er...I...can't...I have to pay cash. I'm not well. My doctor says I have maybe six months. I'm trying to get James ready to be on his own, but he'll need a decent car. What we're driving now is also on borrowed time."

"Who's your doctor?" DeShawn asked abruptly. Twenty years in prison had taught him to suspect con artists, and he needed to challenge her story.

"Elizabeth Reynolds, here in town. Why?" Mrs. Daniels responded quickly, though her eyebrows knit together.

DeShawn broke out a wide grin upon recognizing the name of Dr. Buffington's sister. "Just wanted to make sure you were in expert hands," he affirmed.

"She's been my cardiologist since we moved here 15 years ago, and she's good. But there's only so much that can be done when you have advanced heart disease."

"Mrs. Daniels, when James is done checking out his new car, we'll go inside and find a way for you to drive it home. But I'd like to ask you something. It's obviously important that you make sure James has what he needs to live independently because you're a loving mom. But have you considered what will happen to your soul after you've taken your final breath on Earth?"

"Well...I...I hope...I mean...I've been a good person. I've done more good than bad, and God is supposed to be loving and forgiving. So, I think I'll make it," Mrs. Daniels reasoned through nervous laughter.

"I'm sure you are a good person, Mrs. Daniels. And if that was God's standard to gain entrance into heaven, I'm sure you would. But did you realize God's word says we must be perfectly righteous? Holy. Sinless! And that's a big problem for everyone because we can't meet that standard."

DeShawn let her consider this information and noticed her thin shoulders sag with the weight of it.

"So, you're saying nobody goes to heaven?" she asked after a moment.

"Oh, no! People go to heaven. It's just that we don't go there on our merits. God, the Father poured out His righteous wrath against our sin on His Son, Jesus, when He was crucified. Jesus bore the punishment we deserve for our sins. And the news gets even better! Not only does Jesus take our sins upon Himself, but He gives us His righteous standing before the Father. When the Father looks at us, He sees us as He sees His Son – perfectly righteous. The Apostle Paul explained it this way:

For our sake he made him to be sin who knew no sin, so that in him we might become the righteousness of God. 2 Corinthians 5:21"

"Then, you're saying everybody goes to heaven?" Mrs. Daniels cocked her head.

"Only those who repent and believe," DeShawn corrected. "We need to understand our sins as offenses against the One who created us and turn away from them. We need to believe that Jesus, the Son of God, can save us from the judgment and condemnation we deserve because He took our place. His resurrection from the dead proves His sacrifice satisfied the Holy Father's justice. If we place all our faith in Jesus and none in ourselves, God will save us by His grace, and we will live again as surely as Jesus is now. Mrs. Daniels, do you believe that?"

DeShawn watched as her expression turned from confusion to comprehension.

"I do! It all makes sense. But how come I've never heard this before?"

"I don't know the answer to that. But God made sure you heard it now, didn't He?"

"Yes!" Mrs. Daniels lifted her shoulders and smiled. "Yes, He did. And not too late!"

DeShawn rapped on the vehicle's windshield, getting James' attention and waving him out to follow his mother.

"Let's go inside the office and see what we can both afford to do, Mrs. Daniels," DeShawn invited.

Bobby slid the window shut and sat behind his desk, shuffling papers to appear busy instead of an eavesdropping busybody. He smiled and waved at the group as they came through the entrance before disappearing into DeShawn's office and behind the closed door.

Sitting back in his chair, Bobby marveled at his son's confidence and boldness in sharing his faith with the dying woman who was helped by it. DeShawn's kindness and determination to help her purchase the vehicle she needed impressed him.

"*Yes, indeed,*" Bobby returned to his musing, "*Julia would have been as proud of him as I am. And if Claire weren't so stubborn, she would be, too.*"

CHAPTER FIFTY-NINE

"Going for your evening constitutional before Thursday Meeting, Grant?" Cal asked, consulting the kitchen clock as he and Marcus finished cleaning up after a supper of Cobb salad and biscuits.

"Not today. It's hot enough to melt rocks outside, and I don't need a heatstroke," Grant shook his head.

"Dat's a good call," Marcus agreed, wiping the island countertop with a wet dishcloth in one hand and a dry towel in the other.

"But I was thinking about taking Marie to the flavored ice truck by the ball fields later when it cools down. Are you guys interested in making it a household outing with the girls?" Grant suggested.

Cal and Marcus looked at each other and shrugged.

"Why not?" Cal responded. "We're big spenders!"

"Good! Let's save the thrill for them till after the meeting," Grant joked.

Twenty minutes later, the household settled in the living room for Thursday Meeting, including Mercy, who stretched her body on a section of cool hardwood floor near the piano.

"Dis may be da shortest meeting we've ever had unless someone has business I'm not aware of," Marcus began.

"I have something," Marie began, raising her hand for attention. "I have a favor to ask of Cal." She turned to look him in the eye.

"I was talking to Shelby today, and she mentioned Will is ready to move his things over to the gray house. However, he has to find a rental truck for his and the boy's beds and their kitchen set. Cal, would you be willing to loan Will your truck to spare them that expense?"

"Everybody loves the guy with a truck when they have to move," Cal muttered, then looked to June to gauge if he'd spoken selfishly or honestly.

"Since God's blessed us with a truck, I'm sure Cal would happily pass on the blessing. Wouldn't you, dear?" June encouraged him, un-condemning.

Cal nodded his head in affirmation.

"Since that's settled," Ava jumped in, "I have a favor to ask of Grant."

Grant lifted his bushy eyebrows, curious.

"Nelly Sullivan came into the church office today and told Pastor Jefferson she's ready to pass the volunteer bookkeeping torch to someone else. She said her old eyes just can't do the job anymore. Because of your accounting background, you're her most likely successor. I told Pastor I'd ask you if you'd be willing to serve the Body of Christ in this capacity," Ava informed Grant.

"Willing to serve the Body of Christ?" Grant repeated with a chuckle. "So, no pressure to say 'yes,' right?"

"You are free to deny your Savior and His church the God-given talents and abilities that provided you and your family food, clothing, and shelter for 45 years. Don't give it another thought!" Ava spread it on thick.

"Since you put it that way, I guess I'll be doing it," Grant consented, rolling his eyes.

"Thank you, Grant. I was sure you would," Ava laughed.

"Does anyone else have a favor they'd like to shame someone into?" Elodie asked, scanning the room over the top of her glasses.

"I suppose that completes the bullying for today. Don't you, Ava?" Marie cocked her head, looking satisfied.

"For today," Ava agreed, grinning.

"We hate to reward bad behavior, but we planned to ask you ladies to be our guests at the Icey Breeze truck this evening. About 7:30?" Grant invited.

"Our first group date!" Marie exclaimed.

"Group dates are the only kind I go on," Elodie muttered.

"That's not our fault," Ava responded, goosing Elodie's bum and making her smile.

Icey Breeze was on the mind of many Faircourt residents in the stifling heat, and the friends had to stand in a line 15 deep from the ordering window.

"Didn't imagine it would be so crowded now that the kids are back to school," Ava griped.

As they waited their turn, Marie's eyes fell on the back of a small woman seated alone at a picnic table on the edge of the property.

"That might be Christine Williams over there," Marie pointed the woman out to Grant. "Order for me – pina colada, please. I'm going to go over and say hello to her."

"Should I come with you?" Grant offered protectively.

"No. She seems to be extra-defensive the more people are around. I can approach the lioness on my own though." Marie declined his offer and made a beeline for the woman.

"Mrs. Williams?" Marie inquired when she was still several yards from the table, not wanting to startle.

Christine turned toward the voice, surprised to be greeted in the community. Her face softened as she recognized her neighbor.

"I thought that was you sitting here," Marie returned her soft expression with a smile.

"It's hot," Christine said, raising the cone of green-colored flavored ice in her hand to explain her presence.

"That's what we all thought," Marie nodded toward the line.

"Got the entire house with you, do you?" Christine asked, shoulders tensing.

"Yes. I just came over to say hello, though. I won't keep you." Marie turned to go, realizing the proximity of the entire household tribe in an uncontrolled setting was too much for her neighbor.

"Um, before you go, could I ask your opinion on something?"

"Sure!"

"Do you believe it's appropriate to intervene when the welfare of a child is at risk?" Christine asked as if testing.

"If the primary motive is the welfare of the child, then it's absolutely appropriate," Marie agreed, adding the qualification.

"I agree. Enjoy the shaved ice with your friends," Christine dismissed her.

"When it comes out, she'll know I was concerned for the child. Besides, who is able to judge primary from secondary motives?" Christine justified herself as Marie walked away.

CHAPTER SIXTY

"Well, Lov, what do you think?" Shelby asked her niece after giving her a complete tour of the gray house.

"There's hardly any furniture!" Lovie responded bluntly, her mouth stained with spaghetti sauce from supper.

"It's just Will's things for now. But we'll make it comfortable and homey before you know it," Shelby assured.

"It's kind of small, too."

"It's smaller than your house, that's true. Do you think Will and I should look for a bigger place somewhere else?" Shelby challenged her playfully.

"Oh, no! Right here is perfect!" Lovie backed away from her critical comments.

"Agreed. Right here is perfect." Shelby walked to the living room window and extended an arm toward Lovie, who came to her side.

"It's nice to have a home filled with lovely things. But how happy would you be if it wasn't filled with love first?" Shelby began. "We can be sure Mrs. Williams' big house next door is filled with beautiful antiques and expensive furniture, but she's all alone. Do you imagine she's happy? I don't. This house may not have much, and it's not large. But, Will and I are going to fill it with love first, then we'll see what else we have room for."

"Will you have room for a bed for me so I can sleep over sometimes?"

Lovie asked expectantly.

"I know! Maybe we'll put wheels on your bed at home and roll it back and forth across the street," Shelby joked, pointing out the window toward the Norman house.

As they giggled at the notion, Shelby observed an unfamiliar white sedan pull into the Norman driveway. A man and woman in business casual attire rang the doorbell next to the front door, and Chase ushered them inside.

"Do you have any snacks in the cupboards yet?" Lovie asked, unaware of the visitors at her house. She darted toward the kitchen to investigate, and Shelby, abandoning her curiosity about the strangers, hurried to catch up with her. She'd ask Chase or Micah about them later.

Lovie and Shelby rummaged through what little food Will had stocked in the kitchen. The sardines, crackers, coffee, and honey-mustard pretzel pieces were of little interest to either of them. Then Lovie opened a cupboard containing a box of Ding Dongs.

"Here we go!" Lovie shouted. "Jackpot!"

They sat at Will's kitchen table, each polishing off two chocolate-covered cakes, discussing whether Will would notice the pilferage. And then they heard Chase shouting angrily across the street.

Shelby rushed to the front door, flinging it open, Lovie on her heels.

"I'm not going! You can't do this! Dad, do something! Daaaad!" Chase shouted as the male visitor put Chase in the back seat of the strange car and slid in next to him.

Shelby transferred her gaze to Micah, standing in the house's doorway, unmoving.

"Stay here!" she warned Lovie as she sped down the porch steps of the gray house barefoot.

When she reached the street, the woman was backing the white sedan out of the driveway.

"Chase!" Shelby screeched to her nephew in the car. She glimpsed his frightened face as the sedan pulled away, disappearing down Cedar Street.

"Micah!" Shelby shouted at her immobile brother, still standing in the doorway. "Micah, what is wrong with you? Who took Chase, and why did you let them?"

She stomped toward her brother, and as soon as she reached the top of the porch steps, she could smell the alcohol.

"They said I'm unfit," Micah stared past her with glassy eyes, slurring his words.

"And right now, they're not wrong! Are you proud of yourself? I watched you let your son be taken away without so much as lifting a finger. You just stood there like a statue. I'm glad I'm not your child! Well, they haven't got Lovie. I have her over..."

Shelby turned to look across the street and saw Lovie standing on the porch behind her. After witnessing Chase being taken away, she followed her aunt to the house. She'd heard every word yelled at her father.

Time froze for an instant. Shelby fixed her eyes on her niece, straggly blonde locks falling around small shoulders covered by a red tank top. Spaghetti sauce still stained her open mouth, and blue eyes widened with fear as she stared past Shelby at Micah. Most notable were Lovie's trembling hands dangling at the sides of her cut-off blue jean shorts.

"Oh, Lovie! I'm so sorry, baby," Shelby knelt to embrace the child and shield her from further trauma. She stroked the hair of the shaking child, whispering promises she'd fix everything quickly and hoping she could make good on them.

Across the street, in the upper guest room window, Christine Williams watched the scene unfold to its dramatic conclusion, biting the knuckle of her index finger in astonishment.

"It wasn't supposed to go this far. They shouldn't have taken him and terrified the little one. How did this get so out of hand?" she worried.

Shelby called Will and related, through sobs and tears, what had happened. Will, in turn, called Joe Jacobs and Marcus. By 7:45 PM, Shelby was meeting Joe at the Child Protective Services office. Through Joe's legal connections and his sister-in-law, who managed the local agency, he was able to arrange emergency custody for Shelby so they could pick Chase up that night.

"I didn't know what else to do with Lovie," Will explained to Marcus, Grant, and Cal as they sat around the kitchen table in the friend's house. "The person she feels safest with, next to Shelby, is June."

"She's always welcome here. And my Junie is happy to love her up and comfort her," Cal assured.

"How did CPS land on Micah's doorstep?" Marcus, bewildered, wondered.

"I don't know," Will shook his head.

"I have an idea," Grant offered. "After you spoke to Marcus and told him what happened to Chase, we were all in shock. But then Marie told me Christine Williams had asked her a few days ago if she thought it was appropriate to intervene if the welfare of a child was at risk. She wondered if it could be connected."

"Of course, it was that woman!" Cal refused to say her name.

"But how did she know Micah was drinking? Shelby didn't even know!" Will wondered.

"We knew," Cal admitted. "I took his keys from him Father's Day weekend. We talked about it the next day, and I thought he was finished with it. I guess I hoped he was."

"Why didn't you tell me?" Will demanded, hands pressing the table top.

"Same reason he wouldn't tell Micah your business," Grant defended

Cal.

"Like I said, I didn't think it was an continuing problem," Cal reiterated.

"Yeah, okay," Will relented with a heavy sigh, releasing the tension in his arms.

"What about Micah?" Marcus asked cautiously.

"What about him?" Will snapped. "Shelby and I are getting married in seven days, and now she has emergency custody of his children. Micah is at the bottom of my priority list at the moment."

"Yes, but he's not at da bottom of dos children's list," Marcus replied.

"You're right. Kids come first. Help me process through this then," Will agreed, lowering his head.

"Chase and Lovie should stay in their own house and beds," Grant recommended.

"Then where does Micah go?" Cal wondered. "He can't stay in the house, can he?"

"Nope," Will sat back in his chair.

"We should put him on that woman's doorstep. She created this mess," Cal muttered.

Will allowed himself a tiny smirk at Cal's suggestion before answering. "I guess he can stay with me across the street for the week. It might be less than that if we can get him into rehab quickly."

Since nobody had another suggestion, Will stood. "If he's coming to my place, I better get him there before Shelby and Chase return. Any volunteers to help?"

"I'll go," Cal offered and stood. "Guess he's my son now."

"He may be your son, but your knees still don't do stairs. We'll go too," Grant volunteered himself and Marcus.

"Dear Lord, help us be as kind to our neighbor as You have been to us," Marcus prayed the single sentence aloud as the men headed toward the unpleasant task ahead.

Chapter Sixty-One

"Let's ditch the school bus today. I'll drive you," Shelby suggested to Chase and Lovie.

"I don't want to go to school," Lovie whined, although she was already dressed to go.

"I know, Lov. But I've got to sort things out with Dad today. Besides, you'll get to be with Addy and Lena at school. You always have fun with your besties," Shelby coaxed.

Lovie walked out the back door to Shelby's car, followed by Chase, who expressed no preference for anywhere or anything. He'd been unusually but understandably quiet since the previous evening's drama. His answer to any question asked of him was either 'no' or 'fine.'

Shelby grabbed a box of mini-muffins and two apple juice boxes for the kids to eat in the car as she drove. She dropped Lovie off first and then Chase.

"I love you. I'm going to fix this for you," Shelby promised as Chase gave her an expressionless glance and closed the car door.

When she arrived back at Cedar Street, Shelby parked in her usual spot in front of Micah's garage and walked across the street to the gray house, unsure of what awaited.

Fumbling and dropping her key, she unlocked the front door and stepped inside.

"Hey, babe," Will hurried down the staircase to greet her with a kiss.

"Will! I assumed you'd be at the post office by now," startled Shelby babbled.

"Thought you might need me here more," Will lowered his volume.

"How is he?" Shelby matched it.

Approaching from the kitchen, coffee in hand, Micah answered her question: "He's sober and humiliated."

"Good on both counts," Shelby turned to face him.

She ran her eyes over her brother who looked homeless. He wore the same clothes as the previous day, only rumpled now and splashed with minor orangey stains. A 24-hour beard poked from an ashy chin, and though his shaggy brown hair had been finger-combed, it still looked disheveled. His light brown eyes were red-rimmed, though whether it was from crying or a hangover, Shelby didn't wasn't sure.

"I'm still unpacking and organizing the bathroom upstairs. If you need me, just shout," Will retreated up the staircase to give the brother and sister some space.

"Any more coffee?" Shelby hinted.

"Yeah, sure," Micah answered and shuffled to the kitchen.

"How long have you been secretly drinking?" Shelby sat at the table and began the discussion.

Micah splashed some vanilla creamer in a mug of coffee and handed it to Shelby before sitting down.

"It's been a couple of months," he answered without making eye contact. "I can't imagine how disappointed Dahlia would be in me for how I've screwed things up."

"Oh, I can! But we're not going down your self-pity path. Save that for a counselor. Chase and Lovie are my number one concern right now, and they should be yours as well," Shelby rebuked. "Just to make sure I have the entire picture, is there anything else you've been into that I should be aware of?"

"No," he looked her in the eye at last.

"Then what will it be: the booze or your kids? You can't have both."

"You know it's the kids," Micah responded with a whine in his tone.

"Yesterday morning, I would have said, 'I know' my brother wouldn't stand passively by while strangers took his son away. So, let's not rely on what you presume 'I know,'" Shelby challenged, trying to curb her angry tone.

"I want my children. They're the most important thing," Micah corrected himself.

"Glad to hear it. So, rehab then?"

"I searched this morning and found a local AA chapter that meets at St. Anthony's tonight at 6 PM. I'll start there. You understand what going to rehab will do to my career, which won't be good for anybody depending on me. But if the AA doesn't help me, then rehab it is. I promise."

Shelby took a sip of her coffee and sat back in her chair, thinking about Micah's proposal.

"Okay," she agreed. "I have temporary legal custody of the kids until you can prove to the court you've got yourself together. But you remember I'm getting married on Monday, right? I'd rather not cancel my honeymoon, so I need someone to stay with Chase and Lovie for the five days we're gone. My first thought is Dahlia's parents."

"But the kids might talk..." Micah objected.

"Aht!" Shelby interrupted, holding up her hand. "Perhaps they'll need to talk. They have been traumatized. It's kid's needs first, not yours, remember?"

"I'm such an..." Micah folded his arms on the table and buried his head in them, muffling his words.

Shelby let him be and sipped her coffee. For the first time in 15 hours, she relaxed and released the stress she'd been reining in. Now, the liquid stress streamed down her cheeks. She reached across the corner of the table and patted her brother's arm.

Micah looked up at his teary sister and vowed: "This will never happen again."

***

Marie waited until the housekeeping crew at Christine Williams' house departed. As they drove down Cedar Street, she marched down her porch steps toward Christine's.

"Hello, Marie!" Christine answered her doorbell in an overly friendly manner.

"May I come in?" Marie was direct.

Christine stepped aside and widened the entry so her visitor could pass through. Marie scanned the exquisite interior as her hostess led her to the living room.

"Please sit," Christine invited.

The women sat across from one another on matching white sofas.

"Why?" Marie asked.

Christine respected her neighbor and liked her enough not to put up a pretense of ignorance regarding her question.

"He is allowing the boy to associate with the felon. Unsupervised! That's irresponsible. You said so, yourself."

"You asked me if it was appropriate to intervene when the welfare of a child was at risk, and I said it was if the child's welfare was the primary motive," Marie corrected. "But in this case, the primary motive was to get DeShawn McBride ostracized from the community so he'd tuck his tail and leave – which would make you happier, no?"

"I didn't think they would take the boy from his father," Christine deflected. "That shouldn't have happened."

"But it did because Micah was intoxicated when CPS arrived, and Chase was home alone with him. It was take Micah and leave the child alone – which they couldn't do – or take Chase and leave Micah," Marie explained.

Christine's thin hand flew to her face, covering her mouth, as she processed the gravity of facts she hadn't foreseen.

Recovering, she asked: "Well, if the father has a problem with alcohol, maybe it worked out as it should."

"Cal, Marcus, and my Grant have been working with Micah and knew about the problem. Did they manage it perfectly? No, they made an assumption and a mistake. But they didn't put the children through the traumatic situation your method accomplished. If you were concerned about Chase associating with DeShawn, why didn't you speak to his father instead of letting weeks go by until CPS came by to do it for you?"

"The gentlemen are involved in this?" Christine deflected once more, raising an arched eyebrow.

"Yes! That's what neighbors do for one another. They get involved – not just to celebrate the good times, but to be a blessing and a help in the messy times, too," Marie defended with some exasperation.

Christine lowered her shoulders and tilted her head as a new realization dawned on her.

"Is that why you're here with me? To be a blessing and a help in the mess I've made?" she asked in profound hope.

Marie managed a smile. "I'm trying my best, but you don't make it easy."

"You are the only person who has ever tried at all. For that, I thank you, Marie."

Before thinking about it, Marie was on her feet and sitting beside Christine. Hugging her.

CHAPTER SIXTY-TWO

"The total of checks and cash does not match what's recorded on the deposit slip in the night deposit bag. Sometimes it's more, sometimes less, but it's never accurate. It used to happen occasionally, but now it's a regular mistake that is surely making your bookkeeper pull their hair out. That is, if they're reconciling statements and catching them, I just wanted to alert you about it from our end, Mr. McBride."

"I appreciate your bringing this to my attention, Sarah. I'll take care of the matter personally," DeShawn assured the manager of Faircourt Savings Bank and hung up the phone.

"Dad?" DeShawn called from his desk to get his father's attention. When no reply was forthcoming, he walked into his father's office and saw him talking with a customer outside through the office window.

DeShawn turned back toward his father's desk and picked up a well-worn business card file. He flipped through it, hoping to find the contact for McBride Motor Mart's bookkeeper. Having located it, he copied the number and returned to his office. He decided he'd tell his father he was curious to learn more aspects of the business and request his approval to speak with the bookkeeper. Confident he wouldn't be denied, DeShawn called and made an appointment for that afternoon.

In the meantime, he'd see if he could assist his dad with the customer on the lot. He was just about to head out the front door when he heard the back door of the sales office slam. A chair in the break room was flung across the room, and a mild expletive grumbled. DeShawn changed course and headed to the break room.

"Sounds like you're lettin' off some steam. Hope it helped," DeShawn sympathized as he recognized Shorty, an employee who worked in the detailing building.

"Sorry, boss. Didn't think anyone was in here," Shorty apologized.

"Anything I can do?" DeShawn offered.

"Nah," came the terse response from the stocky, middle-aged man, who was still aggravated.

DeShawn figured whatever set him off had something to do with his coworkers in the detail shop, and he let Shorty keep it to himself. If he'd learned anything in prison, it was to respect the guy who refused to snitch.

"How's your father doing?" DeShawn switched gears. All he knew about Shorty's personal life was that he'd never married and took care of his aging father.

Shorty shook his head and looked at his feet.

"I'm sorry, man, if he's not well," DeShawn sympathized.

"I don't know how much longer I can do it. My father really shouldn't be left alone anymore, but I don't have a choice. I need to work. We have to eat and pay rent," Shorty admitted.

"I don't mean to get into your business..."

"No, go ahead. If you have any ideas, I need 'em."

"If he shouldn't be left alone, is it time to get him full-time care? A nursing home?"

"To be honest, I need his Social Security to keep up the rent. It's not a fancy place, but I can't do it on what I make," Shorty tried not to sound ungrateful for his job. "A nursing home will take everything he gets."

"Are you open to having a roommate?" DeShawn asked, trying to push through the obstacle.

"A roommate? Maybe," Shorty considered the idea. "But Faircourt is a small town. I've no idea who.

"I might have a contact who'd be interested," DeShawn offered, considering young James Daniels, whose mother was terminal. "I'll make an inquiry. No promises, though."

"Okay," Shorty brightened with a glimmer of hope.

"You might need this if it's going to be a late night," Mariana suggested as she placed an insulated mug of black coffee on her husband's study desk.

"Thanks," DeShawn responded, lifting the mug to his lips.

"I'll leave you to your books then," she said, turning to go.

"Hey, babe," he called her back. "Got a minute?"

"Always for you," Mariana smiled and sat on the second-hand rocking chair they'd added to the room at her insistence.

"I've been doing some praying and, um, some thinking..." he began unsteadily. "I know I made plans; we made plans that you'd work while I worked part time and went to school part time. But that was before...before things changed. I just don't know anymore. I'm wondering if I have to adjust the plan."

"Oh?" Mariana invited his explanation.

"Well, I've been working full time at the lot for Dad, learning the business, and finding out there's more he can't do. Today, I spent half the day with our bookkeeper trying to sort out a bunch of errors he made with the bank deposits and getting educated on the basics of accounting. I feel like I need to be all in at the lot or all out – one or the other. But if I'm all in, I can't do this too," DeShawn gestured to the pile of theology books before him. I'm not saying I'll never take classes, but perhaps now isn't the time."

"The heart of man plans his way, but the LORD establishes his steps," Mariana quoted Proverbs 16:9

"Exactly!" DeShawn agreed, relieved his wife understood. "I know you married me with the idea I was someone you could go into full-time Christian ministry with, but..."

"No need for 'but,'" Mariana cut him off. "I married you because I love you. That's it."

"You are the best wife I could have hoped for." DeShawn reached for her hand across the desk, and she placed hers in his. "Guess what?" he added.

"No clue," Mariana shrugged.

"Today, I also spoke with a guy who works in the detailing shop. There are needs there, Mariana. Our employees have physical, emotional, and spiritual needs – a built-in mission field in my workplace's backyard. I realized I don't have to be in professional full-time Christian ministry to be in Christian ministry. God can use an amateur like me in the last place I thought I wanted to be."

"That's right, baby. Just respond to God's leading. That's all I ask you to do. Right now, I'm being led to bed. Long day on my feet. Tired." Mariana responded in shorter sentences before yawning and shuffling toward the bedroom.

CHAPTER SIXTY-THREE

"What a week!" Ava declared, tucking a foot under her bottom as she sat on the couch, ready for Thursday Meeting.

"You're not kidding," Marie agreed, smoothing the skirt of her yellow shirtwaist dress.

"Elodie and I got to see Lovie today for the first time since Monday night. It's amazing how resilient kids can be. She's just going with the flow, knowing her dad is staying across the street with Will for a while," June shared.

"How's Chase doing?" Marcus asked, curious.

"We didn't see him. Shelby said he was in his room and has been holed up since, you know..." June trailed off.

"Yeah, not everyting bounces back when trust is broken," Marcus shook his head slowly.

"I'll be spendin' next week with Chase and Lovie while Shelby and Will are on their honeymoon. Shelby said she asked Dahlia's parents first, but the father had a heart attack two weeks ago, and they're not ready to take on full-time child care for children just yet," Elodie informed the friends. "It won't be too bad because the kids have school most of the day during the week."

"I can help you on Saturday, and the newlyweds will be home Sunday," June volunteered.

Elodie nodded, accepting the offer of help.

"Are you ladies all set for Monday's big event?" Grant asked, hopeful of a positive response. He was nervous about being roped into more responsibilities than he was prepared for.

"We're all set. You can relax, Grant," Ava soothed.

"Your wife has checklists for checklists," Elodie groaned. "She could run receptions as a side business."

"Do not give him any ideas!" Marie warned.

"Here's a question that I am not certain if anyone has the answer to," Ava spoke out. "Is Micah allowed to attend his sister's wedding since the kids will be there?"

"He's coming," Cal spoke up. "He said Shelby threatened to disown him if he didn't, seeing it's her first and only wedding. I guess he can see his kiddos. It might have to be supervised. I'm not sure how it all works from a legal standpoint, but I told him to tell Shelby my eye will be on him since she'll be busy."

"You've talked to Micah, den?" Marcus asked, more to express his surprise than confirm.

"Drove him to his first AA meeting Tuesday evening. Taking him again tomorrow evening," Cal confided.

"That's where you were! I thought you went to bed early 'cause you didn't want to watch Gunsmoke reruns with Marcus and me," Grant chortled.

"Just giving the boy some fatherly support and encouragement. He feels like the rest of the world hates him or should. He knows I can dish out the tough love, so I thought he should see some of the, well, friendlier love," Cal explained.

"Did you mean to say 'tender love' instead of 'friendlier love'?" Marie attempted to correct to feminine standards.

"No! We're still dudes," Cal scowled at her. "Dude love is friendly, not tender, right, Marcus?"

"It's barely even friendly," Marcus agreed.

"How nice," Marie scoffed before adding: "I wasn't planning on it, but I showed Christine Williams some womanly tender love the other day."

"You what?" Grant raised his eyebrows.

"Whose side are you on?" Cal wondered.

"Chase and Lovie are our priority because they're young and vulnerable. I am firmly on their side. So, I marched myself across the street to give Christine the dressing down she was due. But somehow, the Lord flipped the script on me when I was over there."

"You were inside her house?" Grant asked, disbelieving. "First my mother, now you go traipsing into the lion's den."

Marie held out her arms for inspection. "Not a scratch. Back to my story. I ranted a bit about how neighbors get involved in good times and bad in order to be a blessing in both. Then she got this strange look on her face and asked me if that's why I was there – to be a blessing to her. It wasn't, but what flew into my mind was Matthew 5:46

For if you love those who love you, what reward do you have? Do not even the tax collectors do the same?

"Next thing I know, she's thanking me, and I'm hugging her!" Marie concluded.

Grant began shaking his head, and Elodie joined him, adding, "Mmm, mmm, mmm!"

"Good for you, Marie!" June exclaimed. "So you didn't plan to go there to show her love. But when the Holy Spirit brought Scripture to your mind, you pivoted in obedience. That's the best any of us can hope for when God scrubs our motives with His word. That Scripture should convict to all of us. It's easy to love the Norman children because they return our love. The reward comes for loving the likes of Christine Williams."

"I guess we all need to adjust our attitudes about our neighbor across the street and try to show her love instead of focusing on the trouble she causes," Ava suggested.

Ava looked at her husband, expecting him to nod in agreement with her. Instead, he was gazing inattentively out the front window from his chair across the room.

"Marcus, are you alright?" Ava wondered aloud, her body leaning toward his.

Marcus turned to Ava, refocused. "I was just tinking about dat Scripture and what June had to say about it. As we've seen for ourselves, dat verse is straightforward but extremely difficult to obey in our flesh. For da past few months, I've been discontent – looking for a ministry to challenge and satisfy me. Maybe dis is da season for me to apply myself to my own sanctification – which, I'm convicted now, is challenging enough. Pray for me. Ask for da Holy Spirit's power and blessing to produce spiritual fruit and a harvest of righteousness."

"Amen. Me too," whispered Grant in agreement.

"That's for all of us!" Elodie declared.

"I never thought about God using our discontent – which seems like a complaint against Him – as a sanctifying tool to make us long for spiritual fruit," June was mulling over Marcus' words.

"He faithfully uses our worst to produce His best. And thank God, not every trial has to be a major drama. Sometimes, it can be just a nagging...void," Ava observed, placing a hand on her husband's knee.

"Whew! For a minute there I thought you were going to say God will use a nagging wife," Cal chuckled.

"What would you know about a nagging wife?" June pouted semi-seriously.

"Nothin', darlin'," Cal grimaced, scrambling to remove his foot from his mouth.

Chapter Sixty-Four

"What'll it be, guys? Two Coconut Snowballs?" Five approached Will and Shelby for their order at a sidewalk table.

"Ha ha, not today, Five. Two sweet teas and a pimento cheese sandwich to split. Much as we love them, even we can't do Coconut Snowballs with pimento cheese," Shelby grinned at their favorite server.

"Coming right up!" she answered, stuffing the order pad in her apron.

"Hey, girl!" Shelby caught her attention again. "Your hair is extra bold and pretty today."

"Just re-did the pink dye yesterday. It was getting drab. Thanks for noticing," Five smiled before heading to the kitchen.

When she was through the cafe's door, Will asked, "Do you think her hair is 'extra pretty' with the new dye job, or were you just being nice?"

"Testing my sincerity, are you? The answer is yes and yes," Shelby replied. "Pink hair is not for me, and frankly, would look terrible with my complexion – like a newborn mole or rat. But she rocks it with confidence. And if you're going to have pink hair, then don't have drab pink hair. It has to be bold and kept up. And yes, I also wanted to be nice. Miss Ava says, 'If you think it and it builds up instead of tearing down, you should say it.'"

"Words to live by. Shelby, you look beautiful this September afternoon, and I can't wait to see you in the church in your wedding dress in three days," Will proclaimed.

"Same. I mean, I don't hope to see you in a wedding dress, but at the church when I'm wearing mine," Shelby giggled and then grew serious.

"How's Micah doing?" she asked, lowering her gaze.

"You know he returned to work yesterday and went today, too. It's good for him to get back to his routine. He's still a little awkward around me, but then, it's been a little awkward between him and me since we started dating – so I guess that's nothing new. He says he misses the kids and wants to apologize to them, especially Chase."

"I'm sure Chase needs to hear it," Shelby conceded.

"They'll both be at the wedding, and I think the day will go smoother if they talk beforehand. Could we work that out, maybe this evening or tomorrow?"

"Let's try."

Five arrived table-side with their tea and sandwich. "Here you go. Big day coming up soon, right?" She inquired with a sly grin.

"Three days," Will and Shelby answered in unison.

"Congratulations three days in advance, then. I hope you have a perfect day and a perfect life together," Five wished sincerely and left the couple to share their lunch.

They consumed their tiny meal in ten minutes, and Will left the payment and tip on the table. It took another 20 minutes in Will's car to reach the Oldham County Courthouse in LaGrange to obtain their marriage license.

"Hey, Joe!" Will greeted the newest member of his Sunday School class as Joe Jacobs exited the courthouse in a sharp navy suit.

"Will! Shelby!" Joe stuck out his hand to shake theirs in turn. "Here for the marriage license, I'll bet."

"You'd win the bet. Must see a lot of this place in your line of work," Will guessed.

"You're right as well. Only today, I'm here on business of a more personal nature. Our county representative to the state legislature is retiring, and I'm considering running for his seat. We met to talk about it," Joe confided. "Wanted to look the part," he added to account for the suit.

"Politics? Really?" Will raised his eyebrows.

"Ever since I attended that first Sunday School class, and we discussed Christians being instruments of doing God's will on Earth, I've been considering using my abilities to help shape policy issues. If I run, I hope I'll have your vote. And yours, too, Shelby."

"Sounds like you're getting a running start on your campaign now," Shelby noted.

"Well, my meeting encouraged me, I'll say that. But I've never run for office before and have much to learn. I know God is sovereign and raises leaders to fulfill His purposes, but that's no guarantee I'll win. I'm a little nervous about falling on my face so publicly if I lose. I mean, I feel at peace about doing this, but...See the thing I said about being nervous?" Joe hesitated and laughed.

"Joe, can I pray for you now?" Shelby asked.

Without waiting for a response, she tugged on Joe's arm to move with her a little farther from the courthouse's front door so they wouldn't impede foot traffic. Will shuffled over to the edge of the sidewalk with them. Shelby reached for both men's hands and prayed:

"Father, we come before You in agreement to ask for Your favor and blessing on Joe as he seeks Your will to be done on Earth as it is in Heaven. Thank you for Joe's willingness to run a public campaign for state office. I pray You will give him all the wisdom and fortitude he needs for such an endeavor and that he will glorify You in all he does. Keep him humble. Keep him from the temptations of political office, whatever they may be.

May Your protection be on Joe, Allison, and their children as they become open to public scrutiny. May they as a family stand faithful to You and above reproach. Father, we bow before You as the sovereign King of Kings and submit ourselves to Your perfect will. We ask these things in the name of Jesus Christ our Lord. Amen."

"Amen! Shelby, thank you so much for praying for me and my family. Win or lose, I'm going to do this!" Joe exclaimed. "Well, I'll let you guys get that paper you're after. I can't wait to go home and tell Allison I met you guys here, and we prayed right on the street corner!"

As Joe walked away, Will turned to Shelby and stared at her.

"What?" she asked, grinning.

"Nothing." Will returned her grin. "You just surprise me sometimes, that's all."

"Miss June doesn't wait to pray. She does it when needed, and I thought that was a good idea after I got over my initial astonishment."

"Okay," Will took her by the hand again to enter the courthouse. "Let's get a marriage license!"

"As they walked, Will began to chuckle.

"Now what?" Shelby demanded.

"Miss Ava says this, Miss June does that. Sounds like your neighbors have had quite the influence."

"Is there a problem with that?" Shelby stopped to look Will in the eye.

"None," he responded.

CHAPTER SIXTY-FIVE

Chase sat at his kitchen table, chewing a tiny piece of dead skin from his thumbnail, waiting for his dad to walk over from Will's place across the street. Shelby relayed a message from his father the previous evening, asking if he could talk to Chase. Although Chase gave no outward hint of enthusiasm at the prospect, he agreed.

At 8:30 AM, Micah knocked on the front door of his own house. Shelby welcomed him and informed him Chase was in the kitchen and that she and Lovie would be assembling wedding favors in the living room so the guys could have some space.

"Hey, bud," Micah entered the kitchen with a smile for his boy.

"Hey, Dad," Chase copied the greeting.

Chase studied his father carefully as he pulled the back of a chair from the table to sit. His dad wore a navy and white striped golf shirt, cargo blue jean shorts, and leather sandals. It was an ensemble his father defaulted to in the summer months and quite familiar to Chase. Yet, the clothes seemed more familiar this morning than the man wearing them. For the first time in his life, Chase felt awkward with his dad.

Micah sat kitty-corner from Chase at the table. He'd rehearsed an apology but, at the moment, struggled to recall the words.

"I'm so sorry I let you down, son...let Lovie and Aunt Shelby down...myself," Micah began, stammering.

Chase said nothing, unsure if his father's statement was complete and not knowing how to respond if it was.

Micah continued. "I shouldn't have turned to alcohol to numb my feelings. I should have gotten counseling instead, like I am now. It's a sort of a relief now not having to hide the things I did – acknowledging it.

"You didn't hide it very well. I knew. I wondered why you started spending so much time alone in your room instead of with us like you used to. After you left for work one day, I went into your room and saw the bottle on the shelf in your closet. I'd smell it on your breath too when you thought you covered it up with mouthwash," Chase closed his eyes, remembering. "Mint and bourbon."

"You went through my room?" Micah raised a single eyebrow.

"Your closet door was open, and there it was."

It was Micah's turn to be silent. He raked his fingers through his hair, trying to find a direction that wouldn't stir up more confrontation.

"Remember last fall when I told you Trevor's father found weed that his brother had stashed under his mattress? You said it was a good thing because a man was responsible for knowing what was going on under his own roof. Well, I needed to know what was going on under my roof," Chase continued to defend his actions.

"Fair enough," Micah conceded the point grudgingly. He realized it wouldn't be productive to argue about ownership of the roof.

"Dad, I'm still angry you let those strangers put me in that car and take me away. I begged you to help me, and you didn't, and now I can't trust you," Chase declared his feelings but without malice.

"For as long as I live, I'll regret that, Chase." Micah momentarily looked his son in the eye and then lowered his gaze, ashamed. "I wasn't myself."

"You were drunk," Chase defined the situation succinctly, with an even tone.

"I was drunk," Micah admitted. "I saw what was happening that evening, of course, but I feared I would fall if I let go of the door jamb.

And if I fell, everyone would know what I still believed I was getting away with. Another part of me wondered if I deserved to lose you."

"So, all your concern was for yourself and none for me," Chase had listened carefully.

Micah exhaled. "I'm not going to add lying to you on top of everything else. Yes, at that moment, it was all about me. I'd like to tell you it was one hundred percent the effects of the alcohol, but I'm not sure. Maybe it was just selfishness, or maybe a bit of both. I'll find out though, because I'm not going to drink anymore. I've joined a group to help me with that. So, I'll see what's left in my head when nothing is competing there. That's as honest as I can be, Chase. Now, how can I help you? What are you dealing with, and what do you need from me?"

"Tell me what made you drink in the first place. Help me understand," Chase asked, his brown eyes imploring.

"Wow, that's a good question." Micah rubbed sweaty palms on his shorts. "Okay. In no particular order, here are a few things that come to mind: Things just seemed to get harder. You are growing up – blazing a path of your own that I'm not on. I miss your mom and came to the end of my strength, I guess. I just wanted to run away in my own house, if that makes sense. Mother's Day was brutal this year. Work is challenging at the moment. And then your Aunt Shelby fell in love with Will, and I was jealous. Am jealous. You're not supposed to say you're sad about your sister's happiness. I took the coward's way out, and instead of dealing with each issue, I numbed them with alcohol so they wouldn't hurt."

Chase knew his father's reference to him blazing a path of his own meant his becoming a Christian and the changes it was making in his life. But while he'd been comparing his father to the Christian men at church, he understood now that his father had been hurt by his pulling away. Chase had been the first one to change, not his dad. Plus, all the matters his father dealt with that he hadn't known existed.

"Dad, I'm sorry, too," Chase apologized. "I understand what you mean about different paths, and I want you to know I don't mean to hurt you by following Jesus."

Chase stood and closed the one-step gap that separated him from his dad. Micah stood too and embraced his son. They clung to one another, erasing the previous awkwardness and tension.

"I love you, son. I'll never let anyone take you away from me again. I'm done drinking, I swear," Micah pledged.

"I love you, too," Chase reassured. "And Dad, I've missed you."

CHAPTER SIXTY-SIX

DeShawn and Mariana crossed Tamarack Street on the cloudless Sunday morning and added the Rennigers, Van Zants, and Elodie to their walking party. At the end of the next driveway stood Shelby, Chase, and Lovie, ready to join the group for the three-block walk to Grace Fellowship Church.

Over the spring and summer, without the benefit of a discussion of rules, the custom developed of treating the walk to church like a dance from a bygone era. Only instead of dancing, the partners engaged one another in conversation. Partners could switch if the person they wished to speak with was agreeable.

Lovie, who was making the best of the change in her regular Sunday morning routine of pancakes with Dad, walked with Elodie since June wasn't an option. Chase, as was lately the case, sought DeShawn, which edged out Mariana. However, Shelby swooped in beside her, taking her by the arm.

"It's my last Sunday walk to church as a single woman!" Shelby squealed. "We won't be returning to Faircourt until next Sunday afternoon, but Sunday after that, I'll be on Will's arm for the church walk, and I'll stink-eye anyone who tries to take him away from me."

"Thanks for the warning," Mariana laughed. "I love your peach dress – my favorite color. Is it new?"

"It is. I planned to wear it for the rehearsal dinner this evening and decided I might as well wear it to church, too."

"What did you guys decide on for your honeymoon? Is it going to be Niagara Falls or Gatlinburg?"

"Niagara Falls. There's just something traditional about it. It's where people went when marriages lasted. And, neither of us has ever been, so it's a place we can discover together."

"How old do kids have to be to work at your dad's car-cleaning business?" Chase quizzed DeShawn as they walked together.

"The detailing shop? Sixteen. That's when I started. How old are you now?"

"Turned fourteen a couple of weeks ago," Chase groaned.

"No promises, but we might allow a mature 15-year-old to have a shot at a job."

"Really?" Chase brightened. "I'm mature. I want to save my money and become a customer, too."

"Oh, yeah? What kind of vehicle are we trying to get into?"

"I don't know that yet. I only know what vehicle I'm trying to stay out of: my dad's minivan. Maybe a truck would be cool," Chase thought out loud.

DeShawn laughed. "You've seen my dad's beater S10. There's nothing cool about it."

"Yeah, it would have to be bigger than that," Chase agreed.

"Can I take your walking partner?" Marcus nudged DeShawn's arm.

"I'm out, Freshman," DeShawn lifted his hands helplessly in the air. He moved forward in the group to chat with Grant, displacing Marie.

"I haven't seen you since last Sunday, and I know you've had quite da week," Marcus aimed straight at the heart of his concern for Chase.

"You could say that," Chase acknowledged. He would have been embarrassed if anyone else but Mr. Van Zant had brought up his trouble.

"How are you feeling?" Marcus asked point blank, shifting the Bible to his other arm.

"Better since I talked with my dad yesterday. He had a lot of stuff going on," Chase offered in defense of his father.

"Dat's usually da case."

"Mr. Van Zant, was your father a Christian?"

They walked several paces before Marcus answered. "I hope he was. He said he was. But his life produced little evidence dat he was. Why do you ask?"

"I thought you must have had a great dad. But at least you're a great dad to your kids," Chase concluded.

Again, Marcus took his time before responding. "I wouldn't be so sure about dat either. I have tree daughters, and only one of dem will speak to me."

"You're joking?" Chase was incredulous. He looked at Marcus with an expression of disbelief that wouldn't budge.

"When I talked wit you and DeShawn the oder week about your faders, I asked you to focus on being a godly son. But I understand you're trying to figure out faders – what makes a good one and what makes a bad one, and how being a Christian man influences dat. It's more complicated den you imagine. Just because a man isn't saved doesn't mean he's a lousy fader. And just because a man is saved, dat doesn't guarantee he's a good one.

Chase, dere is only one perfect Fader. All da rest of us are failures at times. It's da same wit being a son. Dere's one perfect Son. Do you agree wit dat?"

"I'm not a perfect son," Chase acknowledged.

"So, we should give as much grace as we want to be given for our failures, no matter if da person is a Christian or not. In eternity, it won't matter who was da best fader, da best student, or da best ice cream salesman. What will matter is dat God is glorified because any of us are dere."

"I think I'm getting it. I should want my dad to be a Christian so that he'll be saved, not just because it might make him a better father to me. And when he fails as a father, I should remember that I failed too and forgive him. Is that right?"

"Dat's right, but I tink you said it better dan I did," Marcus clapped the boy on his back.

The group arrived at the main entrance doors of the church and exchanged raised eyebrows upon spotting Christine Williams standing outside. Waiting, it seemed. When Chase passed by her, she made a slight motion toward him as if she wanted to say something to him. But then, she didn't.

Chapter Sixty-Seven

The Rental Scapes truck parked along the Tamarack Street side of the Cedar Street house, and a crew of four men, three in their mid-twenties and one in his early sixties, set about erecting the large reception tent in the side yard.

Marie monitored the progress, ready to jump in with directions for the arrangement of lights and tables once the tent was up. She assumed the older man was in charge, a lanky gentleman with weather-beaten skin and a full head of wavy gray hair. However, after several minutes of observation from the second-floor guest room window, Marie concluded he was the group's rookie. He'd clearly never put up a tent before if the constant stream of instruction and correction from his coworkers was any indication.

Marie felt sorry for the guy. Here he was, starting a new job when many men his age were thinking about retiring. She wondered what his personal circumstances were that necessitated employment requiring heavy physical labor.

It wasn't long before the reception tent was erected, and it was time to unload and arrange the next phase of the setup. Marie hurried down the stairs and out to the side yard before the men could take a breather.

"There's an electrical outlet on the porch where you can run your cord for the strings of patio lights," Marie intentionally deferred to the older man. Standing closer to him, she noted the scent of cheap aftershave. It seemed strange since he clearly hadn't shaved in several days.

"Oh, I don't do the electrics yet," he replied. "Hey, Mike! She wants to talk about the electrics," he called to a young man with tattooed calves.

After the lights were hung and extension outlets were placed for the DJ, it was time to arrange the tables.

"Two 6' tables go here for the buffet, one goes over here for the cake, one here for the DJ, two up front for the bridal party, and the last one goes here for gifts," Marie instructed with a flying pointed index finger. "Then fill in the middle with the round tables."

"Wait. What? Could you say that again?" the older man asked while his coworkers walked to the truck, comprehending the first time they heard the arrangement.

Marie repeated herself for the man's benefit and stepped aside as the younger guys carried tables in and unfolded them .

"I'll just get the chairs," the older man muttered, slinking to the truck.

"I don't give him a month," a young goateed man wearing a navy sweatshirt with cut-off sleeves laughed. Mike and the other guy joined in.

"I wouldn't be so smug about your proficiency in your chosen career," Marie wanted to rebuke them in the old man's defense. Instead, she repeated to herself: *"The fruit of the Spirit is self-control. The fruit of the Spirit is self-control. The fruit of the Spirit..."*

When the tables and chairs were situated, Mike retrieved a box of rented linens from the truck. "Would you like us to put these on the tables, or do you want to do it yourself tomorrow?" he asked Marie.

"If you wouldn't mind carrying the box to the porch and setting it there, I'll do it myself tomorrow."

"Say, that's a pretty house across the street from you. I wonder who lives in such a grand place. Not that your house isn't nice, too," the older man babbled to Marie while he waited for Mike.

"She's a very private woman over there. And thank you; we like our house, too. I just want to say I appreciate your hard work today. You did a great job. I'm going to give Rental Scapes a 5-star online review. Can I mention your name in particular?" Marie replied.

"Oh, no, mam! That's not necessary."

"Hey, old man! Let's go!" Mike yelled, already back at the truck.

"What took so long?" Grant asked as Marie slid into the seat he'd saved for her at the rehearsal dinner - a fresh plate of antipasto salad and a dinner roll before her.

"So long? I thought the men got it set up pretty quickly for all there was to do."

"Well, glad you're here now," Grant acquiesced, taking a bite from his plate.

"I had no idea Latte Da had this upstairs space available." Marie looked around, taking it in.

Accessed through a side door, the second floor used to contain two apartment units. One unit had been gutted into a multi-purpose, open-concept space with a galley kitchenette on one side wall and two single bathrooms on the opposite wall. The walls were sealed exposed brick with rustic beams separating the second floor from the gable roof, and large south-facing windows flooded the room with natural light. For this evening's event, three 8' tables had been arranged end-to-end down the center of the room.

"I don't think they advertise it – which is a shame. Will said their friend who works here told them about it."

"Business must be good if they can afford to let an asset like this go to waste," Marie remarked.

"Look at you! Evaluating the return on investment!" Grant beamed at her.

"Being married to a CPA all these years, something was bound to rub off," Marie chuckled before turning her attention to Shelby and Will, seated next to one another at the middle table.

"Don't they look happy? Considering the heartache they've been through separately, I'm glad they found one another. I'm confident the inevitable parenting challenges with Will's boys won't swamp their boat, but I pray there's not much bailing to do. I just don't want it to be hard for them," Marie leaned over to whisper.

"No doubt there will be all kinds of challenges. But after a year and a half in Will's Sunday School class and his intermittent appearances at Garage Cave night, I'm sure he has the spiritual maturity to remain steadfast under trial. Remember how spiritually green I was when we got married?" Grant shook his head, laughing at himself.

"Both of us. It was God's grace that kept us then and now," Marie patted her husband's back. "We could have given up twenty times without God's steady hand on our hearts. We know we don't deserve any of the credit. But I will tell you this, Grant Renniger: I wouldn't change any of it because our struggles were sanctifying. God used it all to humble us, stretch us, and display His faithfulness to us. What more could we ask for?"

"Then maybe some hard in a marriage is not so bad after all," Grant said and gently kissed her cheek.

"Hey, you two!" shouted Will, catching the public display of affection at the end of the table out of the corner of his eye. "More eating and less kissy-face, alright?"

"No promises," Grant shouted back with a grin.

CHAPTER SIXTY-EIGHT

"It's my wedding day!" Shelby cheered to herself the second she opened her eyes. She threw the summer bed covering off, sat upright, and was startled to see a vase of flowers on her nightstand, which wasn't there when she went to sleep. She counted eleven white roses surrounding a single red one. Tucked into the flowers was a card:

My darling bride, for the rest of our lives, I aim to display the love Christ has for His bride in the way I love you. I will be flawed but faithful. Yours, always and all ways, Will

She pressed the small card to her heart and closed her eyes.

"Father, thank you for Your goodness to me. Truly, You've given me abundant life – eternally as well as in this world. I am undeserving and grateful for both. Please help me be an excellent wife to Will. Help me bring glory to Your Son in all I say and do. Thank You! Thank You! Thank You! Amen."

Mixed with the scent of the roses was the unmistakable aroma of coffee wafting under her bedroom door. She threw a pink cotton robe over her blue knit nightgown and headed toward the kitchen, where she heard male voices.

"What was it like when you married Mom?" Chase asked his visiting father.

Shelby stopped short of the kitchen and stood unseen in the hall to listen to her brother's answer.

"A lot different from your Aunt Shelby and Will," Micah began. "Your mom and I knew each other since we were kids, but she was four years older – Shelby's age. I would have liked to have gotten to know her better starting in junior high, but she didn't pay any attention to me. That changed when I was almost finished with college and had another girlfriend. I dropped that other girl like a bad habit the second I thought I might have a chance with your mom. She was prettier than ever and amazingly unattached. I realized after our first date I wanted to marry Dahlia Bergman. The week after I graduated from college, we did. We went to the courthouse and were married by a Justice of the Peace - just your Aunt Shelby and a buddy of mine for witnesses. Your Grandma and Grandpa Bergman had a fit because they wanted their only daughter to have a big Jewish wedding. But your mom didn't want it. She said it didn't mean to her what it meant to them. Eventually, they got over it."

Chase pursed his lips and then grinned, imagining. "So, the woman I marry someday might be a freshman in college right now?"

"Theoretically," Micah laughed at his son's takeaway from his story.

"Too bad I don't know her now! Hot college chick," Chase mused.

"Son, right now you're jailbait for hot college chicks," Micah reminded.

Pulled back from his fantasy to reality, Chase asked: "Dad, do you think you'll ever get married again?"

"Do you know any hot college chicks?" Micah joked.

"Dad, seriously!" Chase rolled his eyes to the ceiling.

Micah thought for a moment. "I loved your mom. Loved being married to her. If I could find the right woman, I would like to get married again. But for now, I'm not the right man for anyone. I need to get myself in a better place – first, for you and your sister, then maybe for someone I could love and who could love me."

Sensing the conversation had concluded, Shelby breezed through the kitchen entrance.

"Who was the stalker who crept into my bedroom while I was sleeping to put a vase of flowers on my nightstand?" she demanded with a twinkle in her eye.

"Me!" Chase confessed with pride. "Will said he bet I couldn't do it without waking you, but he was wrong."

"Well then, good job." Shelby walked over to the counter and poured herself a mug of coffee, splashing it with creamer. "Where's my junior bridesmaid? Don't tell me she's still sleeping?"

"Oh, no. She was out the door half an hour ago to help the ladies next door decorate the tent. I was told to expect your reception to be a purple and periwinkle paradise," Micah responded, raising his coffee mug to toast his sister.

"Yeah, it's nice having her out of the house once in a while. It gave Dad and I a chance to have a conversation without all her interfering nonsense babbling," Chase asserted, pleased.

"Chase, sweetie," Shelby started.

"What do you want me to do? Whenever you need me to do something, you always start by saying, 'Chase, sweetie.'"

"I was just about to tell you what I wanted when you interrupted. I'll start again. Chase, sweetie, would you go next door and tell Lovie I need my junior bridesmaid at home? We've got things to do here."

Chase stood up without complaint to retrieve his sister. When she heard the front door close, Shelby sat in his vacated chair.

"I have a confession. I overheard your conversation with Chase about Dahlia and whether you'd ever remarry. I've got a few comments if you'll allow me," Shelby admitted.

"I guess we have more than one creeping stalker in this house," Micah snorted, giving his permission with a smile.

"First, did you see how happy Chase was when he walked out of here? I haven't seen that face on him for a while. He just enjoyed talking with you and having your attention. That's medicine for his heart. You are his medicine.

Second, I want to say how glad I am that you're my brother. When you told Chase about your history with Dahlia, I considered it from my perspective. You and Dahl included me in your family when I had no family of my own to go home to. You never made me feel like a third wheel, and I'll never forget that.

The third thing is, I hope you do find someone you'll love as much as Dahlia and who will love you as much as she did. I want you to be that happy again, and I think you will be happy after you've made those few tweaks in your life.

Last, I hope you'll let Will into your life as a brother. He already loves you because you're my brother, and I love you. Love is a decision, and he's made it. He's not judging you. That's it. That's all I want to say," Shelby laughed and added, "for now."

"Thank you for everything you just said. You've always been good at putting air in my emotional tires," Micah reached for his sister's hand and squeezed it.

"And you always have the weirdest analogies. When you get married again someday, don't put that one in your vows – You put the air in my emotional tires." Shelby mocked, pulling her hand away. "So, how about we get one of us married today? My turn!"

CHAPTER SIXTY-NINE

Grace Fellowship Church was Will and Shelby's local family, and the members dispersed evenly on both sides of the center aisle for the ceremony. As they waited for Shelby to make her entrance, guests admired the bridal party already standing in place and adjusted themselves to the unaccustomed sight of their pastor in the best man's position.

Kesha, Mariana, and Lovie wore satin, tea-length dresses with scoop-necked lace over-bodice and three-quarter sleeves, matching the color of the satin underneath. Mariana and Lovie's were periwinkle blue, and Kesha's, as the matron-of-honor, was lilac purple. All three wore strappy nude sandals, their hair styled in French twists, wispy tendrils pulled out, and they held small bouquets of blue and purple flowers. The junior bridesmaid could not contain her nervous excitement standing in front of the assembled guests and rocked rhythmically from foot to foot.

Jonathan, Sam, and Silas were decked out in navy suits, with their shirts and ties being monochromatic—Jonathan's lilac to match his wife's and the boys' light blue.

Will wore a light gray suit with a white shirt and tie and a boutonniere with a sprig of ivy, baby's breath, and a tiny white rose. His smile rivaled Bobby McBride's, who sat as a guest on the groom's side.

In the middle of the group stood the officiant, Marcus Van Zant, in a single-breasted black suit that served for either weddings or funerals. Clutching his Wedding Manuel, Marcus nodded to Ava, standing at the back door and serving as an unofficial coordinator. When she saw the signal, Beth Ann Sharp played the traditional wedding march on the platform piano, and Ava opened the door for the bride to enter the sanctuary.

The guests stood as Shelby walked down the aisle unaccompanied to meet her groom. She wore a long-sleeved, high-necked, tea-length dress of white lace with a sleeveless satin under-bodice and an A-line skirt puffed out with several layers of fine toole under the lace. Her hair was arranged in a loose up-sweep with baby's breath tucked in the back, and her natural-looking makeup was expertly done. On her pedicured feet were dainty white sandals with a modest 2" heel, and she carried a bouquet of white roses and baby's breath.

"How simple yet sophisticated!" Marie remarked to June, who was standing next to her.

"Breathtaking!" June agreed.

When she reached the bridal party, Shelby turned to Will and curtsied to him in a gesture of respect. He moved to her side, and together, they faced Marcus to hear his wedding charge and say their vows to God and one another. Twenty-five minutes later, Marcus pronounced them husband and wife to the applause of their friends and guests.

"If you have your DJ play a big band song, I guarantee you won't believe what will happen," Marie whispered in the bride's ear after the cake was cut and consumed.

Shelby, ready to sit for a moment, was intrigued. She sat next to Will and asked Lovie to make the request to the DJ. Two songs later, a Glenn Miller classic rang out from the speakers, a decidedly different genre than previous music.

While engaged in conversations with other people at the time, the music caught the attention of Elodie and Bobby, who instantly sought eye contact. When they connected, they smiled and met on the dance floor. Bobby held out his hand to Elodie, and the two began to swing dance like they'd been partners for years—stepping and twirling, with feet and arms flying in rhythm.

"What is happening?" Shelby laughed.

"I did not know he could do that," Mariana, sitting next to the bride, commented, slack-jawed.

"Or her!" Will slapped his knee and laughed.

"Did I lie?" Marie asked over Shelby's shoulder.

"You did not. I can't believe what I'm seeing," Shelby answered, still laughing.

When the song finished, everyone clapped enthusiastically for them, including the DJ. The winded pair grinned at one another and looked for a place to sit.

"That was fun," Bobby said through ragged breaths to Elodie.

"We're gonna hurt tomorrow, but yes, that was fun," she agreed.

The DJ wisely chose a slow-tempo song to follow the energetic one. Nearly everyone paired up to dance, including Ava and Marcus, Shelby and Will, Grant and Marie, Jonathan and Kesha, and even June and Cal on his bad knees. Halfway through the song, Lovie tapped Shelby's elbow to complain.

"No one will dance with me!" she whined.

"Not true!" Will let go of his new wife and held out his hand to Lovie, who brightened.

Shelby stepped away to accommodate her niece and was tagged by her brother.

"May I dance with the bride?" Micah asked.

"You may," she answered, putting her left hand on his shoulder and her right hand in his.

"Congratulations, Shelby. I'm really happy for you and Will. I mean that. And you know, I think I might like him after all. How bad could he be if he landed you?" Micah conceded.

"He's a great guy, Micah. You'll see. So much better than I deserve."

"Wrong. You're too hard on yourself. You've got so much to offer a man. I'm sorry you had to wait so long to find your guy, but God must have had a reason."

"Did you just attribute the biggest blessing of my life to God?" Shelby challenged.

"I guess so. I'm not used to being this sober lately," Micah tried to downplay his comment.

Shelby took it in stride as they continued to dance. She suspected God was at work in her brother's life, even if he wasn't.

"I'm sorry you didn't have all this for our wedding," DeShawn apologized to his wife as they danced.

"You'll never hear me complain about that. Besides, I got something else I'm pretty happy with," Mariana smiled weakly.

"Long day. How are you feeling?" DeShawn asked, concerned.

"Tired. And this dress is getting tighter by the hour," she exhaled and laid her head on her husband's shoulder.

"I'm glad we can tell it after Will and Shelby leave on their honeymoon. Dad will be out of his mind to learn a baby is coming in February," DeShawn whispered, patting Mariana's back.

I'm so thankful for the support I've gotten for this series. My primary goal is to clearly articulate the true gospel of Jesus Christ to the fiction reader. I also aim to demonstrate discipleship principles through the lives and situations of warm, funny, flawed, and, most importantly, relatable characters. That's why there are no lonely hotel heiresses or Amish woodworkers included. (My apologies if you are a hotel heiress or Amish woodworker.) These fictional stories are meant to edify and encourage real, everyday people.

If you're enjoying this series and would like to support it, please review this book on Amazon or Goodreads and then pass it along to a friend. I'll be grateful.

1. Marcus frets about the ministry opportunities he's missed since committing to the Faircourt Friend's household. What Biblical truths soothe our "what if"s and "if only"s?

2. In chapter 12, Will explains to Shelby the parable of the wheat and tares and the potential for unbelievers to create havoc and stress in the assembly of believers. Thinking biblically (relying on Scripture,) discuss mixing worship and evangelism.

3. Marie wants to be more "people-y" like June, whose heart melts over everyone. Are you more like Marie or June, and have you made peace with your bent?

4. Mariana shared with her neighbor ladies that it was difficult for her to stop being her husband's advocate and voice now that she didn't have to. Why is it good for believers to share their struggles?

5. G-Lu advised Grant to quickly get fired again for sharing the gospel, knowing he doesn't need a job to provide for others. How would you advise Grant if he were 35 years younger and providing for a young family?

6. In Chapter 24, Ava and Grant wish they had been better pre-pared to meet their trials. Think back to a trial you've come

through. What was the biggest lesson learned?

7. Joe Jacobs is intrigued by Will's lesson in Romans 13 and the class discussion of Christians being politically active. How do you think being a citizen of heaven impacts our national citizenship?

8. DeShawn is determined to bless and not curse Christine Williams after she tries to get Mariana fired. Most of us are content not to curse our enemies. Have you ever tried to bless one? How?

9. In chapter 47, Cal realizes Micah is not apologizing for his previous behavior. What does a real apology look like?

10. Shelby confronted Micah, and Marie confronted Christine in chapter 61. How is Christian confrontation a demonstration of love?

AVAILABLE NOW

COMING IN 2025